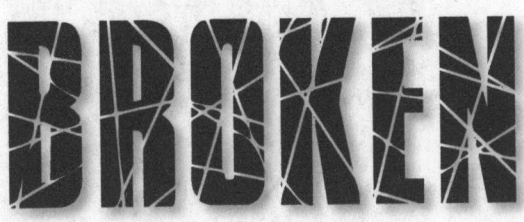

Tony McFadden

Beach Nut Press

ISBN: 978-0-6485628-6-3

DEDICATION

For Al.

The best father I've ever had.

DISCLAIMER

All characters in this book are fictitious. Any resemblance to real people is entirely coincidental.

This book is set in Australia, and written in Australia. It has Australian sayings and spellings.

And swearing. A decent amount of swearing.

You have been warned.

ACKNOWLEDGMENTS

The journey I've followed over the past slightly more than a decade is on the back of the feedback I get from you, my readers.

Thank you so much.

And Stephen. Your input was invaluable.

Chapter One

Nick slowed his car and eased to a stop in the middle of the narrow street. He was in front of his parents' house. The driveway was packed, and cars littered both sides of the street. His parents had been married forty-five years today, and everybody who wanted to kiss his father's arse was out in force.

He looked at the gift-wrapped present sitting on the passenger's seat, sighed and drove ahead to an empty spot on the kerb half a block away. He poked the button on the dash to stop the car and the heat from outside started overpowering the now dormant air conditioning.

He grabbed the gift, the keys from the centre console and got out of the car. His shirt immediately stuck to his chest. Humidity was abnormally high, and the sun sat high in the sky. The local weather lady had informed the country that it was ten degrees warmer than average for November 15th, and there was no sign of a cooling trend in the immediate future. It wasn't even summer yet.

His parents lived in a tidy two-storey house in Rose Bay, with Sydney Harbour across the street from them, and the Royal Sydney Golf Club butted up against their backyard.

The front lawn had been recently tended to by someone professional. As long as he'd remembered, neither parent showed the slightest interest in gardening.

He walked in the front door. There was an underlying hubbub from beyond the foyer. He couldn't see anyone yet, but it was clear it was a full house.

There was a large floor vase, about a metre tall, in the front foyer almost filled with golf balls retrieved from their backyard. Nick had often thought of dumping them onto the fourth fairway in the middle of the next tournament held at the club, just for shits and giggles.

He wandered toward his parents' patio, nodding at vaguely familiar faces as he passed through the house. A crowd was building. A table at one end of the broad patio was loaded with presents. He placed his gift on the pile and stopped by the bar. It was his father's pride of place, the focal point of most of his gatherings. "They running an open bar?"

"Sure are. What'll ya have?"

"Schooner of whatever's cold."

The young man behind the bar shook his head. "Only got wine an' liquor. The white is chilled."

Nick shook his head. "Double Jameson on a lot of ice."

He took the drink and eased his way through the crowd of his father's colleagues from the law firm, and the very odd family friend, until he found his parents. They were sat on the bench in the backyard under the Jacaranda tree. Most of the blossoms had fallen, leaving a carpet of purple on the grass under their feet.

His father noticed his arrival and tapped his wife on the arm. "Susie, Nicky deigned to show up." He raised his glass to his son. Gin and tonic, if Nick were to guess.

Susie interrupted her conversation with a plump Italian woman Nick didn't recognise and smacked her husband on the arm. "Be nice, George." She smiled at her son and raised her wine glass. "Thanks for coming by Nicky. It's a pleasant surprise."

"Wouldn't miss it for the world."

"It's not like you've got anything else going on," said George.

Nick nodded, smiled and took a healthy drink of whiskey. "I'm getting some food. We can catch up when the crowd clears."

His mother held out her hand to stop him. "James is around here. He hoped you'd show up. He wants to hire you."

George snorted. He shook his head and returned to his G&T.

Nick leaned down and got into his father's face. "It's a real job, pops." He stared at the spiderweb of capillaries on his father's nose, shook his head and stood up. "I'll be around."

He acquired another whiskey and angled toward the food. He tucked a napkin under a small plate and loaded it with small lamb chops, satay chicken skewers, peanut sauce and a handful of cucumber slices. He looked around the expanse of the back yard. It was impossible to stand and eat with a drink in one hand and the plate in the other, unless he grazed like a cow, something that didn't work at all well with skewers or chops. He either needed somewhere to sit, or at the very least a place to park his plate.

Half a dozen tables stretched along the low fence separating his parents' property from the golf course. The aforementioned James was sitting at one of them with a couple of junior associates from the law firm. He assumed. They were too young to be real lawyers. Nick grabbed the remaining chair and sat across from James.

"You were looking for me?" Nick picked up a chop by the bone and removed the meat with one bite. He pointedly ignored the look of disgust from one of the associates.

James shovelled a fork full of potato salad in his mouth and nodded while he chewed. "Your father mentioned you were a P.I. Thought I'd throw you some work."

"You did? He did?" Nick nibbled the remaining lamb off the bone and dropped it on his plate. "Surprises me."

James chuckled. "He wasn't bragging." He pointed at the two youngsters. "Have you met Josh and Kelly? Fresh out of law school. Didn't think they had the balls to show up here. Kids, this is Nick Harding." He chuckled and shovelled more potato salad in his mouth.

"Nice to meet you," said Nick. "Don't let my father intimidate you. He was in your shoes once."

Kelly sat up a smidge taller and pushed her hair behind an ear. "Mr Harding is your father?"

4

Nick nodded.

"And you're a lawyer at the firm? I haven't seen you there," said Josh.

"I didn't follow in his footsteps." Nick turned to James. "What's the job?"

James sipped some wine and made a face and abandoned the glass. "Nothing goes with potato salad, if you were wondering." He wiped his mouth and sat back in his chair. "I've got a client who is on death's door. He's well off and tells me he wants to settle things with his son before he goes."

"Nice of him."

"Except he can't find him."

"How old is your client?"

"He'll be 83 next month."

"So, his kid is in his 50s? Not really a kid, is he?"

James shook his head. "Had him late. Randy old geezer. The son is 35." He held up his hand to stop the next question. "Yeah, still not a kid. But the cops won't spend a minute looking for him. He's not officially missing. He's off the grid. He'll pay you a decent day rate and expenses to track the kid down."

"How do you know this guy? Why is he your client?"

"I'm executor of his will. His regular lawyer dropped dead a couple of months ago. Older than him. I'm coming in green. Firm handed this, and half a dozen other peaches, over to me last month." He shovelled another fork full of potato salad into his mouth. He spoke while he chewed. "He wants to see him before he dies." He wave his fork. "Might be within the month. Something to do with the Last Will and Testament, I expect."

"You haven't seen it?"

James shook his head. "Not yet. On the list. Up to my neck with new shit. No rush. I'll get to it before he dies, I'm sure."

Nick nodded and picked up a chicken skewer. "Email me the details, okay? I'll start tomorrow."

James handed Nick his phone. "Put your address in here."

Nick had emptied the plate. Twice. He was on his third drink and the crowd was finally starting to thin. He grabbed a chair from one of the tables and dropped it in front of the bench under the Jacaranda and perched backwards on it. He rested his arms on the back of the chair.

"Happy anniversary, folks. Forty-five years." He shook his head and looked at his mother. "How have you managed to restrain yourself from putting a pillow over his face every single night?"

His mother's cheeks were flushed, and her eyes glittered with amusement. "I could never. Thank you again for showing up." Her speech was deliberately slow and slightly slurred.

"You've had a bit, mum." He smiled. "May you and pops have another forty-five."

"Oh, Christ, I hope not," she said.

His father leaned forward, his elbows on his knees and a seemingly fresh G&T in his right hand. "I should thank you for coming by. I appreciate it. But you're wasting your life. Your job with the AFP had clout. Financial crimes. Growth industry. I still can't understand why you quit and started doing this bullshit detective work."

"Because that great job with the AFP was boring my tits off, pops. I couldn't do it anymore. At least I get some variety as a private dick." His phone rang. "Enjoy the rest of your night. I need to take this."

Nick looked at the number on his phone. He recognised it but couldn't quite remember who it was. "Hello?" He walked back toward the table James had been sitting at. Kelly and Josh were still there. Not billable. His father would be pissed.

"Nick, how you doing, mate?"

Nick wracked his memory, trying to place the voice. "Doing fine. You?"

"It's Scott. From the bank. Remember?"

Nick remembered. One of his contacts while he was with the AFP. Scott Smith ran the enterprise risk management team at one of Australia's big three banks. "Scottie. Still riding?"

"Got a new bike last month. Evie and I are riding to Adelaide next month."

"Cool. What's this about?"

"A woman named Lucy should be calling you tomorrow. She's in our collections department. Works for one of my people." He named the financial organisation he was with. Not with one of the Big Three anymore.

"You've moved. What happened? Easing into retirement?"

"An opportunity came up I couldn't say no to. Smaller organisations are more agile, things move faster. I get more freedom to do what needs to be done."

"And Lucy?"

"She found a client who hasn't been paying his bills."

"No. Hell, no."

"Please. For old times' sake. He's a serial deadbeat who has been stinging us like crazy. Multiple aliases, keeps switching email and mobile phone numbers. The latest is an 80-series BMW convertible. $130,000 car. Somehow faked a good enough background to get the loan approved, then disappeared. Three months, hasn't made a single payment. Before that was a high end Lexus Sedan."

"And she's going to call me and ask me to find him."

"Got it in one. Thanks a million."

"I didn't say I'd do it."

"You're intrigued. You wouldn't pass on this for the world."

Nick resigned himself to the inevitable. "Tell her to call. No guarantees. These types are tough to find."

"I have absolute faith in you."

"I'm not cheap."

"We pay well."

Nick sighed. "What's Lucy's last name?"

"Simpson. Thanks a million, mate."

"Thanks, Scottie." Nick wandered back toward his parents. "I appreciate you throwing work my way, but you owe me." He terminated the call and returned to the chair across from his parents.

"So, pops, when are you going to retire? You're 65. Must be time to stop now."

George ran his tongue over his top teeth and smiled. Not a friendly smile. "I'm not a quitter. There's lots of fight left in me."

"I'm sure there is. Mum would probably love another trip to Tuscany before she's too old to enjoy it, though."

His mother sat back against the arm on her side of the bench, and looked at her husband, waiting for him to answer.

George glanced at her, then looked away. "A vacation would be nice."

"Hell, pops. I know how much money you have. I don't expect any inheritance. Spend it all. I don't need the money. Buy a villa there and make it a retirement home." His phone vibrated with a message. It was from Lucy. He held up the phone. "See this? That's a new job. Private investigator stuff." He smiled at his parents. "Thanks for pointing James my way, pops. Great seeing you again. I'll see myself out. Fingers crossed, I don't drive myself into a tree."

"No," said Susie. "You're in no state. Stay here."

Nick shook his head. "Oh, no. I can't stay here. But I'll Uber home. I'll come back tomorrow for my car."

His mother walked him to the door. "You're doing okay?"

Nick nodded and gave her a hug. "Living my best life."

She gently pulled out of the hug and held him by the shoulders. She looked into his eyes for a minute. "You call me if you need anything, okay?"

"I'm fine, mum. Business is great. Both of these cases are people reaching out to me because of my experience and reputation. There's no need to worry."

"Be that as it may, I'm a mother. I'm legally allowed to worry. Obligated to, really."

Nick's phone chimed. "My ride's here. I'll stop in tomorrow when I come back for my car."

His mother looked over her shoulder. "George will be out."

"Perfect."

Her smile was sad. "I wish you'd make an effort to reconcile with your father. We're not going to be around much longer."

"You've got decades left. And he's got to meet me halfway."

She shook her head. "Maybe you'll have to go a little further than halfway to meet him. He's got your stubbornness."

"More like I've got his."

Chapter Two

The share ride dropped him at his unit block. There were eight units, four down and four up, like a really small motel. He walked up the stairs at the side of the building to the upper level and unlocked the sliding door of the third unit.

It was about the same size as the apartment he lived in when he lived in Stanmore, but nicer. Cleaner, newer, and in Bondi Junction. A thirty-minute walk to Bondi Beach, if he took his time. He had a tight kitchen, a place to use as an office and a nice view over a local park. And the neighbours weren't nosy. Or noisy.

He did miss having Davie close by.

His phone vibrated with a message. Lucy, again. It was almost 11:00 p.m. "Jesus." He grabbed a beer and sat at his desk. He ran his tongue over his teeth, deciding whether to call now or in the morning. "Screw it."

He put his headphones in, took another drink and called.

"Lucy Simpson speaking. Is this Nicholas Harding?"

"Just Nick, please. Yes. Scottie told me you'd call, but I wasn't expecting to hear from you until tomorrow." He leaned back in his chair and took another drink.

"I could call back tomorrow, but since you just called me – "

"Returning your calls."

"And I really appreciate that. I wonder if I could meet you tomorrow, early."

Nick stifled a yawn. "What's your definition of early?"

"Before I get to the office."

He didn't bother stifling the yawn this time. "Apologies, it's been a long, long day. There's a nice cafe near my place. You buy me breakfast, and we've got a deal."

"Give me the address. I'll be there at 7:30."

"Can we make it 8:00?"

"I do have a lot to do tomorrow."

Nick chuckled. "Me asking if we could do it at 8:00 was me telling you that you can get there at whatever time you want, I'll be there at 8:00. I'll see you tomorrow morning, Lucy Simpson." He terminated the call before realising he didn't know what she looked like.

The cafe opened at 6:00 am and was well populated with the morning crowd by the time Nick arrived. At 8:00. He nodded at Lisa, the barista, and looked around for what he thought a Lucy Simpson might look like.

"She's the red-head in a navy suit at the back," said Lisa.

"Whazzat?"

"There's a Lucy something or other who came in about half an hour ago and sat in the back. Told me she was waiting for you, and to let you know where she was sitting. And she bought you breakfast. Eggs Bennie will be ready shortly." Lisa held out a large take-away cup. "Here's your long black."

Nick took the cup and just stood there.

"You okay?" Lisa smiled and nodded toward the back. "She's been here almost half an hour. Don't make her wait any longer."

"Yeah. Right." He hoisted the cup. "Thanks."

Nick wound his way through the tables until he reached the small two-seater near the back, against the window. He approached Lucy Simpson from behind. She was tall, red-headed like Lisa described her, and visibly nervous. She sipped at her coffee, the cup rattling as she placed it in the saucer. She tapped the middle finger of her left hand on a pocket file folder. She glanced at the time on her phone, then picked it up like she was going to call or text someone.

"I'm right here." Nick passed her and sat in the opposite seat. He saluted her with his coffee cup. "Thanks for the coffee. And the breakfast." He put his coffee down and glanced at the folder. "What's this about?"

"Mr Smith didn't tell you?"

Nick shrugged. "All Scottie told me was that this was essentially a skip trace. Someone is managing to get around whatever safeguards your bank has and then stiffing you for the repayments."

"In a nutshell." She held out her hand. "Thanks for meeting with me."

Nick shook it. "Scottie's an old friend. I owe him." He held up a finger. "That doesn't mean I'm not going to charge the bank $1500 a day for this, though."

She didn't reply, instead extracting a dozen sheets of paper from the pocket file. She looked at Nick, her eyebrows raised and held them out.

"What's this?" Nick fanned the pages. Each was a separate client profile the bank had put together. Different addresses, different names, similar credit scores. Three had similar looking photos clipped to them, grainy black and white headshots of a Caucasian man with varying lengths of hair and facial decoration. The loan amounts varied but were all six figures and none had been repaid.

He handed the pages back. "Close to five million. How sure are you?"

She handed them back to Nick. "Look at the names. And the birthdates."

Nick took the papers and leaned back as his eggs Benedict was placed in front of him. "The names?" He thumbed through the pages. "Terry Graves, Tony Garret, Tim Greaves, Thad Grealish." He looked up. "Because they all have the same initials?"

"And?"

He checked them again. "And their birthdays are all on the 13th of different months, 1992."

"And the photos that we could actually get are all close enough to be the same guy. Overweight, dark hair, same beady eyes."

"How'd you get the photos?"

Lucy smiled, a self-satisfied smile. "I got security to go through any footage we had in branches where he showed up to sign documents. These were the only good ones they could find, but it was the piece of information that got me approval to engage you."

He handed the papers back and ground some black pepper on his eggs. "You okay?"

Lucy slid the sheets of paper back into the folder. "Why?"

"You're shaking like a chihuahua."

She took a deep breath and clasped her hands together. "I'm fine. Are you going to help me? Us?"

Nick nodded while he chewed. He took a drink of coffee. "I'm not cheap."

"If we can recover even a tenth of what this dick has taken, it's more than worth it." She glanced at what was left of his breakfast. "I should have eaten."

"What's the rush? Grab something. They do a good omelette here, too."

Lucy looked at her watch. "I can't stay. I have a meeting with our risk team first thing this morning."

"I would imagine." Nick pushed his plate to one side and motioned for the file. "I've got a bit of experience with financial fraud. How in the hell did this get past your compliance department twice, let alone twelve times?" He pulled the paperwork out and thumbed through it.

"Look at the credit reports." She crossed her arms and leaned back in her chair. "Tell me what you see wrong with them."

Nick pulled half a dozen of the reports from the file and fanned them out on the table. He carefully scanned each of them, frowning. "Nothing remarkable about any of them. Not a single red flag. I'd give any one of these guys fantastic interest rates."

Lucy nodded. "I don't know how he's doing it. He's got full, solid looking credit histories. They're all the same. Unquestionably rock solid."

"He must have someone at the agency." He slid them back together and added them to the file folder. "Or has good hacking skills."

She raised an eyebrow. "Hadn't thought of that."

"Yeah," he smiled. "I know a guy who might be able to help."

Lucy took a folded piece of paper from her computer bag. "Our agreement. Include your bank details and we'll deposit three days' retainer. Invoice us against that at the end of the week. If you have to bring on a cyber security expert, give me their details, including rate, and I'll make sure they're included."

"David Sangster. I'll text you the details."

She handed him a business card as she stood. "E-mail me. We're going to need an auditable trail for all of this." She collected her computer bag. "Thanks for meeting me." She stood. "Don't get up. But I need you to meet the team I'm reporting to. My boss, her boss, who is your friend, I believe, and the head of compliance. Can you be at my office at 10:30? The address is on my card. It'll be a quick introductory meeting."

"Yeah, sure. Understandable, given the scope of the fraud." He stood with her and tucked the folder under his arm. "You got this already? The breakfast?"

"All paid for. Enjoy."

"Thanks. I'll have a closer look at these and see you at 10:30."

Lucy's financial services company occupied three floors of a building on Harris Street in Pyrmont, just south west of Sydney's city centre, near the waterfront. Visitor parking was underground. Nick took the parking lot ticket with him to reception.

The area had an aura of successful competence. Their corporate logo was backlit against oak panelling behind the receptionist station. The desk faced a waiting area with half a dozen black leather chairs. At the far end of the waiting area was a meeting room. It had clear glass walls, stainless steel and black leather furniture and a large monitor on the opposite wall to the door.

Nick slowly turned a full 360 degrees, admiring the layout. "Nice."

He stepped up to the reception counter. "Hi there. I'm here to see Lucy Simpson. I'm Nick Harding." He held out the parking ticket. "Do you guys validate?"

The receptionist took the ticket, ran it through a reader and handed it back with a smile. "Gives you two hours. Lucy has been expecting you." She pointed over his shoulder. "The meeting will be in that room in about three minutes. Go on in. There's coffee, ice water and muffins. Help yourself." She started typing on her console. "I'll let her know you're here."

Nick nodded thanks and pushed open the door to the meeting room. There was a white carafe of coffee on a tray with six upside down porcelain cups. Beside it was a pitcher of ice water, condensation collecting on the outside, and six glasses.

And, as promised, a basket of muffins. Nick poked through them. They were warm. Orange poppyseed. Sultana bran. Something that looked and smelled very much like banana walnut.

He poured himself a cup of coffee and snagged one of the banana walnut muffins and sat at the head of the conference table. He peeled the top off the muffin and took a bite. High concentration of walnuts. "I approve." He took a sip of the black coffee. Perfect temperature, and a rich, full taste with no bitterness. "Double approve."

Lucy came in, three people following. She flipped a switch as she entered, and the clear glass walls turned opaque. They took seats around the table.

Nick stood until they sat. "Lucy, you need to tell me where that coffee came from. It's perfect." He sat with the rest of them.

She smiled, a nervous smile. "Nick Harding, this is Catherine Moss, my immediate manager. Her manager is Scott Smith. I believe you know him already. And that's Brad Williams, Head of Compliance." She held up her hands. "We're not expecting any results yet. After all, I just met you this morning. This is an introductory meeting."

Nick nodded. "And by way of introduction, my name is Nick Harding. I run a small Private Investigations operation. My background is in financial crime. I spent a number of years with the Australian Federal Police, put in some time on some money laundering task forces, until I resigned." He nodded at Scottie. "I worked with Scottie, but across the table, on a number of cases. We go way back." He spread the files Lucy had given him across the table, like playing cards. "Lucy has provided a good base of information. I'll be engaging an IT expert to help me."

"David Sangster," said Lucy.

"Exactly. He's very good at what he does. He and I will be meeting this afternoon to put together a plan of attack." Nick looked at each one of them in turn. "Any additional information you might have would be very beneficial." He took another sip of coffee. "And you really need to tell me what coffee this is. It's exquisite."

Nick used magnets and pinned the twelve profiles to the whiteboard by his desk. All the same man, twelve names with the same initials, and birthdays on the 13th of each month. He shook his head. "Always the stupid, smart-arsed things that trip these morons up."

He called his friend. It went to voicemail after three rings, so he hung up and sent a text message. "Davie, if you've got a week's leave, take it. I've got a job I'm going to need you on. I can get you $850 a day."

He thought for a second, then scrolled through his contacts until he found who he was looking for.

"Richard Moffet speaking."

"You delete my number or something, my friend? Nick here. You still the compliance dude at that joint?"

"Nicky, good to hear from you. Kinda smashed right now. Something quick I can do?"

Nick leaned back in his chair and looked at the twelve clean credit reports with Moffet's organisation's logo, all of them fraudulent. "It's not going to be quick. I'm working for a client who has been on the receiving end of massive fraud, supported in large part by falsified, but seemingly good, credit reports issued by your mob. Twelve of them."

"For the same person?"

"Same person, different names, completely different reports, all of them with credit scores of 880 or better."

Nick heard Richard's long, slow exhale over the phone. "Well, crap." He heard papers rustle. "Can you come by my office this afternoon at 2:00? And bring those reports with you. I'll see what I can find. That work for you?"

"Still in North Sydney?"

"I am. Got to run. See you then."

"Later." Nick hung up and his phone rang. He poked the green button to answer. "Davie."

"Buddy, you've got a gig for me?" asked Dave Sangster.

"I'm fine, Davie. Thanks. How are you?" Nick smiled and leaned back, putting his feet up on his desk.

"Yeah, yeah. What's the deal?"

"You have leave?"

"Already booked out the rest of the week."

Nick kicked his feet off his desk and leaned forward, waking up his computer and entering the password. "Are you able to meet me at my place in about an hour?

"See you there."

He hung up and checked his mail. There should have been something in there from James, about a missing heir. But there wasn't.

Chapter Three

Nick arranged for an Uber to go pick up his car. It dropped him at his parent's house. His car was still half a block away. And it was still hot out. He stood at the bottom of the driveway, debating whether to pop in for a cool drink or just get the hell out of there, when the front door opened and his mother stepped out.

"You just going to stand there or are you coming in for a coffee?"

Nick sighed. He took too long. "Coffee would be good." He glanced at his car, then joined his mother.

They sat on the back patio with their cups of coffee and freshly baked banana-walnut bread. Rainbow lorikeets sat on the railing twittering for a piece. Always in pairs, always raucous. The noisy rainbow bitches of the bird kingdom.

"I've got to make this quick, Mum. I've got a job. I need to meet up with Davie at my place and be in North Sydney in an hour or so."

"You've got a little time. Thanks for stopping by last night. Your father may not have shown it, but he was happy you came."

Nick snorted. "Could have fooled me." He picked the pieces of walnut out of the banana bread and popped one in his mouth. He tossed a corner of the banana bread at the pair of lorikeets. They hopped off the railing and onto the patio, fighting for the bread.

"Oh, I wish you hadn't done that. They'll be expecting me to feed them now."

Nick chuckled. "Sorry, Mum. Do you have James' number? I was expecting to hear from him today and I haven't."

"You wait here. I'm sure he's in your father's Rolodex."

So Nick waited. He watched the lorikeets fighting over crumbs. They flitted back to the railing, loudly proclaiming their unhappiness at no more banana bread.

A golfing foursome, which had to be made up of piss-poor golfers to be taking their second shot that close to the tee, stood almost directly across the fence from him, debating which club to use.

He stood and leaned on the chest-high railing. The lorikeets gave up and flew away. He had a better look at the golfers. Their average age was around eighty, by his estimation. They were still spry, and laughing at the golfer's predicament, two large trees between them and a clear shot of the fairway. He revised his opinion of their abilities. If he could even get vertical at that age, he'd be happy. He smiled and sat back in his chair.

His mother returned with a slip of paper. "Here's his number. What are you smiling about?"

"When's the last time you and dad hit the links?"

"Hardly ever, lately. And yet, that's why we bought this house." She smiled, a little bit sadly. "Still, it's a nice home."

Nick finished the banana bread and dusted the crumbs off his fingertips. "Thanks for coffee and the phone number, mum. Got to run." He held up the sheet of paper. "Two cases at the same time. I'm in the big leagues, ma."

Susie laughed. "Stop by any time, Nicky. Maybe we'll play a round or two together."

Nick started his car and called James.

"I'm glad you called."

"I was expecting an email." Nick pulled away from the kerb and idled down the street.

"Better than an email. The old guy wants to meet with you. Today, if possible."

Nick looked at the time on the dashboard. "It'll have to be later. I've got a couple of meetings today set up already. Won't be freed up until maybe 3:00. Does that work?"

"I'll arrange it. I'll text you the address. Where are you going to be at 3:00?"

"North Sydney."

"I'll allow travel time."

"Thanks." Nick hung up and pointed his car home.

He tapped a button on the steering wheel. "Call Davie."

The call burred through the car speakers and was answered on the first ring. *"What's up mate? We still on?"*

Nick glanced at the GPS on the centre console. "The digital bitch says I'll be there in about 15 minutes."

"Am I on the clock?"

"You are. See you shortly." Nick thumbed the 'call end' button on the steering wheel. Fifteen minutes. He still didn't know the brand of coffee.

He called Lucy.

"You've got something for me already?"

"I'm not a magician, Lucy. Give me a couple of hours. It was a delight meeting you, and I understand the importance of this case to you, but far more important for me is knowing the brand of coffee you had at your office. It was brilliant."

She laughed. *"I'll ask around and let you know. And you let me know as soon as you know something."*

"You got it." Nick terminated the call. He was a couple of minutes from his flat.

Then Davie called. *"Hey, I'm sitting on your stoop and you're not here."*

"I don't have a stoop."

"Okay. I'm sitting on the floor in front of your door. How far away are you?"

Nick turned off the road into his marked parking spot. "Just arrived." He took the steps two at a time and found

Davie on his arse in front of his door, trying to open a padlock with one of Nick's old lock pick sets.

Davie kept his concentration on the task at hand, speaking without looking up. "You said this was easy." He was applying tension to the torsion bar and trying to set the pins with a thin, hooked pick. Unsuccessfully.

"Yeah, but you think what you do is easy, and I can't even begin to fathom how you do it." Nick reached out a hand. "Get up. You're blocking my door. I'm sure there's a 'No Loitering' sign around here somewhere."

Davie grabbed his hand and grunted as he pulled himself up. He pocketed the lock picks and swung the padlock around his index finger. "You're going to have to show me how you do this."

"Some other time. We've got work." He handed the file folder to Davie and turned on the kettle. "Coffee?"

"Always." Davie spread the paper out on the kitchen table. "What am I looking at?"

"You tell me."

Davie leaned over, his arms crossed, scanning the documents. "Making me earn my money?"

"Keep looking."

He uncrossed his arms and rapidly flipped through the pages. "This is the same person. Same initials, stupid changes in birth date. Excellent credit scores."

Nick raised his eyebrows. "It took me a lot longer than that to figure it out."

"Bow before my greatness. Any idea what his real name is?"

"Nope." Nick poured hot water into the French press. "That's why we're getting paid. That, and where he is and how to collar him."

Davie slide the pages back into the folder. "Where do we start?"

"We're going to meet a guy I know who works at the place that produced those credit reports. We can go in separate cars, or we can travel together, but after the meeting I'm going to another meeting, and you'll have to make your own way home."

"I'll go with you. Take the train back."

They came out of the underground parking garage in North Sydney into the hot noon sun.

Nick plucked his shirt from his chest. "We've got a bit of time. Lunch on me."

Davie patted his stomach. "There's a Greek place on Walker that makes a mean lamb gyro."

"Never been. Lead the way." He walked with Davie and sat in the shade at an outside table. Davie was as stereotypically IT as one could get. Wiry red hair in a tiny ponytail, a bit overweight, pale skin and a permanent scowl. He was dressed up, by Davie's standards, in a collared shirt and pressed chinos.

"I didn't know you owned an iron." Nick sat across from him and placed the file folder on the table. "Gyros for both of us?"

"Hell yeah."

A server appeared out of nowhere and they ordered.

As soon as he left, Davie nodded at the folder. "Pretty slick con. Would probably have gotten away with it if he'd been a bit more original."

Nick smiled and sat back as drinks were delivered. His was a cola with a slice of lemon floating in it. Davie's looked like sparkling water, another departure from the Davie norm.

He leaned back again as a lamb gyro with sweet potato fries was placed in front of him. The server hovered while Davie moved the folder then placed an identical plate in front of him.

Davie opened the gyro and spread it out on the plate. He dug the sweet potato fries from underneath the wrap and tossed them on the lamb and salad. "Those credit reports. They look perfect." He jabbed his fork into the salad and started eating.

"You okay? Just the salad? No wrap?"

"Tell me about this case. Who are we meeting?"

"The compliance guy at the credit report place," said Nick. He pointed at Davie's plate. "You're really starting to worry me."

"There's this girl. Just started in the office." He picked at the lamb. "Cute, and really smart." He pointed at Nick with a fry. "Tell me more about this case."

"Friend of a friend at the finance company this guy has bilked a dozen times. They finally twigged after a dozen."

"Hey, to be fair, I only noticed because they were all in one pile. Spread them through a few thousand others, I'm surprised it was found at all. Eat."

"True enough." Nick picked at the food. "Really. No carbs?"

Nick and Davie met Richard Moffet on the ground floor and rode with him up the lift to the twelfth floor, through security and on to Moffet's office.

"Show me those credit reports, Nick. I've been sweating since you called." He took the pages and spread them across his desk. "What do you do, Mr Sangster?" He logged into his terminal.

Davie stared at him a second. "Oh, me? I'm Nick's IT guy. Along to pick up whatever information I can."

Richard nodded as he clicked through screens, referring back to the credit reports. "Shit."

"What kind of shit, Richard?" asked Nick.

"The bad kind." He closed down his terminal. "Can I make copies of these? The ones I checked aren't appearing in our system, but the reference numbers look real." He held up a hand. "And we the three of us know they aren't." He sighed and shook his head. "I don't know if it was someone inside or an exceptionally good breach, but it has to be one of the two."

"My thoughts, as well. Go ahead. Make copies. I'm not here about the breach, though. That's your problem." Nick smiled. "I'm trying to find that magical person with at least twelve names and addresses. Can you do some analytics on your database and see if you can unearth any other instances?"

Richard stacked the pages on the copier in his office and watched it spit out copies. "I'm getting heartburn. If there's more than these dozen, I'm going to have a heart attack." He handed the originals back to Nick. "Give me a couple of days. We've got a lot of files. I'll have the data analytics team drop everything and do this." He stood. "Hate to rush you out, but this is everything I'm doing now. Thanks for bringing it to my attention." He took a deep breath. "It gives me a chance to say I found it, head things off at the pass." He smiled. "I'll call you as soon as we've run the data."

"You trust this guy?" asked Davie. They were walking through Greenwood Plaza, heading for the parking structure. They stopped at the point where a right turn took them to parking and straight ahead led to the train platform.

"Pretty much. He was part of the money laundering task force I was on when I was with the AFP, as an industry rep. He impressed me then. You taking the train?"

"Sure as hell not walking."

Nick checked his watch. "Can you poke and prod the credit reporting's system? Don't actually breach because that would be illegal. Just let me know if you think it would be very difficult."

"I'll be gentle. What's the other case?"

"Another missing person. An heir. I'm meeting the client to get whatever details I can."

"The client?"

"Lawrence Goulding."

Davie raised his eyebrows. "Damn. I didn't know you operated in such rarefied air."

"Friends in moderately high places." Nick checked his watch again. "Really got to run."

"I'll drop by tonight. You can feed me a beer or two."

Nick clapped Davie on the shoulder. "Deal."

Chapter Four

The address James had sent to Nick was in Darling Point. A couple of suburbs away from his parents' house. But nicer. Millions nicer. He drove the narrow streets, passing houses worth many millions until he reached his destination, a curving dead-end street with a house worth tens of millions at its end.

The plot of land was at least 2000 square metres, on a hill overlooking the water. A low white wall surrounded the property, less security than decoration. A wrought iron gate barred entry. Nick typed a message in his phone to James, and before he had the chance to press 'Send', the gate swung inward.

He idled his car into the driveway and followed the curve down to the house. He could see Sydney Harbour over the roofline. The front of the house presented as a small single-storey bungalow, but as he slowly drove down the driveway along the side of the house, he saw that it was dug into the hill, three stories on the water side. A railed balcony stretched the width of the back and up the side of the house on the top level.

James was leaning against a Lexus convertible, waiting. Nick parked beside him.

"I think I'm early."

"The old guy has nothing better to do."

Nick nodded. "Tell me something about him before we go in."

"Lawrence Goulding. Mining money. Worth, conservatively, 80 million. Possibly more. He's in his late eighties and has terminal pancreatic cancer. It's spreading fast."

"And he can't find the son he wants to give it to?"

James nodded toward the door.

Nick looked and saw a suited man standing just inside a glass door.

"That's William. His business manager. And lately his carer," said James.

"Then let's talk to the man."

William held the door open for them. "Thanks for seeing me, gentlemen. I know James, so you must be Nick. Good at finding people, Nick?"

Nick glanced at James, bemused. "I've had some luck in the past. What can you tell me about the son?"

William led them to the lounge room. Sliding doors at the far side of the room opened to the broad patio overlooking the bay. An elderly man sat in a recliner, bottle of whiskey on the table beside him, and a couple of ounces in the glass beside the bottle. A folder sat on the table behind the bottle. An oxygen mask hung off one of the handles of an oxygen tank cart. "Mr Goulding will share that information with you. But he needs to be convinced you can do the job first."

Nick raised his eyebrows. "Card tricks? Poetry recital? A bit of soft shoe? What's he expecting?"

"Just meet with him."

"That's why James brought me here." Nick pushed ahead and walked onto the patio.

He extended his hand. "Mr Goulding, my name is Nick Harding. I understand you're looking for your son."

Goulding worked something from between his gums and upper cheek with his tongue. He hadn't shaved in a couple of days and white stubble covered his jaw. His eyes were sunken, with dark rings around them. His clothes hung loose on his frame, a clear sign of recent and rapid weight loss. He sniffed and took a sip of whiskey. "You any good?"

"You trust Jimmy?"

"James? He's okay, I guess. As good as any legal hack can be. What did he tell you?"

Nick pulled a patio chair closer and sat, leaned over, elbows on his knees. "That you have aggressive pancreatic cancer, a shed load of money and a desire to get some of it to your estranged son. Am I close?"

A small smile almost cracked his lips. "No nonsense. To the point. I like that." He grunted as he reached for the folder on the table and handed it to Nick. "Everything I can remember is in there."

"Thanks." Nick pointed at the whiskey. "Think I could get a shot?" He looked at Lawrence, then at William. "Lubricate the brain muscles?"

Lawrence nodded. William grabbed a glass off the table and poured him a light shot. Nick tapped the edge of the glass and looked up at him.

William sighed and doubled it.

"More like it." He leaned back in his chair and opened the file. A headshot of a thin, bearded man was clipped to the top page. "Gareth Goulding."

"He goes by Gary. At least he used to."

"Okay. Gary." He sipped a taste, appreciating the quality, then put the glass back down. He read through the top sheet. "Complete and concise. For what it's worth. Old address, old phone number, old vehicle description." He turned the page over and looked at the back. Blank. "Anything new?"

Lawrence grunted and leaned back in his chair to look at James. "He's the best you could find?"

Nick glanced up at his friend and smiled. "I am the best he could find." He pulled a pen from his pocket. "When's the last time you saw him, or spoke to him?"

"A little over three years ago." Lawrence made an exploding motion with one hand. "Then poof, he was gone. Mobile phone disconnected, rental unit vacated, even dropped his girlfriend."

Nick flipped through the pages. "Girlfriend? She in here somewhere?"

Goulding topped up his glass and took a mouthful. "Nothing about her in there. Penny something. Sorry, I don't remember much about her." He clasped his hands together in his lap and stared at them.

"You had a falling out with your son?"

He glanced at Nick, then returned his gaze to his hands. "Not relevant. Can you find him?"

Nick closed the file and tapped it on his hand. "It's thin but give me a couple of days and I'll let you know what I find out."

Goulding leaned forward and grabbed Nick by the wrist with a surprisingly strong grip. "Not good enough, kid. I need you to find him. And be careful." He wheezed and sat back in his chair. He fumbled for the oxygen mask. William jumped in and helped place it on his face. He adjusted the flow, then motioned for Nick and James to step back into the house.

James waited until the door was closed. "How long does he have?"

"A couple of weeks, at most," said William. "Do whatever you can, okay?"

Nick called Lucy from the car on his drive home. "Hey, it's only been a few hours, but I thought I should give you an update."

"I appreciate that. What do you have?"

"Got a pencil?"

"I'm recording the call. I'll have a transcript a minute after we're finished talking. What do you have?"

Nick laughed. "Early days. I met with the guy running compliance at the reporting agency. An old colleague. I've shared with him the profiles you gave me, in confidence. He's going to do a deep dive on them and see if there's anything he can dig up. I've also got Davie digging into whatever background he can find. On all of the aliases. It's only a matter of time."

"Okay. Good. Not expecting a resolution on the first day. I do appreciate the call, though." She let out a held breath. "Do you think you'll be able to track him down?"

"Davie and I can. Trust me."

"Okay. Thanks again for the call and keep me across everything that's happening, okay?"

"Absolutely. Take care." Nick terminated the call and immediately called Davie.

"How's it going, boss?"

"Hate that word. Partner. Feel like pizza for dinner?" Nick accelerated onto the motorway. "I'm buying."

"I'll bring the beer. Your place?"

"I'll be there in an hour. Working dinner. The deadbeat and the heir."

"Sounds like a shitty TV show."

Nick closed the door after paying for and receiving the deliv-ered pizza and opened it again immediately when a meaty fist pounded on it.

Davie was balancing a flat of beer on one hip, his fist raised to hit again. "Hey. Am I late?"

"Pizza just got here. Come on in." He slid the two pizza boxes out of the way and made space on the counter for the beer. "Plates in the cupboard above the dishwasher."

Davie took his pizza and bottle of beer and sat in front of Nick's laptop. It was on a blonde oak desk, sitting in a dock-ing station connected to two large monitors. He put the beer down and tapped the spacebar.

Nick lifted the beer and placed a coaster under the bottle. "Philistine."

"So, what's the plan?"

"I was thinking just the deadbeat, but since we've got two cases, let's split them up. I'll take the deadbeat; you see what you can find out about the missing heir." He took the folder from his desk and slapped it on Davies' chest. "All the info I've got." He nodded toward the sofa. "And this is my work-station. Make yourself comfortable over there."

"What are the odds these two are the same person?"

"You'd think, right? Perfect twist. But I doubt it. The heir is named Gary. Unlikely he'd use aliases with the initials T.G. for the past three years."

"I can hope." Davie opened his laptop and stretched out on the sofa.

"Shoes, mate."

"Fucking hell." He kicked them off and re-settled himself. He pulled the side table around so he could access the pizza and beer and flipped open the Gareth Goulding file. "Where do you want me to start?"

"History informs decisions. Dig into his past. See if you can find a reason why he might have disappeared off the face of the earth."

Davie cracked his knuckles. "Behold my awesome Google-fu."

Nick chuckled and leaned back in his chair. He sorted the deadbeat files in time order, oldest to the left, most recent to the right. He entered relevant details in a spreadsheet. Names chosen, birthdate, address on file...

He frowned. "Hey, does this make any sense?"

Davie twisted on the sofa. "What?"

"This deadbeat is giving valid street addresses. Why couldn't they find him?" He pored over the files. "It doesn't make sense."

"Sure it does. Everything else is fake, why shouldn't the address be?" Davie thought a second. "Probably the right general area though."

Nick held up a handful of files. "They're all over the place. One of the first ones was just outside of Wollongong. Almost 100km south of here." He picked another off his desk. "The latest is in Wyee." He slapped it down. "The same distance north. The rest are scattered quasi-randomly throughout the city."

Davie was paying less than half attention. He had his own work to focus on. "Right-o. Let me know if there's something I can actually help with."

"Yeah, yeah. Keep digging into Gary's past for me. I'll work on this." Nick put Google maps up on the larger monitor and plotted the twelve addresses. The ten not in Wollongong or Wyee followed a broad curve around the western outskirts of Sydney. A half toroid about thirty kilometres wide, the furthest west was in Penrith and the closest to the city in Parramatta.

He sorted them by time. Pretty much south to north, with some zigzagging through Western Sydney. There might be some deeper meaning in the deadbeat's decision-making process, but Nick couldn't figure it out.

"No rhyme or reason."

"Check this out." Davie sent a photo to the printer and hopped off the sofa. "I think maybe I found something."

Nick grabbed the paper off the printer. It was a grainy newspaper picture from twenty-five years ago. Two kids sat on the edge of an outdoor swimming pool. The caption identified them as Gary Goulding and Penelope Larson, winners of their respective swimming contest. Four older guys, adults, stood behind them, looking to be cheering them on. Nick pointed at the four. "Any idea who these guys are?"

"Didn't look into them. Not really important. Got Penny's last name, right? Larson?"

Nick nodded. "Yeah. Childhood friend. Seems even stranger that they've split."

"Childhood flings don't last that long."

Nick shook his head. "Friendships that start that young tend to last, though." He leaned back and stretched. "Tomorrow I'm going to check out the last three or four addresses the deadbeat used. It'll take me the better part of the day. Can you do more digging? Timeline up to when he disappeared."

"Not a problem, boss." Davie looked up from his screen. "Sorry. Partner. I'll text you if anything surprising shows up."

Chapter Five

A hundred kilometres north of Sydney, in a town so small it has no traffic lights and only one bottle shop, Terry Graves was waiting for his pizza.

"How much longer, Lauren?"

The mother of the family that owned the only pizza place in Wyee looked at the oven. "Five minutes, probably?"

"I'll be right back. Keep it warm for me." He pushed the door open, leaving the chilled air for the late afternoon sun reflecting off the asphalt parking lot. "Son of a bitch." He tugged at his T-shirt and winced in the light.

A diagonal path across the parking lot took him to the bottle shop. He grabbed a flat of Cascade and lugged it to his car. He puffed as he balanced the box of 24 beers on one hip while he opened the back door of the Lexus. The thought of exercising to get in some sort of shape never entered his mind.

He wiped the sweat off his forehead with his forearm, and the forearm on his shorts. He pulled the door to the pizza place open and smiled as the cool air hit his face. "Ready yet, Lozz?"

Lauren slid the large pizza off the warming shelf. "Perfect timing. See you tomorrow."

Terry waded through the thick air back to his car, tossed the pizza on the passenger seat and gingerly held the hot, black steering wheel as he drove the four minutes to his house.

He pulled in between the hedges bracketing his driveway and angled left to the front door. The house he was leasing sat on twenty acres of scrub land, three of it cleared and covered in lawn that he begrudgingly kept mowed.

He parked between a BMW convertible and a Toro ride-on mower. He waddled to the front door with the pizza balanced on top of the flat of beer. He pressed the case of beer against the wall, balancing it while he unlocked the door.

He stumbled into the house as the door was pulled open by a young woman. "You could have knocked."

"Carol. I thought you'd be out back by the pool. Didn't want to disturb you." He pushed the door shut with his arse.

"Pizza, again?"

"Not a lot to choose from up here. I think the chicken at the chicken place was cooked last week. Maybe even older." Terry grunted the case of beer onto the kitchen table and slid the pizza into the table beside it.

"Maybe you could cook?" She hugged him from the side, kissing him on his neck, and running her finger over the scar on the side of his head. "You can cook, right?"

Terry shook his head. "You wouldn't want that. Hey, we'll be out of here in a few weeks. Back into the city with better restaurants. And I won't have to mow the fucking lawn." He flipped open the pizza box. "You got any blow left?"

"Almost all gone."

"That won't do." He scrolled through his messages until he found the one he was looking for. The last exchange was two days ago. He sent a new message. "Need more of the same. Same place. Same price?"

He waited for a second watching the three dots dancing as his supplier tapped out a response. Then "Mate, you're so fucking far away. 10% delivery surcharge."

Terry did some mental math, taking longer than it should, the sent back a thumbs up emoji.

Three dancing dots, then "See you in about an hour."

He tossed his phone on the sofa. "We're good." He grabbed a slice and a beer and headed to the pool. "Grab the rest of the pizza, Carol. We've got an hour before the Candyman shows."

"Your phone is vibrating."

He slowed his walk. "Who is it?"

"Number isn't in your contacts," she said.

"Bring it out to the pool. Don't answer it." He put his beer on the edge of the pool and pulled off his shirt, holding the piece of pizza in his mouth. Then he dropped his shorts and underpants and walked down the steps in the shallow end.

He was waist-deep in the cooling water when Carol stepped onto the back patio and tossed the phone to him. "Heads up."

"Huh? Shit." He jammed the rest of the pizza in his mouth and dove sideways, grabbing his phone before it hit the water. "Bitch."

Carol laughed and returned to the house. "Water must be really cold."

He lifted himself and sat on the edge of the pool. He had a mouthful of beer and looked around. "You bring out the pizza? Bring out the pizza!"

He looked at the missed call, took a breath and called it back. "Whadaya want?"

"You know that thing you wanted me to tell you about?"

"Pretty vague." Terry leaned back and closed his eyes. "Oh yeah."

"They found twelve of them. Including the one you're using now."

"The address is different," said Terry. "I've got a little time."

"I wouldn't bet on it."

Terry looked around at his surroundings. "Shame. I like this place." He cleared his throat. "Okay. I'll need new papers and a clean history."

"There's got to be an easier way to steal money. Parameters?"

Terry took a long draw on the beer and tossed the empty in the pool. "Same."

"You're out of months."

"January, the next year. Keep it rolling." He stood and walked naked back into the house. Carol was on her way out, a baggie of marijuana held between her thumb and index finger. He pointed her back into the house. "Same initials."

"That's how they found you. Change it up a bit more than that. Make it difficult."

Terry pulled the phone from his head and glared at the screen. "Fuck." He slapped it back to his ear. "Be like Nike, champ." He hung up and grabbed the baggie and called the number he had just texted.

"I'm on my way."

"Yeah, got a different question for you. How much cash can you get me for a hot BMW convertible, 80-series, and a Lexus LS500? Fire sale."

"Tonight?"

"Gotta be."

"So, I've got you over a barrel."

"Don't push your luck," warned Terry.

"Easy, now. sixty grand. I'll have to turn around."

"Sixty? This is over three hundred thou in car I'm talking about."

There was a long silence on the line. "Best I can do on short notice is ninety. And I'll have to turn around."

"It'll have to do." He put the baggie down. "Meet us at the Morisset train station. Bring someone to help drive the cars."

Carol opened her mouth to say something, and he held up his hand to stop her. "When will you be there?"

"Gotta turn around, find some friends to drive the cars, make it ninety minutes."

"Don't be late." He tossed the phone on the table. "Bug out time. Pack light. Take anything important." He grabbed a T-shirt and a pair of board shorts from his bedroom. Took his wallet off the dresser and his watch. "Fast, Carol." He headed to the garden shed.

"What do you mean?"

He stopped. "Which part? Pack? Fast?" He lifted two full 20-litre jerry cans from the shed and carried them into the house. "We don't have all night. Grab the keys for the Beemer and the Lex. We're taking them with us."

"When?"

He raised his eyebrows. "Now. Jesus. How many times do I have to tell you?" He unscrewed the top of one can and poured petrol down the hallway to the bedrooms. He saturated the carpet and bedding. "You want any clothes, you better get them now."

Carol watched him, shaking her head. "Fuck it. I'll buy more." She wrinkled her nose. "The landlady is going to be pissed."

"You have the car keys?"

She nodded and grabbed her phone and wallet. "I'm driving the Beemer." She tossed him the keys for the Lexus. "Morisset station?"

He threw them back. "Hang on to these until I'm finished."

He watched her leave out the front door. Poured more petrol in the kitchen and lounge room.

The second jerry can followed the first. The house stunk of petrol. He turned on the gas on the stove top and looked around. Ignition was going to be a trick. One spark now and he'd be instantly barbecued. He picked up one of the jerry cans and sloshed the fuel in the bottom. Should be enough.

He pulled a sheet out of the cupboard and unfolded it. Then he grabbed a tea towel and a couple of bottles of beer and walked out the front door, pulling the sheet behind him.

Carol was in the BMW, idling. She tossed the Lexus keys back at Terry.

He sidestepped them and held up the two bottles in one hand and the jerry can in the other. "How in the hell do you expect me to catch them? In my mouth?" He looked around on the ground until he spotted them. He put the jerry can down and pocketed the keys. He twisted the top off one bottle and poured the beer on the ground. Repeated it with the second bottle. He poured the remaining petrol in the two bottles and tore the tea towel in half, stuffing the halves in each of the beer bottles.

He looked over at Carol. "You have a light?"

She tossed a disposable lighter at him. He grabbed it out of the air. "You upset?"

"Tired of being uprooted like this."

Terry shrugged. "Not much longer. Getting close to my target." He picked up one of the bottles. "You should get out on the street. Wait for me though. If this goes wrong, I'm going to need a lift."

He waited until she pulled through the hedges. He flicked the lighter, looked at the Lexus, then extinguished the flame. He left the bottles standing, rags sticking out of their necks, and moved the car to the end of the drive.

He walked back to the bottles. The front door stood open, the king-sized sheet pulled halfway out of the house. He lit the rags in both bottles and underhanded them to the edge of the sheet. They broke on the pavement, spilling petrol onto the sheet. The burning tea towels lit the fuel, then the sheet. The flames licked up the cotton sheet and into the house.

He ran back to the Lexus and accelerated out of the drive. He pulled up beside Carol. "Morisset Station. Far end of the parking lot. Drive normally and when you get there, turn off the engine, leave the keys on top of the driver's side front wheel. Wait in the station. Buy a one-day ticket with cash. I'll meet you there."

"Where are you going?"

"I'm still fucking hungry. Picking up some of that shitty chicken. Want me to get you something?"

Carol wrinkled her nose. "No way."

There was a mighty WHOMP as the house exploded, brightening the sky. A shock wave hit them almost immediately, rocking their cars. Terry ducked. "That's our cue."

Chapter Six

The driveway was at least 400 metres long; 300 metres down a hill, a right turn for 50 metres, then a left for another 50 metres to the house. A stand of tall, mature pine trees lined the final 50 metres on the side of the driveway opposite the house.

Nick rolled down the gravel drive and parked his car behind a Mercedes, blocking it in. He got out and stretched. It was hot. He was in the Hills District northwest of Sydney. Miles from cooling ocean breezes. Bell birds pinged in the distance. The chimp-on-crack laugh of a kookaburra rang from the line of gum trees on the other side of the house.

He checked the list of registrations on his clipboard, a list of vehicles bought or leased by the phantom fraudster. None matched the car in front of him.

A slightly balding man strode out of the house, two young kids in his wake. "Can I help you?"

Nick looked down at his clipboard. The three photos Lucy had sourced were arrayed on top of the papers. He looked up at the approaching man. Chalk and cheese. No way this was the same guy.

He stuck out his hand. "Apologies for bothering you. My name is Nick Harding. I'm a Private Investigator. I'm trying to find a man named Terry Graves." He flipped the clipboard around to show the man the pictures. "He may be going by a different name, but with the same initials. He used this address in some of his transactions. Do you recognise him, or the name?"

"That's not me."

"I know that sir. Do you recognise any of the men in the photographs?"

He pointed at the photographs. "That's all the same man."

Nick nodded. "Correct. Would you know who it is?"

"Not a clue. Look, I've got to get my kids to school. I've got to ask you to leave now." He handed the clipboard back to Nick and unlocked his car.

Nick checked the date on the lease associated with this address. "Thanks for your help. Just one more quick question, did you move in here within the past eighteen months or so?"

"We've lived here since before my son was born, and he's eight."

"Thanks again for your help." Nick got in his car and backed out to a spur in the driveway at the first corner and turned the car around. He drove out and turned left as he exited onto the main road then pulled over to the shoulder. He typed the next address into his GPS. He saw the Mercedes leave the driveway in his rear-view mirror, turn left and pass him as the dad took the kids to school.

He finished entering the address and the GPS plotted the route. He sighed. An hour north and east. "Jesus."

Davie called when he was about halfway there.

"What's up?" asked Nick.

"Found a bit more about Gary. Not much there though. Poking and prodding the credit agency's network."

"Any luck with that poking and prodding?"

"It's pretty tight. But not impossible. I can access it with a bit of effort, but I'd leave traces. To get in and out without anyone but the very best knowing would be quite the challenge. Want me to start?"

"Oh, Jesus, no." He paused. "At least not yet." He changed lanes and passed a large dump truck struggling to make it up a hill. "Set up an account with them. Premium level. The kind that gets regular credit reports and alerts. Whatever the top end is. Keep the receipts. I'll reimburse you."

"Yeah, sure. Why?"

"Something might be useful later."

"No problem. Where are you?"

"On my way to the mid-north coast. The last of the many, many addresses this arsehole has used. It'll be as much of a dead end was every other one I've checked so far, but I've got to cross them off the list." Nick activated the cruise control. "Long drive, but an easy one. I'll be back later this afternoon. I'll give you a call then."

"Anything else you want me to do in the meantime?"

"Yeah. Take the list of names this arsehole used and dig through any other database you can think of. See if you can find any traces."

"Easy as. Talk to you later."

Nick pushed the button on his steering wheel and dropped the call.

Twenty minutes later Nick slowed as his GPS told him he was reaching his destination. Wyee was a small town, with one main road through its centre. He pulled to a stop in front of a house two streets off the main road. A rusted chain-link fence bordered a dilapidated single-storey wood-frame build-ing. One of the front windows was long broken and the space filled with weathered plywood.

He sighed as he got out of the car. The gate screamed against the rust. He stepped onto the cracked walk to the front of the house and stopped. No point even knocking. The house was falling down. Nobody had lived there for years.

He returned to his car and drove back to the main road. There was a small shopping plaza, an L-shaped building bracketing an adequate-sized parking lot. At one end was a bottle shop. At the other end, a pizza shop. Between them was a small grocery, a dry-cleaning shop, a coffee shop and a couple of vacant store fronts.

He walked into the pizza place. The smell reminded him of his university days. He made a lot of his spending money delivering. Back then his car permanently smelled of pizza.

The middle-aged woman behind the counter picked up a pen. "Good afternoon. What can I get you?"

"Hi. I'm Nick Harding. I'm a private investigator looking for this guy." He placed the credit report with a headshot stapled to the top corner on the counter by the cash register. "Your name is?"

"Lauren Haskill." She picked up the sheet of paper. "Terry Graves? Yeah, he comes in here all the time. What's this about. He kill someone?"

"I'm trying to track him down, for an inheritance." Nick smiled. A little lie, now and again, wasn't a crime.

Lauren's eyes brightened. "Oh, that's good news for him, then. He lives just up the road. The big house behind the really tall hedges, or shrubbery, or whatever it's called."

"Do you know if he lived there alone?"

Lauren furrowed her brow, concern or thought, Nick couldn't tell. "Yeah, there was a girlfriend. She came in with him a couple of times. She was tall, like you. Long blonde hair. She was thin, had a lot of ink." She pointed at her nose. "A ring in one of her nostrils. Right, I think."

"Do you know her name?"

"Carol...Carol Burkowski. Burzinski. Something like that." She shrugged. "Sorry, not that helpful. I only heard it once."

"You'd be surprised how a tiny seed of information can grow into something big. Thank you very much." He handed her a business card. "If anything else comes to mind. Thanks."

Nick drove in the direction Lauren had pointed. He navigated a large, banked corner around a stand of trees and slowed to a stop.

A tall row of juniper blocked the view of the house from the street, but Nick guessed the tendrils of smoke from the other side of them wasn't a good sign. A Highway Patrol car, lights flashing, blocked the road ahead, near the entrance to the driveway.

Nick pulled over and parked. He walked up to the driveway, nodding at the constables milling by the hood of the car. He angled to walk past them onto the property and was stopped by a very large arm.

"Pal, where do you think you're going?"

Nick looked down at the arm. Then at the name tag. "Good morning, Constable Arnold." He pulled his identification wallet from his back pocket. "Private investigator. I'm looking for a man who is supposed to be living here. Terry Graves." He slid the ID back into his back pocket and peered into the driveway. Only a small part of the house was visible. Or what was left of the house. It was a smouldering shell. Two Rural Fire Service trucks were standing by. He could see a couple of firemen walking around the perimeter of the house, looking for stray embers.

"Yeah, well there's nobody in there now. The place was empty when it went up."

"Do you know who was living there?"

Arnold dropped his arm. "The landlady just left. Mate, she was ropeable. The lease was in Terry Graves name. He was three months behind in his rent. She must have told me that a dozen times." He raised his eyebrows. "Def not getting his security deposit back."

Nick chuckled. "No bodies at all?"

"None."

"Accident?"

Constable Arnold shook his head. "More accelerant than the firies have seen in quite some time. Looks like the cooker gas was turned on, petrol splashed all over everything, then lit up. There were two 20-litre jerry cans melted in there."

Nick frowned. "Someone had practice."

"How do you figure?"

"It's a trick to light that up and not get caught in the fire."

"Some kind of fuse was used. The fire started out in the driveway. The arson investigator thinks it was a petrol drenched sheet. Couple of broken beer bottles on the drive, also."

"Ah," said Nick. "Molotov cocktails to start things off. There's nothing here for me, then."

Arnold cleared his throat. "What information do you have about this Graves fella?"

Nick looked back at his car. "Hang on a second." He retrieved the array of photographs with accompanying names, as well as the list of addresses, and brought them back. "This is the guy. He's in the wind, now. Somebody warned him." He held the sheets of paper up. "I'll give you these if you give me the landlady's details."

Arnold shrugged. "No problem." He extracted the small notepad from behind his Kevlar vest. He copied the information from one page to a clean one, ripped it out of the notebook and handed it to Nick. "She was very angry. If you tell her you're trying to track the guy who did this to her beautiful house, I'm sure she'll tell you anything you want to know."

He handed the cop the papers and grabbed the piece of paper. "Thanks."

He plugged the landlady's address into his GPS and was relieved to see it was only fifteen minutes away. He looked at the phone number on the piece of paper. "Well, I'm up here." He dialled.

"Good morning?"

Nick glanced at the paper. "Michelle Wilson?"

"Yeah, who's this?"

Nick let out a slow breath. "Nick Harding. I'm a private investigator trying to track down Terry Graves."

"How did you get my number?"

"One of the constables at your recently burned down house pointed me in your direction. Do you have a few minutes? I'd like to sit down with you and get any information you might have."

"Now?"

"I'm up here. If it's not too much trouble."

Nick heard a long sigh. "Yeah, why not. You find this shit, maybe I'll give you a cut of whatever I can extract from him."

"Not necessary."

"Where are you now?"

Nick looked at the tendrils of smoke rising above the tall hedge. "At the house."

"I'm at the bottle shop around the corner. There's a coffee shop right beside it. I'll text you the address."

Nick's phone chimed and he nodded. "I know the place. See you in a couple of minutes."

He sat in the parking lot for minute watching who he assumed was Michelle Wilson sitting at an outside table, a bundle of nervous energy. She picked up her cup twice and put it down without drinking. She checked her watch and looked around.

Nick approached the table. "Ms Wilson?"

"Michelle. Harding?"

He sat across from her. "Nick. Sorry about your house."

"It's insured." She shook her head. "I'm not going to be financially hurt by losing the house, itself. It's the rental revue that has dried up for however long it's going to take to rebuild and get it back on the market."

"You probably have insurance for that, too."

She waved that off. "Yeah, I've got to get past the arson investigation before any of that comes through. If you're ordering, you need to do it at the counter."

"Nothing for me."

"Okay. What do you want to know?"

"I've been engaged by a financial services company to track down Terry Graves, or whatever alias he's using now."

"Graves is his real name, though, right?"

Nick placed his file on the table. "No. Have a look."

She pulled it closer and opened it. "But his credit report came back almost perfect. Shit. I should have known it was too good to be true." She thumbed through the pages in his file. "Damn. Prolific. I'm almost impressed."

"He's got some contacts somewhere. Is there anything you can tell me about him?"

She held up Graves' credit report. "Identical to what I got. I don't think I can add anything."

"Was he with anyone? Any personal information not on these pieces of paper?"

Michelle pointed to the end of the shopping plaza they were in. Nick twisted to look. "He'd buy pizza there on the regular. Almost daily. You're going to have to hurry, or he'll be dead of a heart attack soon."

Nick made a note. "Anything else?"

"There was a girl living there. She wasn't on the lease, so they tried to hide it the couple of times I stopped by, but there were signs."

"Carol?"

"Don't even know what she looked like, let alone a name. Sorry I couldn't be more help."

Nick took the file and stood. "Nonsense. You've been a great help. Is this the only shopping option around here?"

"Unless you drive to Morisset. About ten minutes from here."

"Thanks again. And good luck." He handed her a business card. "If anything else comes to mind, give me a call, okay?"

Chapter Seven

Nick plugged Morisset into his GPS. She hadn't lied. It was a nine-minute drive, mostly north. It was a long shot, but since he was this far away from home, a little extra drive wouldn't hurt.

Morisset was a metropolis, compared to Wyee. Three sets of traffic lights, a KFC and McDonalds, and a decent sized train station.

Going door-to-door wasn't an option, and wouldn't produce anything, anyway. The house burned down last night. TG, whoever he was now, would be getting as far away as possible. He must have been warned that he was a target. Would have gotten rid of the cars, too.

And found a new ID.

He parked at the train station and took the three pictures to the ticket counter. He waited while the attendant finished a phone call and came to the counter.

"Where to?"

"Nowhere."

"Well, you're at the wrong place, hun."

Nick smiled. "I'm a private investigator looking for this man." He slid the photos across the counter.

She picked them up and scrutinised them, stopping at the one with the long greasy hair. "Yeah, I've seen this guy around. At the pub about a week ago. Started a fight with the bouncer. Lost. Bad." She slid them back and shrugged. "Can't tell you much more than that, though."

"Was he around here last night?"

"Wouldn't know, hun. My shift started at 6 this morning. After three days off. I can ask around, if you want." She held out a hand for the picture. "I'll make copies."

Nick slid the photos and his card back to her. "Thanks. Number's on the card. Call me any time."

She walked the slow walk of a government worker across the room to a copier. Took an interminable amount of time to arrange the photos on the platen before closing the lid and pressing the button to make a copy.

Then walked the same pace back to the window. "Here you go."

"Thanks for all your help." He took the photos back and returned to his car. Called Davie as he pulled out of the parking lot and pointed his car back to Sydney.

"Nicky, how's the trip going?"

"Not a total waste of time. I'll tell you more when I get back. My place in an hour or so?"

"I'll be there."

"Okay. So, what did you learn up north?"

"The deadbeat is a psycho." Nick turned on the kettle. "Where are you setting up?"

"I'm just going to hit the sofa again. This is going to get confusing."

Nick plugged his laptop into the docking station and started it up. The two monitors flashed to life. "What is?"

"Two cases, looking for two people." Davie sat on the sofa, leaned again the arm and swung his feet up.

"Mate. Shoes."

"No worries." He kicked them off and settled in, powering up his machine.

He looked at Davie, "Any luck breaching the credit agency?"

Davie waggled his hand. "Not breach. There are some weaknesses I could exploit but chose not to. It would take a lot of careful effort to get in and out without being noticed."

"So it's possible."

"It's also possible someone from the inside was helping."

Nick nodded. "Or both."

"Or both," agreed Davie. "You want to press on?"

Nick shook his head. "Shifting to the heir. You got anything yet?"

Davie sat up from the sofa. "Yet? I just bloody started." He grinned. "Check your email."

Nick scrolled past the spam the perpetually filled his in-box until he found Davie's email. He opened it and moved it to the largest of his monitors.

"Wow. Old Facebook posts, girlfriend's name, mobile phone number. This case will be over before it even gets started."

Davie swung his feet to the floor and left his laptop on the sofa. He stood behind Nick and crossed his arms. "Oh, you wouldn't believe how wrong you are."

Nick twisted and looked over his shoulder. "How's that?"

"Call the number."

Nick punched it into his phone.

Davie tapped him on the shoulder. "Put it on speaker."

"Hello?"

"Is this Gary Goulding?"

"Oh, for fuck's sake. Stop calling this number. There's no-body here by that name. Hasn't been for the fifteen years I've had it. Take me off whatever fucking list you have me on."

"Whoa, mate, apologies. I'm a private detective looking forb gyro Gary. He's obviously been giving out a fake number. Really sorry to have bothered you."

"You're blocked. Get fucked." The recipient of the call hung up.

Davie grinned. "I got almost exactly the same reception. Facebook hasn't been updated in over two years and the girl-friend is no more."

"She's dead?"

"Jesus, no. She's no longer his girlfriend. Any kind of friend. She hasn't talked to him in over two years. References some other bloke over the past three or four months." He waggled his hand. "On and off."

"Huh. She say why? He's not an ugly man."

"Ugly can go deep."

"Have you talked to her?"

Davie shook his head. "No luck reaching her, so far."

Nick scanned the email. "Do you have her phone number?"

"I would have had an actual voice conversation with her if I had her number."

Nick stood and pointed to the chair. "See if you can get a number for her."

"I can ask her. Don't know if she's online right now, or if she'll give it to me though."

"Come on man. Do your digital magic. See what you can find." Nick patted him on the shoulder. "I know you can do it. Want a beer?"

"Do I want a beer? Really? I thought you were a smart guy. Of course I want a beer. Get me a beer while I do some digital detecting."

Nick chuckled and twisted the top off a bottle. He grabbed a coaster from the kitchen counter and dropped it on his desk. "You're going to use this." He placed the bottle on the coaster.

Davie took a drink from the bottle and carefully, with more precision than was absolutely necessary, slowly placed the bottle dead-centre on the coaster. "You, my friend, have changed."

"That desk cost me almost a grand. Use the coaster."

"Yup." He opened Facebook and navigated to the old girlfriend's page. "This is Penny Larson. Let's see what we can find."

Nick crossed his arms. "Damn. Those are the greenest eyes I've ever seen."

"Probably contacts. They don't look real." He clicked the 'About' link. Nothing. "She has to accept my Friend request before I can see anything there."

"Dead end?"

"Not even close." Davie scrolled through Penny's pictures and stopped on one with her and an older woman. The caption linked to her mother, Lorraine Larson. Clicking on the link took him to her page.

"Mum's not as security savvy, it seems." He clicked on the 'About' link and was presented with a wealth of information. "Okay. Mum lives in Penrith, works at Flower Power and was born in February, 1966." He nodded approvingly. "She looks good for," he counted off on his fingers, "her age."

Nick chuckled. "You can dance through the web like Baryshnikov, but you can't do maths in your head." He rested his hands on Davie's shoulders. "Fifty-five, mate. What do ya got?"

Davie opened the online white pages and entered Lorraine Larson's name and suburb. There were no results returned.

"Strike one."

"Easy on, boss." Davie found the Flower Power in Penrith and called them. He put the call on speaker.

"*Flower Power Penrith. How can we help you?*"

"I'm looking for one of your employees. Lorraine Larson? Is she available?"

"*We're pretty busy right now. I can leave a message for her, if you want.*"

"Would you have her home number, you know, so I can call her after work when she's not so busy?"

Nick quietly chuckled.

"*Um, sorry, no. That's definitely against company policy. I'll leave a message for Lori, and she can call you back if she wants. Is this number okay?*"

Davie looked back at Nick who shook his head and pointed at himself.

"No," said Davie. He gave her Nick's number.

"*And what's it about?*"

"It's an inheritance issue. If you could ask her to call back as soon as possible, it would be very much appreciated."

"*Goodness, has she come into money?*"

"That's a matter for me to discuss with Ms Larson. Thanks for your time. Please pass on the message." Davie poked the 'End' button and sat back in his chair.

"That's it? Leave her a message and hope for the best?" Nick smiled. "I could have done that."

"Oh, you of little faith." Davie opened a new tab on the browser. "Give me a minute or ten. She's got a loyalty card of some sort."

"I'm going to grab some food. Want me to get you something?"

"Lamb gyro, if you could."

"A man of habit. Back in fifteen."

Nick walked into his apartment, bag of hot food in hand. Davie was standing in front of him, waving a piece of paper in his face.

"Took me five minutes."

Nick handed him the food and took the paper. "Have you called her?"

"That's for you, boss."

Nick looked at his watch. "Well, we know she's not home, so I'm not going to reach her now."

"We could head to Penrith and stake out the plant place."

"Waste of time." Nick took the bag back and retrieved his meal. "Get some food in you. We'll get back to the deadbeat after we eat. Nothing we can do with the heir until we talk to his ex-girlfriend's mother."

"True." He took the bag out and extracted the gyro. "Thanks for the grub."

Nick spread his chicken wrap out and picked out the onions, the rolled it up again.

Davie watched with a smile on his face. "You should have asked them not to put the onions on it." He took a big bite of his gyro, tzatziki dripping onto his hand. He grabbed a napkin. "Or you could just eat the onions. They're good for you."

"You're eating the bread. I thought there was this girl, or something."

Davie finished chewing and swallowed. "You know what the problem is with a low carb diet?"

"What's that, Davie?"

"No fucking carbs. I need carbs, I've discovered. And if she doesn't love me for all of me, well, her loss."

"You're talking love, now?"

Davie waggled his hand. "A little ahead of myself, granted. But I can hope, right?"

Nick wiped his hands and picked up the paper. "Let's leave her another message."

He picked up the phone and before he had a chance to dial Lorraine Larson, it rang with his mother's number.

"Hey, Ma. This is a pleasant surprise. We just talked."

"Your father is in the hospital. He's had a heart attack. Can you meet me at Royal North Shore?"

"Jesus, Mum? Is he okay?"

All he heard was three tones in his ear. She'd hung up.

Chapter Eight

Nick rushed through the doors to the Accident and Emergency Department of the Royal North Shore Hospital. It had taken him ten minutes to get there, but it felt like hours. His mother was pacing in the waiting room. "How is he?"

"He's in surgery. I'm told he's stable." She rested her hands on her son's arms. "He's going to be okay."

"What happened?"

"The only exercise your father gets is yelling at people. And his diet is terrible. He was on the phone yelling at someone and collapsed."

"Heart attack?"

"Yeah. Not a big one. I think a couple of stents will do it." She looked around. "It's been almost ten years since I've been here. Nothing has changed."

"Do you miss it?"

"Being a nurse? Yes. This place? Not so much." She walked to a chair at the back and sat, motioning her son to sit beside her. "How long can you stay?"

He sat and looked at her, puzzled. "As long as it takes. This takes priority over anything else." He took a breath and looked around. "How long is it going to take?"

"An hour, at most. The surgeon said she'd message me when he was heading to recovery."

"This isn't like open heart stuff, right?"

Susan shook her head. "Thank God, no. And hopefully this is enough of a wakeup call for him to make a couple of lifestyle changes."

Nick chuckled. "Don't hold your breath."

Ninety minutes later Nick followed his mother into recovery. Beds jutted from the walls, heads in, feet to the center. Curtains divided the beds providing the minimum amount of privacy possible. It was quiet. Only two of the eight beds were occupied. His father was in one of them.

The machines connected to him were beeping. The tube feeding oxygen to the nasal cannula was wrapped around his head. The head of the bed was elevated. His father's eyes were closed. To Nick he looked older and frailer than he'd ever seen him.

He looked at his mother, who nodded, then took a step closer to the bed. His father's eyes fluttered open. He looked confused for a couple of seconds.

"Pops. You bionic now?"

His father took a hesitant breath, then a deeper one. "You shouldn't have come."

"Take a deep breath, George. How are you feeling?"

George adjusted his legs and winced. "Shit, that hurts."

Nick pressed up against the bed. "What's wrong with your leg? I thought it was your heart."

George pulled the sheet to one side. A catheter sheath extended a couple of centimetres from the inside of his upper right thigh.

"Damn, that looks nasty." Nick leaned closer to look and his father whipped the sheet back over his leg.

"You're getting a bit too close there, son." He father had a half smile on his face. "That's where they went in to place the stent. Doc should be closing it up soon."

"How did this happen?"

"It was a mild heart attack, Nick. How do you think it happened?" He leaned back in the bed and took a deep breath. "Shouldn't you be out finding lost cats or spying on cheating husbands or something?"

"Jesus, dad. It's my business. I created it. I'm good at it. I've got two clients now, which I should probably get back to."

"Maybe you should."

Nick's mother put her hand on his arm. "Nicky, I'll see you in the waiting room, okay? I need to speak to your father for a minute."

Nick shook his head and left. He took a seat near the back of the waiting room and stretched out his legs. He slid his hands in his pocket and felt the piece of paper with Lorraine Larson's number on it. He checked the time. Dialled the number.

And got her voicemail, exhorting the caller to leave a message.

"Hey there, Mrs Lorraine Larson. I'm Nick Harding. I'm trying to track down Penny Larson, regarding an inheritance matter. If you could call me back at this number when you get the chance, I would appreciate it very much."

He slid the phone back in his pocket and it vibrated with an incoming call. "That was quick." He looked at the incoming number. "Davie."

"You don't have to sound so excited. How's your dad?"

Nick groaned. "He's going to live. The heart attack hasn't changed him a bit. Still a grumpy old shit." He adjusted in his plastic chair. "I think my mother thinks that it will force him into a lifestyle change. Maybe exercise a bit, eat better. Certainly isn't helping his mood."

"Give him some time. He only just almost died today. It's still early."

Nick looked around the waiting room. "You're a dick, Davie. Did you just call to see how I'm doing, or do you have something for me?"

"Nothing on the heir case..."

"I've left a message with the mother of the ex."

"That's a weird sentence. I think I've got a line on the other guy. The deadbeat guy. Maybe a mobile phone number."

76

"Maybe? It's a number or it's not a number."

"I've got a number. It's not disconnected, which is good, but it's going to a blind voicemail."

"Blind?"

"You know. Non-personalised greeting. 'You have reached the voice message system for zero-four-blah blah blah'. That kind of thing. Doesn't say who it is. I've left a message."

"Is it ringing out, or going direct to a message bank?" Nick saw his mother leave the recovery room and raised his hand to get her attention. "I've got to go. I'll give you a call later. See if you can find out where that phone is, okay?"

He hung up and stood as his mother arrived. "How is he, really?" He slipped her arm through his.

She smiled and patted his hand. "Unfortunately, it's like this brush with mortality hasn't changed him the slightest. He'll live. For a while longer."

"That's dark. How long is he in here?" They walked out, into the heat. The sliding doors cut off the cool air.

"The doctor was removing his catheter as I was leaving. He'll be home tomorrow. He'll be sore for a week or so and he has to take some time from work and relax."

Nick laughed. "He doesn't know the meaning of the word. Why in the hell doesn't he retire?"

"Your father's sense of self-worth is tied up in that law firm of his. I'm afraid he's going to die at his desk one of these days."

Terry peeled a couple of fifty-dollar notes off a roll and handed them to Carol. "Get us some food, okay? And some more beer." They were in a small motel room, beige carpet, orange bedspread, dark brown curtains. Lamps either side of the bed cast a dirty yellow glow.

She held up the two notes. "This all?"

"Pizza and beer for the two of us shouldn't cost more than fifty. Get a couple of pizzas. We're going to be holed up in this motel for a couple of days while the new ID bakes in."

"It never took that long before."

"It was always on my terms. Before. Had a comfortable overlap." Terry pulled the curtain aside and looked out in the parking lot. "Got blindsided this time." He took a deep breath. "Not sure what happened. Trying to sort it out." He let the curtain fall closed. "I don't know enough. And until I do, I can't risk showing my face. Grab the food and beer and get back here and we'll pop on a movie and do some coke, okay?"

Carol looked around the room. "Really couldn't find a better place than this?"

"They took cash, and didn't need ID. It'll have to do for now." He dug through the clothes on the floor until he found his phone. "Good beer, right? None of that Lite shit."

Carol saluted, mockingly, and left. Terry shook his head and turned on the phone. It buzzed with messages of missed calls and voicemails. He cleared them without listening or replying to the calls. He didn't know the numbers.

He dialled a number from memory. He paced while it rang out to voicemail. "Hey, it's me. You should have had an update for me by now. Where are my new papers? I needed them yesterday. Call me as soon as you get this."

He slammed the flip phone closed and threw it on the bed.

It rang almost immediately. "You got my stuff?"

"Soon. I've been trying to reach you. There's a private dick looking for you."

Terry sat hard on the bed. "You sure?"

"Bloke named Nick Harding."

Terry stretched out on the bed and crossed his legs. "I'll keep an eye for him. Thanks. Call me when the papers are ready."

"Same dead drop?"

Terry jumped out of the bed. "Oh, no, no, no. I need you to deliver them."

"That doesn't happen."

Terry chewed his thumbnail to the quick. Spat the nail on the carpet. "It has to. I'll pay more."

There was a sigh, followed by a long pause. "Double."

"Oh, hell no. Fifty percent more."

"Seventy-five percent. And I'm strongly against this."

Terry nodded. Bounced on the balls of his feet for a second. "Yeah. Okay. Last and only time. As fast as you can get here." He hung up the call and tossed the phone on the bed. "Son of a bitch."

He thought for a second, then grabbed his phone and googled Nick Harding. He scrolled through the photos from his time managing cases with the Financial Crimes Task Force, while he was with the AFP. There were links to a number of press releases discussing the dismantling of a Russian money laundering ring, a couple of links on a massive methamphetamine ring busted through financial irregularities, and a sex traffic ring exposed in similar ways. He found a couple of photos from his website and clicked through to the site itself.

As he scrolled through the site on his phone, his phone rang, startling him. "Jesus fuck, who the hell is this?"

Nick tapped the speaker button on his phone. "Is this Terry Graves? Or whatever name you're calling yourself now?"

"I asked first. Who is this and how did you get this number?"

Nick looked at Davie and smiled. He leaned close to the phone. "My name is Nick Harding, Terry. I've been engaged by the financial services company you've been defrauding to find you. And it looks like I found you." He looked over at Davie who was at his laptop, aggressively navigating the cellular company's switching system.

"Harding? Nick Harding? What a fucking coincidence. Did you quit the AFP, or did they fire you?"

Nick raised his eyebrows. "Neither here nor there, Terry. I'm flattered you've been researching me. But I'm intrigued that you know my name. Who told you I was looking for you?"

"Neither here nor there, Nicky. How much are you getting paid? I'll double it if you piss off and forget you ever heard my name."

"Come on, Terry. You know that's not how it works. *You'll* forget your name in a week or so. I mean, I'm assuming you're getting a new one set up as we speak. You've been doing this a long time, and successfully. Are you really good at hacking, or do you have someone inside the credit reporting agency?"

"You're in the city, right?"

"Neither here nor there, Terry. Or Tom. Or Todd." He scribbled a note for Davie. How much longer?

"Two minutes," whispered Davie. "But five is better."

Terry laughed over the phone line. *"You're in the city. Look, pal, you'll never find me. You're right. I'm getting new papers in a couple of hours, and I'll disappear into the crowd of legitimates. You're wasting your time, Harding. I hope they paid you in advance."*

Nick chuckled. "You under-estimate both my abilities and my persistence. Make it a bit of a challenge for me next time, okay?"

Terry hung up the phone and dropped it on the bed. "What an arrogant prick." He looked at the contents of his beer bottle, tossed it in the garbage.

Carol pushed open the door, pizza balanced on top of a flat of beer. "Who?"

"What?"

"The arrogant prick. Who are you calling an arrogant prick?"

Terry hauled himself off the bed and took the flat of beer from her. "Not your concern." He grabbed two bottles. He twisted the top off one and handed it to Carol. "Keep the change."

She scowled at him and grabbed the beer and sat in the cheap chair in the corner. "You're welcome for the pizza. There's no way in hell I'm going to last, holed up in here."

"Well," said Terry around a mouthful of pizza, "Have I got great news for you."

"What?"

"New ID should be here shortly. We'll be able to leave this dump."

There was a knock on the door. "Open up. It's me."

"Get the door, Carol. It's okay."

She pushed off the bed and opened the motel room door. She looked at the muscular man in front of her and frowned. "Who's this?"

"You can call me John Doe. JD for short." He had a buff envelope under his arm. "Tom." He proffered the envelope to Terry. "Your new life." He pulled it back a bit as Terry reached for it. "The money first."

Terry grumbled and unzipped a sports bag laying on the floor by the bed. He extracted three stacks of bills. "Fifteen. As agreed."

JD grabbed the stacks and handed over the envelope. "Pleasure doing business."

Terry slid the papers out of the envelope. "Don't go any-where." He grabbed a beer and tossed it underhand at JD. "Hang around a bit." He held up the NSW driver licence. It looked perfect, right down to the holographic coat of arms on the front face. It was scuffed up, like it had been in and out of a wallet for the past couple of years. "Troy Gibson? Troy? Jesus."

"You've got my hands tied with these stupid initials. Give me a bit of freedom."

"What about me?" asked Carol.

"What about you?"

"Do I get a new name?"

Terry laughed. "Why in the hell would you need a new name? Is anybody looking for you?"

"Well, you're getting a completely clean credit history, right?"

"That's not how it works." He took his old license out and compared it to the new one and nodded at JD. "You do a good job." He dropped the old licence and credit cards into the bin under the table and slid the credit cards and a Medicare card out of the envelope, all in Troy Gibson's name. "Limits?"

"All of them at 20k, low balance."

"Nice." He took the cards out of his wallet and added them to the old driver licence. "Time for a fire."

"Ease up there, Troy. Give your new plastic at least 48 hours to gel."

"I fucking hate that name. Why wait?"

"Rush job, right?" JD scratched his chin. "Takes about thirty-six hours for all of your credit info to propagate through the necessary reporting systems and organisations. Give it a couple of days to be on the safe side."

"Terry, I don't understand. What's going on?"

JD looked at Carol, then at Terry and frowned. "Is she good?"

"She's good."

"Nah, I mean it. Is she going to rat if you get caught? Because I can't get caught."

"Yeah, yeah. She's good. What in the hell do you mean, two days? We've got to get out of here tonight."

"You'll have to use cash. Right now, there's a 50/50 chance your credit and cards will trip an alert. That drops to zero percent in 48 hours. So wait, or use cash. And trust me when I tell you I'll take you down with me if I get caught."

He nodded at Carol. "Keep your mouth shut, sweetie." And he left.

"What a dickhead."

Terry waved at her to calm down. "Forget you ever saw him." He looked at the identification credentials and credit cards that were effectively useless for the next couple of days. He grabbed his phone. "Hey, one more thing."

"It'll cost," said JD.

"I know. Find me everything you can about Nick Harding. Who he is, where he is, what cases he's working on, everything."

"It'll really cost."

"Yeah, of course it will."

Nick pulled a chair over and sat beside Davie. "Did you find him?"

"You haven't told me how your father is."

"Mild myocardial infarction. Got a stent. Maybe two. He'll be out, garrulous and unrepentant tomorrow. Mum's going to have her hands full. No question he's going to be pre-scribed exercise and a better diet and he's going to buck that for all he's worth." He cleared his throat. "He'll be fine."

"That's good to hear."

"You find this Terry arsehole?"

"Somewhere in Parramatta. Can't really narrow it down. Too many bounces off the buildings."

Nick leaned back in thought. "He's backtracking."

"New IDs. He knows he's been busted. We've got a day or so. I need to track down the old guy's heir." He looked at the time. "It's getting late. I'll order some pizza."

"You just had a gyro."

"Thinking burns calories. What kind do you want?"

Nick shook his head. "Chicken wings. Hot." His phone rang. "You're going to have to hit the gym." He answered his phone. "Harding."

"Hi, Nick. Lucy here. The team would like a face-to-face update meeting tomorrow morning. 9:30. Can you make it?"

Nick scratched the back of his head. "Already? I'm not a big fan of micro-management, Lucy."

"Well," she sighed. "Well, neither am I. It can't be helped, though. There's a lot of management attention on this. This one person has caused more loss than any other ten in the company's history."

"Ten?"

"Estimate. Can you make it?"

"Do I need to present anything?"

"A verbal update is fine."

"Can I dial in to a conference bridge or something?"

"My bosses requested face-to-face."

"Face-to-face it will be, then. I'll see you tomorrow morning."

"Thanks."

Nick tossed the phone on his desk. "Needy people. I've got to meet the client tomorrow morning."

"TG, right? I heard you mention Lucy's name."

Nick leaned back in his chair. "Yeah. Micro-managing and crapping their compliance pants. I'll be there in the morning. Think you can get an address for the heir's ex before tomorrow morning?"

"Piece of piss."

Carol watched her boyfriend pace, his fists clenched, a terrible scowl on his face.

"I need to get rid of him." He looked around until he found his phone. "I need to end that smug punk today."

"Who?"

He ignored her and called the first number on his speed dial.

The recipient answered with a subdued voice. "Mate, can't talk right now. About to go into a meeting."

"Like I give a shit. I told you I need you to find out where this arsehole Nick Harding is, and where he'll be for every minute over the next 48 hours, and you haven't gotten back to me."

"Have you finally gone completely nuts? No way I can do that right now. And even if I could, I wouldn't. Don't call me again today."

"Son of a bitch." He looked at his phone. He looked at Carol. "How am I supposed to find this Nick guy?"

Carol crossed her arms and leaned against the wall. "He's the guy you talked to, right? The PI?"

"Yeah." He squeezed his phone. "I can't keep gaining unless I get rid of him."

"You've got his phone number. Any way you can track him with that?"

He grabbed the car keys. "You're smarter than you look. We've got to steal a truck."

Chapter Nine

The morning meeting was in the same room as the last time. Nick sat in the same seat, took one of the banana-walnut muffins and a cup of black coffee. He stood when Lucy and Catherine and Scott and Brad entered, and waited until they had taken their seats. Same seats as last time.

Lucy stood at the head of the table. "This will be a quick catch up. Thanks for agreeing to a face-to-face meeting, Nick. Communication is more than just words. Could you please provide us an update?"

Nick looked at each of the attendees, one at a time, taking his time. "Who called this meeting?"

Lucy slowly raised her hand.

"I don't mean who put it in the calendar for everyone to see. Who requested that we meet?"

Brad, the Director of Client Compliance held up his hand. "That would be me. I'm sure Lucy has expressed to you the broad seriousness of this — incident. It's not understating it to say the future of this organisation is held in your hands. A lot of this problem lies at my feet. I want to know all the details, all the time."

"Fair call." Nick sipped coffee. "Latest news for you. Your deadbeat, who went by the name Terry Graves up to the day before yesterday, has undoubtably acquired a new identity. The initials will undoubtably be TG. With a birthday undoubtably on the 12th of the month. Probably January since the last one was December. We know he's somewhere in Parramatta now, but I doubt he'll stay there long. His new identity will probably take effect tonight, based on how long I know it takes to propagate information through the usual financial systems."

"How do you know this? What's his new identity?" asked Catherine.

"Speculation based on the fact that he's just recently torched the house he was living in under the Terry Graves name. I suspect he's also sold whatever vehicles he may have leased under that name, extracted as much cash as he could from the credit cards, and has his contact setting up a new identity for him." He shook his head. "Couldn't hazard a guess what that new identity might be. You folks have any ideas on that?"

He looked at each of them in turn. Nobody opened their mouth.

He took a breath. "He's going to continue doing this until he gets caught. Actual, literal handcuffs on wrists caught. I will continue to work toward that end, and will keep you all current with the case though Lucy." He looked at the time on his phone. "Now if you'll excuse me, I need to meet someone."

Nick checked the message on his phone and confirmed his destination address. The last known address of Penny Larson, Gary's ex-girlfriend.

The street was in one of those recently slapped together neighbourhoods where the houses all look very similar, the driveways were filled with utes, and kid's toys littered the lawns. The last time Nick had been in this neck of the woods, over a decade ago, it was paddock, as far as the eyes could see.

GPS pointed him to a house on the corner of two indistinguishable streets. The driveway was empty. He placed a phone call. "You're positive about this address, Davie?"

"Absolutely. They moved in about four years ago. I can't find any more records of leases or purchases in all of Australia. It's either there, or overseas."

He knocked and rang the doorbell. The house felt empty. The ring on the doorbell camera was lit. He waved at it but got no response. He looked around. A curtain fluttered in the house across the street.

He smiled and walked across. The garden was almost as nice as at the house he just left. Regularly trimmed, with a flowerbed that looked like an English garden. He raised his hand to knock on the door and it opened.

A small, grey-haired woman with glasses hanging off a bronze chain around her neck looked up at him with a smile. "She's not home. Hasn't been for a week. I think she went to her mother's place."

Nick frowned. "You always this free with information to strangers?"

"You look like a nice boy. And I never get any visitors." She smiled. "And Penny hasn't had any boys over since that Gareth boy left."

"It's actually the Gareth boy I'm looking for." Nick took out his investigator's credentials. "My name is Nick Harding. It's an inheritance thing. You wouldn't know where he is, would you?"

"Come in and I'll make you some tea. I never get any visitors anymore."

Nick looked around. The neighbourhood was dead. He shrugged. "That would be nice. Thank you. I didn't get your name."

She stood to one side. "I'm Dora McLeod. My son bought me this place about five years ago. He and his lovely wife," she arched her eyebrows, "and delightful adult children," she shook her head, "bought a huge house less than five minutes from here. Promises of regular visits did not eventuate."

Nick entered a sitting room that had bookcases on three of the four walls. Stuffed bookcases. Hardcovers, mixed with paperbacks. Books lying flat across the top of those standing upright. Three stuffed chairs were placed in good light, with floor lamps as backup. He let out a low whistle. "I'd never leave this room. And who needs visitors when you have all of these friends to talk with?"

Dora smiled. "I knew I'd like you as soon as I saw you. Take a seat and I'll get you some tea."

"That's really not necessary, Dora. I only have a few questions."

"I insist. Sit."

Nick smiled, sighed and picked the chair opposite the one by the window. He picked a book off the table next to his chair. Lysistrata, by Aristophanes. He smiled and returned the book to the table as Dora returned with a tray of tea and shortbread biscuits.

"One of my favourites. Women letting men know who really rule the world." She sat at the window and pulled the curtain to one side and looked out the window. "Why are you looking for Gareth?"

Nick added a teaspoon of sugar and a drop of milk to his tea. "It's an inheritance thing. His father only has a few weeks, they've been estranged for over two years. He wants to patch things up and, I gather, leave him a healthy sum."

"Sad, to go that young. Gareth couldn't be more than thirty or forty."

"His father is late eighties. Gary was a late child."

Dora nodded. She looked out the window again. "I'm not sure how I can help. He hasn't lived here for more than a couple of years." She nodded out the window. "And it shows."

Nick took his tea to the window, looking for what she saw. "How do you mean?"

"That garden. It used to be beautiful." She looked up at him. "And it certainly wasn't Penny. Gareth spent hours working the ground. She tried, but frankly, she had a black thumb. And she freely admitted it. And he was happy to do it. It was his bliss."

Nick smiled and sat back in the chair. "It looks good to me, but I'm not the best judge. Why'd they split?"

"Oh, I couldn't say. That would be gossiping. You don't think I'm a gossip, do you?" She had a small smile on her face and Nick was sure he saw a twinkle in her eye.

"I think, Dora, that you're a very well-read, very observant resident in this neighbourhood. I'm sure you've formed an opinion."

She leaned forward. "The month or so before he left, they seemed strained. She would usually help out in the garden, they'd go grocery shopping together, a genuinely happy couple. But then..."

Nick also leaned forward, raising his eyebrows. "Yes?"

"They seemed to drift apart. One day a ute showed up, he threw a few bags in the back and whoever it was drove him away. He didn't show up again."

"She's okay, though?"

Dora nodded. "She seems to be. Her mother comes by more often. She goes there." She shrugged. "Like I said, I'm not sure how I can help you find Gareth."

"This is a nice neighbourhood. Is she showing any signs of financial problems?"

"Oh, I wouldn't pry." She looked out the window again. "But she gets a lawn care guy by regularly, has her gutters cleaned three or four times a year and doesn't seem to want for anything."

"No idea where Gary — Gareth — went?"

Dora shook her head. "I'm afraid not."

Nick smiled and took out two business cards. "When Penny gets back would you be able to give her one of these and let her know I'm looking for her?"

She hesitated, then took the cards. "No promises. The second card?"

"For you. If anything else comes to mind." Nick smiled. "Or if you need help opening a library."

Nick sat in his car for a minute, weighing options. He didn't have enough information. Usually, the combination of his intuition and Davie's electronic digging got them a lot closer to finding someone. He needed more information.

He glanced back at Dora's house. The curtain pulled back and she was watching. He gave her a smile and a wave and dialled a number. He pulled from the kerb as it started ringing.

"Lawrence Goulding's residence. William speaking."

"Good morning, William. Nick Harding."

"You've located Gary?"

"That's why I'm calling." Nick navigated his way out of the suburb and onto the main road back to Sydney. His GPS promised he'd be home in thirty minutes. "Can I talk to Lawrence? I'd like to pick his brains a bit more. Our first conversation was very brief."

"You also have a very thorough dossier."

"Thorough?" He snorted. "If all that was required to find Gary was the dossier, I'm sure you would have found him by now. Can I stop by and talk?"

"No." William paused. "But I'll put the phone on speaker for you."

The background noise changed. Nick could hear the faint noise of surf in the background.

"Nick Harding? Lawrence speaking. How are you progressing?"

"A lot of dead ends, I'm afraid. I'm still exploring avenues, but your son has done a remarkable job at becoming invisible."

"So, you're giving up." His voice quavered.

"Not even close. My colleague and I are still digging. I'm just looking for any additional morsels of information that could help."

"I don't have a lot of time." Lawrence wheezed out a cough. "Literally. *What more do you want to know?*"

"The file you've provided covers your son's adult life. Up to two years ago. And I've had some luck tracking down his former girlfriend, but it dead ends there. What can you tell me about his childhood?"

"How will that — never mind. I trust this isn't a waste of my time."

"I certainly hope not. Did he play sports?"

"Not well. He was a big lad, but very uncoordinated."

"He have any problems when he was younger? Before he got big?"

"I'm sure there was the odd scrape or two, but he was the biggest in his class since he was eleven." He coughed again. A wet and phlegmy cough. *"And the smartest. Always the smartest."*

"I understand he was great in the garden."

"That boy had ten green thumbs. A horticultural genius. It's like the plants talked to him." He sighed. *"I'm getting tired. I don't know if this helped, but I need to go. I really hope you succeed."*

"I hope so, too. One final thing. You didn't tell me why you're estranged."

"I think we're finished," said William.

"No, he should know." Lawrence coughed. *"We had a bit of a blow up. He started smoking marijuana and that led to some poor decisions. Life altering decisions."* He took a wheezy breath. *"Ironic, now that I'm partaking as a legal method of pain relief. Find him for me, please."*

Nick smiled. "Thanks. I'll keep you and William updated regularly." He hung up and moved into the turn lane. His stomach growled. He waited until the green arrow gave him permission to turn and accelerated into the intersection.

He saw the approaching ute, roo-bar glinting in the sun, just before it hit him.

It caught his car on the rear, left quarter-panel, spinning the front of his car to slam the side of the ute. His side and front airbags deployed, blocking his view of the truck driver.

Nicks ears were ringing, and he tasted blood. "Son of a bitch." The ute had stopped sideways, then straightened and accelerated away in a cloud of burning rubber. Nick got out and took a series of photos as it disappeared.

He took a deep, steadying breath. His hands shook. Occupants from other vehicles were coming over to check on him. He ignored them and walked to the kerb.

"You should sit, mate."

Nick glanced at the stranger. "I'm okay. Thanks." And he sat on the grass verge.

"I've got dashcam if you need it." He pointed at a plumber's ute that was behind him at the light.

Nick looked up at the bearded man. "That would be very useful. Thanks." He dug through his pockets and found a business card. "Could you email it to me?"

"Absolutely, mate." He took the card. "I'm Benny Kovac." He handed Nick one of his own cards. "Call me if you need to."

Nick nodded. "Thanks. I appreciate that." His phone vibrated. He had a new text message.

That was a warning, dickhead. Stop looking or the next one will really hurt.

Chapter Ten

"I thought you were going to kill him?"

He poured a 10 litre can of petrol into the cab and motioned her back to the car. "Unlucky. Get in the car." He lit a disposable lighter and underhanded it through the truck window. Walked back to the car while the truck lit up behind him.

He got behind the wheel. His phone rang. He looked at the incoming number and put the car in gear.

"You going to answer that?"

He shook his head. "Nothing to say to him."

Nick pressed his phone tight to his head, his other hand covering the opposite ear, trying to block traffic noise. The call rang out, with no voicemail. "Burner."

"Excuse me?"

Nick looked up from the grass. "It's nothing, Benny. Thanks for your help." He pulled himself to his feet. A police car, roof lights strobing, stopped in the intersection. Nick leaned against the traffic light stanchion and called Davie.

"How'd it go, boss? Any luck with the girlfriend?"

"I've just been run off the road, and then taunted by the guy who did it. I'm going to send you some photos of the arse end of the truck. They're kinda blurry. My adrenal gland was working overtime. See if you can make anything of it."

"Shit. You okay?"

"I'm vertical. My car is toast. Hey, the copper is coming over. I need to have a chat with her. Let me know what you find out."

"I reckon it was stolen."

"Facts first. Talk later." Nick pocketed his phone and took out his wallet.

As the constable arrived he handed her his driver licence. The name on the shirt was Evans. "Constable Evans, I'm Nick Harding. I believe I was targeted."

Evans looked at the driver licence and handed it back. She held up a breathalyser. "Count to ten for me, Mr Harding."

"Sure." He counted into the device and the constable stopped him at eight. "Okay, you're good. Tell me what happened."

While Nick repeated the story of getting tagged as he went through the green arrow, a tow truck arrived and started loading his car. "I should talk with that guy."

"You'll talk to me for a few more minutes. He isn't going anywhere." The constable poised a pen above her notebook. "Why do you think you were targeted?"

Nick opened his phone to the messages and showed Evans the one he received just after the crash. "Seems pretty obvious."

"Hold your phone still." Evans copied the number, and the time the message arrived, into her notepad. "What's your mobile number?"

Nick told her, then pocketed his phone.

"Obvious question, but you don't know this number?"

"No. And I called it. It rang out with no voicemail."

"Burner."

"I thought the same thing." Nick showed Benny's business card to Evans. "This guy was behind me. Got the whole thing on dash cam. He's going to send me a copy, but for chain of evidence you should reach out to him directly."

Evans took the card. "What do you do for a living?"

Nick handed her one of his cards. "Private investigator."

Evans grunted and stuck it in the back of her notepad. "I assume you're currently on a case looking for someone."

Nick nodded. "How much effort is the force going to put into finding out who did this?"

Evans looked at Nick for a long second. "No cameras at this intersection. You say you were targeted, but that would mean whoever did this would have had to have known you'd be at this intersection at this time. The dash cam might help, but don't hold your breath. I'll have a copy of the report sent to your email address, for the insurance company." She looked toward the tow truck. Nick's car was loaded. Fluid dripped from the battered chassis. "He's waiting for you."

Nick's Uber deposited him at his apartment building, a bit battered and now famished. He rated the driver five stars and limped into his apartment. His leg hurt more the longer he sat in one place. He pointed the key at the lock and the door opened before he touched it.

"You look like shit," said Davie. "You okay?"

Nick hobbled into his apartment and gingerly lowered himself into a chair. "Yeah, it's starting to hit me. Any luck with the ute?"

"Running the rego by some friends. I'll find something out later today." He frowned. "Anybody look at that cut above your right ear?"

Nick touched the side of his head. Winced and looked at the drying blood on his fingertips. "It looks worse than it is. I'm stiff and sore, but nothing serious."

"What in the hell happened?"

"Some jackhole tried to T-bone me. Then he sent me this text." He showed Davie his phone. "Do what you can with the phone number, okay?"

"Or she."

"Huh?"

"You have any scorned girlfriends looking for you?" asked Davie.

Nick chuckled and groaned. "Nah. We're all good." He tapped on the phone screen. "Someone really doesn't want me to find them. So now I really want to find that guy. Unfortunately, I don't know which guy it is who doesn't want me to find them." He stretched and groaned again. "I'm starving. Any pizza left?" He pushed himself out of the chair and limped to the kitchen. He put two slices on a paper plate and stuck them in the microwave.

"What's wrong with you?"

"I think I banged my leg."

"No, the pizza. It's better cold."

Nick opened the fridge and grabbed two beers. He tossed one to Davie. "Go see what you can find out about the number that sent me the text." The microwave beeped and he extracted the pizza. "And give me my phone back." He sat at the counter and twisted the top off his beer and downed half of it.

Davie scribbled the number on a pad and handed the phone back. "Don't hold your breath. It's probably a burner."

Nick grunted and scrolled through his mail. Nothing new. He opened the car insurance app. He entered as many details as he knew and ticked the box for a rental while his car was being repaired.

The pizza had cooled enough to eat. "Any luck? At all?"

"Patience, ass."

Nick sighed and shoved half a slice in his mouth, followed by a large amount of beer. When his mouth was at its fullest, his phone rang.

"Shit." He almost choked. "Nick Harding speaking."

"Hi, there. This is Hertz. You've just filed an insurance claim?"

Nick raised his eyebrows. "Wow. That was fast."

"Would you be dropping by to pick up your replacement vehicle, or would you like us to drop it off?"

"You wouldn't have any green cars, would you?"

"No, Mr Harding, none of that colour. We have white, silver, red and black."

Nick sighed. "No, not colour. Green as environmentally friendly. Hybrids or electric."

The agent chuckled. "Of course, Mr Harding. We have both. Do you have a preference?"

"I don't suppose you have any Dvorak convertibles, do you?" Nick closed his eyes and crossed his fingers. He'd worked for them for a couple of weeks, and they'd given him one to drive while he was on the case. It was too expensive for him to own, but even a week in one would be nice.

"Sorry, sir, no convertibles." Nick deflated. "But there is a sedan."

He smiled. "Would my insurance cover that as a replacement while my vehicle is being repaired?"

"Just, one second." Nick heard fingertips dance over the keyboard. "In fact, yes. You have very good coverage."

"Can you bring it by? I have no way to get there."

The agent confirmed Nick's address. "The car and paperwork will be there in fifteen minutes. Please ensure you have your driver licence ready."

Nick placed the phone on the counter and took another bite of pizza. Picked up his beer, looked at it, and set it back down. "I'm getting a Dvorak."

Davie looked up from his laptop. "Sorry, what was that?"

"Insurance is paying for a Dvorak while my car is getting fixed."

"Sweet. A convertible?"

Nick shook his head. "No. But I don't care. The sedan is nice." He grinned. "Nice bonus."

"When?"

"It's here in fifteen minutes." His phone rang again. "Hang on a second." He poked the green button. "Nick Harding speaking."

"Hello, Nick Harding. This is Dora. From earlier?"

"Mrs McLeod. Delightful to hear from you. What can I do for you?"

"Love, it's just Dora. Penny came home just after you left. I talked to her and tried to give her your card, but she wasn't having a bar of it. But she is home now. I thought you'd want to know."

Nick leaned back and looked at Davie. "Thank you, Dora. That's great news. Do me a favour and don't tell her I'm on my way."

Dora chuckled. "Your secret is safe with me."

"Thanks, Dora." He hung up and gently placed the phone on the counter. "Davie, I'm retracing my steps. Text me if you find out anything about that fucking truck."

That 'fucking truck' was a smouldering burnt out shell. Detective Sergeant Richard Wallace carefully stepped around the chassis, making sure to avoid touching the charred metal with any part of his extremely expensive bespoke suit.

His partner, Detective Senior Constable Elizabeth 'Liz' Lin, snorted. "Come on. Get in. The soot compliments the grey of that outrageously expensive suit." She pulled on a pair of latex gloves and looked in the passenger side window. "Not a lot left."

She took out her phone and photographed the VIN tag on the front dash. "Nothing much else here. Let's leave it for the techs."

Wallace stood in one place and looked up, slowly turning. They were in a small parking lot behind a group of small shops which formed a horseshoe shape around them.

"What are you looking for?"

"CCTV." He pointed at a couple of cameras. "You start at one end, and I'll start at the other. I want to see what they were driving when they left."

Chapter Eleven

Nick adjusted himself in the leather Recaro seat, smiled, and pushed the ignition button. The large screen on the centre console came alive showing the battery at 97%, a map centred on his apartment and a list of music streaming services to choose from. He paired his phone and started a playlist of old Rolling Stones classics.

He selected the address from the history on his phone and started driving.

Six months earlier he had worked for the owner of Dvorak Kars, Kirra Roach. She had hired him to sort out some financial irregularities, and in the process, he discovered who had killed her husband, the founder of Dvorak. During that period of time he had become very fond of driving their cars.

He settled in and pointed north-west. GPS promised a forty-minute drive. He smiled and planned a route that would take closer to an hour.

He parked in the same place as he had the day before. He waved at the curtain flutter in Dora's front window and walked up to Penny's door. The was a car in the driveway, so he was pretty sure she was still home. Nick glanced back at Dora's house. She was in the window, waving him on. He smiled and knocked on the door.

"I can see you, but I don't know you. Who are you?"

Nick took a step back and looked into the camera doorbell. He smiled and gave it a small wave. "My name is Nick Harding." He took out his laminated Commercial and Private Inquiry Agent card and held it up by the camera lens. "I'm a private investigator looking for Gareth Goulding."

"I've never heard of him."

Nick shook his head. "I'm pretty good at my job. I know you two were living together and, for whatever reason, he left you a bit more than two years ago. Look, I can assure you that this is only for his good."

"I've heard that before."

Nick sighed. "I feel kinda weird standing on your front step arguing about this. May I come in?"

He heard a grunt, and footsteps crossing the floor coming through the doorbell as she approached the door. It opened and a tall woman closed the doorbell app on her phone.

The eyes looked legitimately green in person. She was almost as tall as Nick, had brown hair in a ponytail and was decked out in exercise wear.

She crossed her arms and leaned on the doorjamb. "Okay, so I know Gary. I haven't seen him in years. And I haven't been looking for him. No idea where he is." She shifted a bit. "Why are you looking for him?"

"His father has maybe two weeks to live. He wants to reconcile."

Penny let out a slow breath. She nodded toward the interior. "Let's get off the step. We've given Dora enough ammo for weeks of intrigue."

Nick chuckled as he entered her home. "True. You know Dora well?"

A frown pinched Penny's face. "Everyone knows that old bird. She's the neighbourhood CCTV." She motioned Nick toward a chair in the lounge room and sat opposite him on the sofa. "How is Larry doing?"

He waggled his hand. "Not great. He's on oxygen. William, his business manager did most of the talking. Very advanced pancreatic cancer. It was implied he's only got weeks."

Penny's frown deepened. "Larry's a good guy. It broke his heart when Gary turned his back on him." She sat back and crossed her arms. "William is a snake."

Nick chuckled. "No comment on William. It was all 'Lawrence' and 'Gareth' when we met. Formal to the point of ridiculous."

The brow furrows deepened. "Are we talking about the same William? Beefy, tightly wound guy? He was his Business Manager?"

He nodded. "That's how he was described to me. What caused the split between father and son?"

She shook her head. "That's not my story to tell. If Larry wanted to tell you, he would have." She raised her eyebrows. "That said, it'll be a challenge to get Gary to agree."

"Okay. Why did you and Gary split up?"

"I can't see how that is any of your business, Nick. If you find Gary, maybe you can ask him."

Nick leaned back in his chair, getting comfortable. "I guess that's why I'm here, Penny." He had a small smile on his face. "You have a beautiful home, by the way. Although Dora tells me your garden has slipped since Gary left."

She finally smiled. "That old bird. Yeah. He's a whiz with plants. Loves them more than people." She sighed. "He's probably in the Blue Mountains somewhere."

"That narrows it down."

"His girlfriend, his new girlfriend, lives somewhere up there."

"Still not narrowing it down."

She sighed. "Okay. Give me a minute. I've got her address somewhere. Stay here." She disappeared into the back of the house.

Nick stood and wandered around the lounge room. There was nothing cheap on display. And nothing gaudy. Expensive understatement everywhere he looked. He smiled at the small piece of Aboriginal art she had hanging on the wall by her full bookcase.

She re-entered with a slip of paper and saw him examining the painting. "You like that?"

"It's beautiful. One of Kirra's, right?"

"Kirra Roach, yeah. You know art? I'm impressed."

"I know the artist." Nick sat back in his chair. "Any luck?"

She remained standing. "This is the latest address I have for the girl I believe he is currently dating." She handed him the paper. "Patty. This information is eighteen months old, so do with it what you will."

"Thanks." Nick stood and pointed at the painting. "You have very good taste. Do you mind if I ask what you do for a living?"

"I'm a business analyst. With a large accounting firm. Why?"

"I know how much a Kirra painting is worth. And some of the books on your bookshelf look like first editions."

"We're finished here, Nick. I've told you all I can. I hope you manage to give Larry peace, somehow."

Nick read the address as he walked back to his car. He smiled. Bilpin. At least another hour in the car. He waved at Dora's spying face as he got in the car and entered the address in the GPS. An hour and ten minutes. He silently pulled away from the kerb and spoke. "Hey, Siri, call Kirra."

It rang while he navigated his way out of the suburb onto the main road. She answered on the fourth ring. "Nick, Great to hear from you. How are you?"

"Delighted that you've answered. I would have thought your day job would keep you too busy to talk to peons like me."

She laughed. "I learned well from my late husband. I've delegated all but the really fun stuff down as far as I can. And thanks to you, I can rest easy knowing the governance in place helps keep the ship upright. What can I do for you?"

"What makes you think I want something?"

"You don't small talk well."

Nick chuckled. "I'm heading into the Blue Mountains in one of your beautiful cars having left a house of a woman who had one of your paintings hanging on her wall."

"Congratulations on your purchase. Are you liking it?"

"It's a rental while my car is getting repaired. I don't think I could afford one of these. Not yet. I'm calling to see if you could tell me what that painting is worth."

"A case?"

"Yes."

"What did it look like?"

Nick eased onto the freeway. "It's one of your smaller ones. About the size of a laptop. Hung landscape mode. Light blue background with an ever-widening spiral of alternating white and indigo dots starting in the lower left quadrant."

"That's an excellent description. I remember it well. I sold it at my gallery about eighteen months ago for about twelve thousand."

"Holy shit."

She laughed. "It would be worth about double that now. She made a great investment."

"I'm not sure I understand how she afforded it in the first place. Thank you very much for your time, Kirra."

"Don't be so formal. You and Davie need to come by for dinner one of these evenings."

"I'll give you a call. It was great talking with you."

"We got the last of them." Wallace grabbed his laptop and motioned for Lin to follow him into a meeting room at the station. He plugged an HDMI cable into the port on the side and projected on a large monitor. "With the two I got, and the one you found, we've got a measly thirty seconds of vision before the truck is engulfed."

"Ten seconds, times three. We're going to watch mine first."

"Let's watch all three together. Three different angles." Wallace arranged three windows on the laptop screen. Larger versions appeared on the monitor. He started them and they watched as the black truck pulled to a stop. There was noticeable damage to the large chrome bumper. A fender of a follow car appeared on one video, its back bumper on the other two. A man jumped out of the truck, retrieved a 10-litre fuel can from the truck bed and poured petrol into the cab. He lit a lighter and underhanded it into the cab, then ran off screen. Seconds later the edges of the car disappeared from view as the truck was engulfed in flames.

Lin pushed back from the table. "Would have been nice to see the car he took off in."

Wallace scrubbed back one of the videos and froze it on a front on view of the truck driver's face. Screen grabbed the face and sent it to the printer. "Not the owner of the truck." He brought up the driver licence of the man listed as the registered owner of the truck. "Doesn't look anything like him."

The screen grab was Terry Graves, a greasy-haired, overweight white man in his fifties. The picture on the driver licence was a large man with a bald head, from somewhere in the South Pacific.

"We should probably have a chat with Mr Jerome Sosa."

Chapter Twelve

"I found the truck."

Nick slowed before the onramp to the freeway. "Where?"

"Not the truck, but the owner," corrected Davie.

"Got it. Where?"

Davie gave him an address in Parramatta.

"Excellent. That's on my way. What's the owner's name?"

"Hang on a second." Nick heard Davie rustle through papers. "Okay. It's Jerome Sosa. Probably goes by Jerry. I'll text you his number."

"How do you get all this information, Davie?"

"Do you want plausible deniability?"

Nick shook his head. "Are you still at my place?"

"You have better internet."

"Then plausible deniability is a dream. You're doing whatever you're doing on my IP address. Doesn't matter. Just don't tell me how you're doing this." He pulled over to the shoulder and entered the address. "I'm going to Bilbin after this. And thanks again. I couldn't do this without you."

"Tor."

"What?"

"I'll show you sometime. Plausible deniability still exists."

Nick chuckled. "Of course it does." He hung up, checked traffic, and accelerated onto the freeway.

The truck was in the evidence garage and Wallace and Lin were harassing the evidence techs about what they had.

"Nothing, really. The fire did a good job of wiping out any forensics. There was a lot of petrol involved."

Wallace squatted and peered at the roo-bar. Paint flecks were ground into the chrome bar. "You saw this, right?"

The tech grabbed tweezers and a small glassine bag. "Let me look." She picked a few samples off the chrome and stopped them in the bag. "Not sure what this will tell us. Make and model of car this thing rammed, but not much else."

Lin took out her phone and scrolled through her photos until she reached the screen grab from the plumber's dash cam. "We know the make and model." She held out her phone. "We're looking for the person driving it."

"Did you check with the owner? You've got the VIN, right?"

"It wasn't the owner. Maybe a friend. That's our next stop. Let us know if you find anything." Lin got in the passenger's seat of the unmarked car; Wallace got behind the wheel.

It was a shorter drive than Nick preferred in the electric car. He stopped in front of the address Davie had sent him. It was a neat little bungalow in a neighbourhood full of neat little bungalows. The yard had a fence around it, with a little gate off the driveway onto a short walk to the front steps.

Nick scanned for dogs. It was that kind of neighbourhood, where dogs were used as advance doorbells. Sometimes they bit, sometimes they didn't. No point tempting fate.

He knocked on the door. No camera doorbell on this house. There were toys in the yard, though, and the lawn was freshly mowed. Somebody was home.

And he heard that somebody walking across a wood floor, approaching the door.

The inside door opened and a large man with a gleaming, bald pate scowled at him through the screen door. "What?"

"Jerome Sosa?"

"Who's asking?"

Nick smiled his most disarming smile and showed him his identification. "Nick Harding. I'm a private investigator. Do you own a black Toyota ute, big roo-bar on the front?"

"Do you see one in the driveway?"

"Could be in the shop."

"It's not." He sighed. "It was just stolen. I've reported it to the police. Why? What's this about?"

Nick showed him a screen grab from the plumber's dash cam. It was grabbed just before impact. "This it?"

"Oh, Jesus." He opened the screen door. "Come in. Come in." He ushered Nick into a small kitchen. "Coffee?"

"No, Jerome, I'm good."

"It's Jerry. That, uh, that accident you showed me. Was anybody hurt?"

Nick showed him the cut above his right ear. "Not seriously. You reported the theft?"

"Yeah." He rubbed his hand on the back of his head. "I was an idiot. Left the keys in it at the servo. Whoever grabbed it, got it with a full tank."

Nick opened the notes app on his phone. "Which servo? Did they have CCTV?"

"The one just up the road. I don't know about the cameras. The police called and said they'd be here to talk to me," Jerry looked at his watch, "in about ten minutes. You can ask them when they get here." He looked concerned. "You're okay, though?"

"A little rattled."

"And the truck?"

"Better shape than my car. Your truck drove away. My car is being reconstructed from a pile of metal." Nick closed the app on his phone. "Thanks for talking to me." He placed a card on the table. "If you think of anything else, give me a call, okay?"

Jerry nodded as he picked up the card. "Really sorry, mate. I'm not sure how my insurance works if the vehicle was stolen. I'll call them and let you know."

"No need. It's been handled. I have another appointment. I've got to run. Don't leave your keys in the truck when you get fuel, hey?"

"Yeah. You're not going to wait for the police?"

"We try to run in separate circles. Natural antagonists. Thanks for your time."

Nick retraced his steps back to the car. Wallace and Lin pulled in behind him.

"Oh, Jesus. If it isn't the private dick." Lin closed the door to the unmarked police car. "What brings you here?"

"Thought I'd have a chat with the guy who owned the truck that T-boned me."

Wallace leaned against the police car. "We just found this guy. How did you find him?"

"My techs are better than your techs, maybe?" Nick smiled and opened his car door. "You'll find the guy doesn't know anything. But do enjoy yourselves." He got in, closed the door and started the car. He rolled down the window and waved at them as he slowly pulled from the kerb. The servo was a block and a half away, directly in front of him. He needed them in the house before he reached his next potential source of information. He glanced in the rear-view mirror a couple of times, then stopped at the intersection with a very fresh amber traffic light. The taxi behind him laid on the horn. He grinned and waited for the light to turn green, and then another couple of seconds, before pulling away. The cops were in Jerry's house now.

The man behind the counter at the service station was Sikh, with a name tag that read Hardeep Singh. Nick held out his private investigator identification. "Good afternoon, Hardeep. My name is Nick."

Hardeep read the ID, then looked past Nick. "I've got a couple of customers. Let me help them and I'll be right with you."

"No worries."

Nick waited, eyeing the box of glazed donuts by the register and fighting an internal war with himself, finally coming to an agreement with himself they would be his reward if he ever figured out the two cases he was working.

Hardeep motioned him over. "Mr Harding, how may I help you?"

"It's Nick. Please. Were you working the day the black ute was stolen?"

Hardeep smiled. "Forgive me for laughing, but yes. That man, his name is Jerry I think, was ropeable. He was paying for his fuel. Had just paid, actually, when someone jumped in and drove it away."

Nick shook his head. "That would be rough. I noticed cameras over the pumps. Have the police collected the CCTV yet?"

"No, and I'm not surprised. The police have more important things to worry about."

Nick cleared his throat. "Any chance I can get a copy of it?" He held up his hands. "No pressure. Whoever stole that truck used it to drive me off the road, then sent me a mocking text message. Really would like to track that bastard down."

Hardeep raised his eyebrows. "I'm pretty sure I can't give you the footage. But do you have a mobile phone?"

"What?"

"Of course you do. Everyone has one. You could record me playing the video, right?"

Nick slid his phone out of his back pocket. "Nothing personal, Hardeep, but I won't be recording you. I'll be recording the video."

Hardeep chuckled. "Of course. I'm going to let you behind the counter. Don't steal any cigarettes, okay?"

"Deal."

Nick sat in the car and shortened the video down to the clip where the person who stole the truck got out of a mid-sized sedan and into the truck. He selected the clip and sent it to Davie, then called him.

"I just sent you a video. Do your thing, okay? Someone gets out of a car and steals the truck."

"You want a cleaned up face and info on the car?"

"You read my mind. I'm now going to Bilpin. Not sure what mobile coverage is like. Text me when you find something out."

"You are paying me, right?"

"We should open up shop together. We make a great team."

"How much are you paying me?"

"I'll buy dinner tonight." He entered the Bilbin address. "Thanks again."

The police car pulled into the spot to his right. He rolled down his window. "Hey, Lin. Fancy running into you again. And here."

"Detective Sergeant Lin, to you." She exited the car. Wallace got out the driver's side. "I sincerely hope you haven't removed the video. That would be obstruction of justice." She leaned down and looked in the car window. "PI work pays better than I thought it did. Nice."

Nick chuckled. "Wouldn't think of stepping on your toes, Detective Sergeant. Hardeep has what you need. Still a bit confused about why two detectives of your stature in the force feel the need to chase down a stolen truck. Seems beneath you." He started rolling up his window. "See you around, Lin."

He backed out of the spot and gave Wallace and Lin a wave. They seemed pissed off. That was icing on his cake of a day.

"That guy is getting on my nerves." Lin slammed the car door shut. "One step ahead of us on this, every turn we make."

"Let's do something about it."

They flashed their badges at Hardeep and showed him the photo. "This guy look familiar?"

Hardeep looked at the picture for a second, then glanced out the window at Nick's departing car. "Yeah. As a matter of fact." He took them around behind the counter. Pointed out the surveillance system. "It's already queued up. You're not the first person in here looking for it."

"Don't remind me," said Lin. She handed him a thumb drive. "Can you copy the relevant footage to this, or are we going to need a warrant?"

"No warrant needed. The guy who just left recorded it on his phone. No reason not to give you a copy." He took the thumb drive and inserted it correctly the first time. He tapped a couple of keys, waited a second, then handed the drive back. "Haven't seen a theft like that before." Hardeep smiled. "Wouldn't have been fun if it happened to me, but since it didn't happen to me, I find it kind of amusing." He turned the monitor so they could see. He tapped the spacebar and their target got out of a mid-sized sedan, glanced at the interior of the station and pull open the door of the truck. The car pulled out of the frame, the truck started and pulled out of the station as the very large owner ran out after him.

"Did you laugh in front of Mr Sosa?"

Hardeep was blank for a second. "Oh, the truck owner. Of course not. I may work at a servo, but I'm not an idiot. He would have pulled my arms off and beat me to death with them. But he's not here now, and I will smile. Comedy is pain, usually someone else's, viewed from the distance of time. Most times. Generally, the less the pain, the shorter the time required."

Lin held up the thumb drive. "All of that's been copied to this?"

"It has." He moved the monitor back to its original position. "Is there anything else?" He still had a smile on his face.

Wallace showed Hardeep the picture again. "He's never been around here before?"

"Fortunately, no. Sounds like an unpleasant person, hitting that poor Mr Harding, then texting him to mock him."

"He what now?"

Hardeep nodded at Lin. "Mr Harding told me he got a text mocking him right after he got hit."

"Did he tell you what it said?" asked Wallace.

Hardeep shook his head. "Sorry, no."

"Thanks, you've been very helpful." He pointed at Hardeep. "You might want to get your face under control before Mr Sosa comes back, though."

Lin led the way back to their car. "You've still got Harding's card, right?"

"I had Harding's card?"

"That thing with the dead billionaire a few months back. Thought he gave you a card."

Wallace shrugged. "If I do, it's back at the station. Doesn't matter, though. His number is on his website. We'll run it as soon as we get back."

Chapter Thirteen

The car handled the winding round into the Blue Mountains better than any ride Nick had ever driven. He rolled down all the windows, bathing in the fresh smell of pine trees and eucalyptus. Traffic was light. He pushed the car as hard as he dared on the winding road, exhilarating in the silence, tempered by the sounds of wheels on road and singing birds.

As he got closer to his destination small fruit stands started appearing on the side of the road, until he reached the giant one he assumed marked the beginning of the actual town of Bilpin.

He followed his GPS's instructions until he reached a large house on an even larger plot of land, maybe 5 hectares. The driveway was a good two hundred metres long, straight off the main road. Nick noticed security cameras in the pine trees lining the driveway.

He waved at the nearest camera as he got out of the car. Bell birds were pinging in the distance. A pair of lorikeets flew by his head and perched in the gum tree. "Beautiful neighbourhood."

A woman he assumed to be Patty stepped out on the front porch, drying her hands with a tea towel. "It certainly is. Who are you and why are you on my property?"

"Good afternoon. I'm a Private Investigator. Nick Harding. I've been engaged by Lawrence Goulding to find his son, Gareth."

"And you think I know Gareth?"

Nick sighed and looked at his watch. "I've come a long way, Patty. Let's stop the dance. His father is dying and wants to achieve some degree of reconciliation before he passes away." He chewed the inside of his cheek. "Wouldn't you want to patch things up with a kid before you died?"

She threw the tea towel over her shoulder and nodded for him to follow her in.

Nick stepped into the house and let out a low whistle. "I've been transported to the '70s." The centrepiece of the lounge room was an open-hearth fireplace, the grate large enough to handle metre long logs. A two-tiered wrought iron wood rack was filled with split iron bark on the top and pine kindling on the bottom.

In front of fireplace, at a comfortable distance, was a vintage fabric sofa, the four legs ankle deep in a rusty orange shag carpet. A pair of matching chairs flanked the sofa forming a partial arc around a Formica coffee table stacked with horticultural magazines and pamphlets for a fruit and vegetable orchard.

Beaded curtains separated the lounge room from what looked to Nick like a dining room filled with oak slab furniture. Patty sat in one of the chairs and motioned for Nick to sit in the other.

"Interesting decorating choices. I don't think I was born when this sofa was made."

"This is my grandparent's house. It was left to me when my grandmother died. I've tried to keep the place as vintage as possible. Tell me about Larry."

Nick leaned forward and rested his elbows on his knees. "Just so we're clear, you know where I can reach Gareth?"

Patty shook her head. "Gareth? I don't anybody who calls him that. Yes, I know where Gary is. But he doesn't live here. We split a couple of months ago. And no, I'm not going to tell you where he lives now. I'll pass on your message, and if he wants to talk to that old piece of crap he'll reach out. But I doubt it will happen."

"I'm sorry, but I keep getting the message they'll never reconcile, and nobody will tell me why. What happened?"

Patty sat back and considered Nick for a moment. "Tea?"

"Sure." He followed her to the kitchen. "When is Gary home?"

She looked puzzled. "I just told you, he doesn't live here. And even if he did, which he doesn't, it's harvest time and they keep him pretty busy." Patty filled a kettle and put it on the stove.

"Call him. I need to get the message to him."

Patty leaned against the counter and crossed her arms. "I told you I would. Later. After you've left." She shrugged. "Can't call him now, anyway. No mobile phones while working." She poured water into the ceramic teapot and took a couple of cups out of the cupboard. "Milk and sugar?"

Nick placed one of his business cards on the counter beside the teapot. "Give this to him. Ask him to call me, please. I think I'll pass on the tea. Thanks anyway."

"Come on, let's get out of here." Carol watched her boyfriend pace. "There are motels we can stay in that don't need ID, right? I know we got cash."

He stopped. "Why?"

She chewed on her thumbnail. "That guy made me nervous. I don't want him coming back on me."

Terry scoffed. "I've known him since I was a kid. You're good." He nodded. "But I don't disagree."

"Go settle the bill and I'll get our stuff together."

Terry laughed. "Yeah, right. Take only what is important to you or identifies you. We'll get new stuff later. You really think I'd pay for the privilege of staying at this dump?" He grabbed his phone and did a quick scan around the room. Checked and made sure the new licence and credit cards were in his wallet.

Carol grabbed a bit more. She had a small leather pack. Stuffed her makeup and a few other personal items in it. Swung it over her shoulder. "I'm ready. Where are we going?"

"Another place like this," he held up his hand to stop her complaint. "Just for a day, until the cards are clear. Closer into the city. So when they are clear we move into the city." He smiled. "Like that?"

"We're going to settle down soon, right? Jumping around is getting old."

"Almost there." He opened the door and peered out. "Let's go."

"I just got the results from our warrant on Harding's phone." Lin dropped a sheet of paper on Wallace's desk. "Interesting number sent him a text right around the time he was T-boned. Ran it and it's a burner. A pre-pay picked up at a service station on the Mid-North coast about two weeks ago. Before you ask, no GPS, so tracking it is going to require another warrant."

Wallace poked a button on his desk phone, releasing the dial tone. "Let's call it." He poked in the numbers and listened to the ring.

Terry's phone started ringing as he got in the car. He slipped it out of his back pocket and tossed it in the centre console.

"You should answer that."

"I don't answer that phone unless it's someone I've already called and that's not a number I recognise." He pushed a button on the phone and sent it to voicemail. "You know that. Are you expecting a call from someone I should know about?" He glared at her. "Well?"

"No, no, hun." She rested her hand on his arm. "Just the two of us." He pulled out of the parking lot and merged onto the highway. "North Ryde, okay? Close enough to the city."

His phone started ringing again.

"Okay, someone knows this number who shouldn't." He opened the car window as they were passing a large dump truck and threw the phone under its wheels.

"Hey, it might just have been a wrong number."

He shrugged. "Doesn't matter. Phones are cheap. I'll get another one."

"Not surprised he didn't answer," said Lin.

"Doesn't matter. The network will have recorded which sites the phone responded to. We'll get a rough idea where he is." Wallace scribbled the number on a sheet of paper. "I'll put in the request for a more detailed warrant on this number. All locations recorded from the time it was registered. Two weeks, right?"

"Sixteen days. In the past."

He looked up at her and smiled. "Lin, if you know how we could trace the movements of suspects sixteen days into the future, well, you're going to turn police work on its head."

"You know what I mean. We'll know where he's been. We won't know where he is. But it's better than nothing. Past is prologue. Should give us an idea where he might be now."

"With any luck."

Terry, now almost Troy, stopped at a service station and bought a new pre-pay phone. They asked for his ID. He showed them the Troy Gibson driver licence. The clerk had handwritten the information on a form. It would be days, if ever, before it was entered into any digital system. He should be fine.

Carol had her face buried in her phone when he returned. "I found a place."

Terry was sending texts to the three contacts who needed to know his new number. "A what?"

"Motel. Near the Uni." She pulled her head out of the small screen and looked at him with a big smile. "It's got a pool. Same price as the one in Parramatta."

"The one in Parramatta was almost free. And I've got to set up things. I'm not going to have time for the pool. Jesus."

"They must have a new guy on. This was fast." Wallace took the call log from Lin. It listed all of the numbers called and received. Beside each number was a list of the cell sites used and an approximate location.

"New lady. She sent it through almost immediately after she received it." She took the log back. "Most of the calls were placed or received in Wyee. You know Wyee?"

He shook his head. "How do you?"

"Got an uncle up there. Has a nursery providing roses for most of the flower shops around here. Good business." She looked at her watch. "We've still got time today to get there."

Lin pulled their car to a stop in front of the pizza place at the only plaza in Wyee.

"Christ, that was a drive." Wallace got out and stretched. He sniffed the air. "I don't smell the city."

Lin wrinkled her nose. "Hint of something burning, though. I'll start at the pizza place, you start at the bottle shop, we'll meet in the middle." She handed Wallace a print of the man's photo.

Wallace headed to the liquor store, flapping his suit jacket in the heat, and Lin stepped into the air conditioned cool of the pizza parlour. Half a dozen customers sat, in pairs, all of them stopped and watching Lin approach the counter.

The woman behind the counter smiled at her. "Hi there. I'm Lauren. What can I get for you?"

Lin slid the photo onto the counter. "Good afternoon. I'm DSC Lin. We're looking for this man. We have information he may have been in this area. Have you seen him before?"

Lauren picked up the picture, looked at it and handed it back. "Yeah. Terry Graves. Used to live in the big house around the corner. Until it burned down."

"That's what I smell outside. Did he own the house?"

Lauren shook her head. "I don't think so. I'm pretty sure he was leasing the place."

Lin flipped open her notebook. "I've got a couple of questions, if you've got a minute."

The guy behind the counter at the liquor store was completely unhelpful. Wallace didn't push it. There were four other shops to hit. He pushed through the hanging vertical plastic slats at the entrance to the small grocery store next to the liquor store. Immediately to his right was a cooler with a glass front, filled with drums of different flavoured ice creams. Immediately beside that was the cash register, an older middle eastern man piloting the till. Beyond that was a deli display with a couple of customers waiting for an older woman to select which slices of ham she wanted. The woman behind the deli counter looked like she was the man's wife. An immigrant couple keeping the residents of Wyee fed.

Wallace showed the man behind the counter the photo. "I'm DS Wallace. Looking for this guy. I understand he's been around here."

One of the waiting deli customers looked over at the photo and broke out of line. "Yeah. That's the son of a bitch who burned down my house." She clenched her fist, obliterating her grocery list.

Wallace nodded at the man behind the register in thanks and moved out of the way, leading the woman with him. "What's your name?"

"Michelle Wilson. This prick, Terry Graves he called himself, burned my house down."

The customers in the store started to gather.

Wallace guided her gently by the arm outside. "Is there somewhere around here we can talk? Somewhere a little more private?"

"Buy me a skinny latte and I'll sit with you." She led him to the small cafe and sat at an outside table.

"Uh, right." He ordered her drink and joined her back at the table. He noticed Lin leaving the pizza place and waved her over. He sat across from Michelle and used his foot to kick out a chair on the third side of the table for his partner.

"Michelle Wilson, this is DSC Lin. Lin, Ms Wilson owns the building Graves used to live in…"

"…that he burnt down. Got it. Did he leave a forwarding address?"

Michelle looked puzzled. "I already told this to that PI, what's his name, Harding. No forwarding address. And he was behind in his rent." The barista delivered her coffee. "I'm pretty sure there's nothing more I can tell you."

Lin had a mapping app open on her phone. "That's a big house. He lived there by himself?"

"There was a woman there also." Michelle pointed an index finger. "I don't know her name. Someone else around here might now." She sipped her coffee. "If you find that guy, would you let me have five minutes alone with him in a room?"

Lin chuckled. "I'm beginning to think there might be a queue."

"Would you have a copy of the lease?" Wallace held up his phone. "Need a picture of Graves' pertinent details. DOB, Emergency Contact, that sort of thing."

"Are you kidding? No. It's in the office." She thought a moment. "But if you have an email address I can get someone in my office send it to you."

Chapter Fourteen

Wallace and Lin walked back to their car. Wallace had a copy of the lease in his email, and the results of the latest warrant on Graves' phone. "We're going to Parramatta." He entered the location in his phone. "Looks like a shit hole motel."

Lin put the car in gear and left the small shopping plaza. "Put it in the GPS for me, would you?"

The first part of the trip was on autopilot. Up Wyee Road past the smouldering embers of the recently torched house, then left and onto the freeway back to the city.

Wallace swung the onboard laptop in its pedestal toward him and accessed the department databases. He opened the attachment to the email and scrolled to the personal details of the lease. He entered Terry Graves' name and date of birth.

"Finding anything?"

"No priors. Checking some other things." He tapped the keyboard a couple of times. "Driver Licence is less than twelve months old." He tapped a couple more keys. "There's no occupation listed against his Tax File Number, and it appears there never was."

He spun the laptop back, the screen facing Lin. "Who is he now?"

"Who says he still isn't Graves?"

He shook his head. "He isn't."

Nick sat in the car scrolling through fruit nurseries and orchards on his phone until he found the nursery with a logo matching the pamphlets he saw on Patty's coffee table. He entered the address in the car satnav and changed the display to the satellite view. The nursery was roughly a 30-hectare area peppered with long, rectangular greenhouses. At the far end of the property, farthest from the gate, was a large, sprawling house.

The property was at a curve on the road, nestled into the corner. A driveway off the road on the short side of the property led to a gate. One of the long sides of the nursery ran parallel to the road.

He entered the address into the GPS and headed north. The trip took seven minutes. It was a small town.

The gate was barricaded with a padlocked chain. A 'No Trespassing' sign shared space with 'CCTV in Use' and "Beware of the DOG" signs.

"More than one way to skin a cat."

He continued down the main road, turning the corner and driving parallel to the long side of the property. In the gaps in the bush along the side of the road Nick could see a three-strand barbed-wire fence running along the property line. He pulled over to the shoulder at one of the larger gaps and got out of the car.

Through the scrub trees he could see rows of green-houses, side on. They were long half tubes, the top of the arch about two metres above a half-metre tall base, and 30 metres long. There was a door at each end. Nick could count six of them side by side and at least ten of them end to end. Off to his right, through the gaps, he could see the large ranch-style house with motorcycles, and a dirty brown van parked out front.

He pulled the top and middle strand of barbed-wire apart and slipped through the gap, careful not to snag his shirt. He stood and listened for voices, or footsteps or wheels of any kind. All he could hear was birds, and a shit tonne of them.

He angled his approach to the end of the nearest green-house, keeping it between him and the house. A wooden door and doorframe, providing no security, just protection from the elements, was unlocked. He stepped through the door into a warm, humid garden. The plants were on two tiers. Tomatoes were on a shelf about chest height, on either side of the centre aisle. The fruit was still green, but the strong smell of the vine was unmistakeable.

Unmistakeable, but second to the strong, sweet smell of marijuana. Tall plants starting at the ground level stretched up through and around the tomato vines. "Son of a bitch."

He stood in the middle of the greenhouse and slowly turned. He pulled a leaf off one of the tall plants and slowly rolled it between his thumb and forefinger, crushing it. He sniffed the resulting oil on his fingers. "Son. Of. A. Bitch."

He opened the door at the other end a crack and peered out. It was clear. The next greenhouse in line was only three metres in front of him. He darted across the gap and into the next one. It was the same layout. Tomatoes and weed. Nick pulled his phone out of his back pocket and scrolled to Davie's number and dialled. He got three tones. No service.

"That's not going to work here."

Nick spun around. A tall, bearded man, and a stocky woman, both dressed in khakis and navy blue shirts displaying the nursery logo were standing in front of him.

"We got jammers," continued the man. "That thing's useless."

The woman held out her hand. "Give it."

"I think not," said Nick. "Who the hell do you think you are?"

The woman slowly walked closer, looking up at the taller Nick. "Gloria."

"What?"

"I'm Gloria. That there is Charlie. Gimme the phone."

"Piss off."

Gloria was standing directly in front of Nick now. "Don't say I didn't warn you."

Nick chuckled and opened his mouth to say something witty in response when her fist lashed out and caught him in the throat.

Charlie laughed. Nick staggered backward holding his throat, trying to catch his breath.

"She fookin' tagged ya, mate." Charlie danced with delight. "Tagged ya." His face rapidly turned serious. "Ya better gives her the mobile, mate."

"Piss off," rasped Nick. He lashed out with a foot and caught Gloria on the kneecap. She let out a wail and Charlie's face darkened.

"Bad mistake, laddie." Charlie helped Gloria to her feet and moved her behind him. Nick back-pedalled as Charlie advanced. "Ya should never hit a girl."

"She fucking jabbed me in the throat," he rasped. "What did you expect me to do?"

"Give her your phone."

Nick's back was against the door. "What are you, security? I just want to talk to Gary Goulding."

"The boss man isn't taking visitors today. By appointment only." Charlie held his meaty hand out and wiggled his fingers. "Yer phone."

"What's the point, if it doesn't work here?"

Charlie paused for a second, trapped in thought. "Stop asking questions." He swung a fist the size of a loaf of bread at Nick's head.

Nick scrambled backwards and fell out the door onto the mud. He crabbed walked away as Charlie bore down on him.

"Ease up. I'll leave. Tell Gary I'm looking for him." He scrambled to his feet and leaned against the next greenhouse in line. "I'll leave the way I came in. Okay?"

Charlie pulled a gun from the small of his back, cocked it and held it to Nick's head. "Maybe we just use ya fer fertiliser."

The door opened beside him, and Gary walked through. Nick recognised him from the picture in the file. He was balder, and his beard had grown out, but it was him.

Gary held up his hand and stopped Charlie. "No need for heat, Charlie. Take Gloria to the house and get her knee iced."

"But – "

"Charlie." Gary spoke to him like he was chastising a naughty pre-teen. He turned his attention to Nick. "You're trespassing."

"You're a hard man to find." Nick peered in the door of the greenhouse he just left. "And I think I can understand why. There's like a quarter mill of product in each one of these. There's upward of fifteen million in weed here."

"Don't downplay the tomatoes," said Gary. He smiled at the look on Nick's face. "Seriously. A couple mill from them, too. And they legitimise my operations." He sighed. "I don't want to be found. I am both impressed and annoyed you tracked me down. How did you find me?"

"Breadcrumbs. An old picture from a swimming carnival leads to your ex, Penny Larson. A chat with the delightful

Penny points me to Patty and a brochure on Patty's coffee table led me here."

"That was it?"

"Took a bit more than a day."

"Damn."

Nick extracted a business card and gave it to Gary. "I'm good at what I do."

Gary examined the card, flicking the edge of it with his thumb. "Why?"

"Why what? Why am I good at what I do?"

"I'm re-evaluating my opinion of your intelligence. Why are you looking for me?"

Nick nodded. "Right. Your father hired me to find you."

"Get the fuck out. Go the way you came and if I see you back on my property, I'll let Charlie remove each of your limbs one at a time, and let Gloria beat you to death with them."

Nick held his hands up. "Easy on. No need for that."

"Then piss off."

"He's dying."

"None too soon."

"He wants to reconcile, and I've been led to believe there's an inheritance."

Gary snorted. "I don't need the money. Look around you."

"I got the impression your father was more concerned about the reconciliation than the money."

Gary shook his head. "I find that very hard to believe. It was a very irrevocable split."

"If you don't mind me asking, what happened between the two of you?"

"I killed his wife. My mother."

Chapter Fifteen

Gary raised an eyebrow, watching Nick rub his throat. "You okay?"

"Still trying to process that statement."

Gary laughed. "No, your throat." He tilted his head and looked under Nick's chin. "There's a bruise building. Charlie do that?"

Nick shook his head. "Gloria. What do you mean, you killed your mother?"

Gary sighed. "It's not what you think." He checked his watch. "Ah, what the fuck. I'm getting some food. Join me?"

"You're a very strange person." Nick looked at the pot plants surrounding them. "Why not? I have so many questions."

"It's a bit of a walk. I'll give you a lift." He led Nick through the greenhouse he had just left, and out the other end. A high-end electric golf cart was parked in the path between the greenhouses.

"You're very well set up here." He climbed in the passenger side.

Gary grunted and accelerated, bouncing over the dirt track to the driveway, then to the house. He parked the golf cart in front of the large house at the back end of the property. Nick followed him into the house. It was a double brick construction, immediately cooler when he entered the foyer.

"Nice place. Pot pays well."

"You going to narc on me?"

"Not my concern. I was hired to find you, which I've done."

Gary shook his head. "Still a little freaked out at how easy it was for you to do that, by the way. I stay way under the radar."

"And to mediate a reconciliation with your father."

"Good luck." He sat at a small table and motioned for Nick to join him. "I hope you like tomatoes."

"My favourite fruit." Nick slowly took his seat. "I'd really like to hear the story about your mother."

"We eat first."

A young guy placed a low-walled porcelain dish on a cutting board in the middle of the table. Nick's reservation at eating an all-tomato meal vanished as the smell hit his nose. "What is this?"

"Chicken, prosciutto, basil, some mozzarella, and of course, cherry tomatoes. Dig in."

Nick served the prosciutto wrapped chicken onto his ceramic plate.

"Beer?" Gary twisted the top off a bottle and handed it to him.

"Since you put it like that. Tell me about your mother."

"Eat first."

Half a dozen kids were screaming in the shallow end of the pool. The chlorine smell was especially strong. "You really like this?" Terry, almost Troy, shook his head. "We've got lovely beaches an hour's drive from here."

"You won't go, though." Carol was in a swimsuit, stretched out on a chaise lounge beside the motel pool in North Ryde. Mothers with small children looked at her, and her numerous tattoos, with disdain and moved the kids away from her.

"Too much sand. You know how to drive." He dug the car keys out of his pocket and dropped them on her stomach.

She looked over her sunglasses at them, then up at her boyfriend. "A hot car? You think I'm crazy?"

"Then stay here. I'm getting fucking buggy."

"We've been here maybe three hours."

"And I don't like it." He paced the pool deck, a few steps in each direction. "This was a mistake. This place is too – " he struggled for the word, "suburban. We stick out like shit in a punch bowl. We need to get out of here."

"Listen, hun. Your pacing is what's making you stick out. Sit down. Relax. Ditching this joint before we even get bed use would raise even more eyebrows. Don't you think?"

"First thing tomorrow, we're out of here." He lowered his voice. "Should be fully Troy by then. Fuck, I hate that name."

Nick pushed back his plate and finished the beer. "Compliments to the chef."

Gary smiled and pointed at his chest with both index fingers. "It's good, right?"

"Your mother?"

Gary took a deep breath and slowly let it out. "How is this going to help you?"

"Just trying to understand why. Your father is not well and seems to have a genuine need to get the relationship with you back on track, for whatever little time he has left." He shrugged. "Plus, there's the money."

"Look around, Nick. I'm doing okay. I don't need his money."

"He has a lot of money. What's the deal? What did he do?"

"The unexpurgated version?"

Nick nodded. "The best version."

"I killed my mother. Or so he says. And his inability to accept what actually happened has put him on the wrong side of me for the rest of his miserable life."

"Sounds like there's some expurgating going on."

Gary sighed and twisted the top off another bottle. "Ten years ago. I - I let my brother drive my car. My mother was in the front passenger seat, and I was stretched across the backseat." He waggled his hand. "I may have given my brother a taste of the herb," he held up an index finger, "but I didn't think he was impaired. Not even a buzz. It wouldn't have made a difference, anyway. We were heading north out of Windsor, on that windy bit of road near Wheeny Creek, when an oncoming truck veered across the centreline. Apparently, he'd fallen asleep. My brother had a choice — a head on collision that would have guaranteed a forensic team would be tweezing our remains out of the wreckage for weeks, or drive the car off the road."

"You're in one piece, so you obviously went off road."

"Through the guardrail, into a tree, then rolled down an embankment."

Nick leaned forward. "Through the guardrail?"

"It must have already been damaged. It was a rock wall on the other side of the road. That would have been as bad as a head-on." Gary took a breath and rubbed his face. "I walked away from the car without a scratch. My mother died instantly when a large branch went through the windscreen and then her chest. My father blamed — blames — me for, in his words, getting my brother stoned. Wouldn't listen to my story then, and I have no interest in repeating it now."

Gary leaned back in his chair in thought. Nick let him stew while they both nursed their beers. Then something occurred to him.

"You have a brother?"

Gary raised his eyebrows. "Tom? Yeah. An older brother by ten years." He frowned. "He survived the accident but received a bad head injury. TBI."

"Traumatic brain injury? Where is Tom now?"

Gary shrugged. "No clue. He went off the rails about five years ago. Headed out west, I think. Maybe Darwin. No question it was a result of his brain injury. I'd help if he came to me and asked, but nobody has heard from him in years." He grabbed his beer and stood. "And now you've pissed me off. So, thank you for sharing a meal with me and get the fuck out of here." He smiled. "Before I let Gloria loose on you again."

"Can I get a lift back to my car?"

Garry narrowed his eyes. "Make your own way back." He looked at his watch. "I'll give you five minutes before I let people know you're not invited."

Nick pushed his chair back from the table. "Thanks for the food. And the beer. I need to piss."

"Make sure you do it off my property. You better hurry."

Nick stepped out of the house and oriented himself, then pointed to the east. "My car is that way, right?" And he set off at a brisk walk.

He dug his phone out of his pocket and tried to make a call while he wended his way through the greenhouses. No signal until he reached the property line. "Hey, William. I need to meet your boss. Face-to-face."

"When?"

"Right bloody now."

"How far away are you?"

"Be there in an hour."

"Just around the next corner." Wallace pointed. They were in Parramatta. It had been a long drive.

"I know," said Lin. "GPS."

"Right." Wallace's phone chimed. He read the alert and scowled. "Keep driving. Back to the station."

"What's up?"

"Unclear. But it's flagged urgent."

An alert flashed on the laptop screen. "We're here. Like literally 100 metres away." Lin grimaced and pulled a U-turn and stomped on the accelerator.

"We'll be back." He looked at the time. "Tomorrow."

Chapter Sixteen

The car silently rolled to a stop outside of Lawrence's, or Larry's, as Nick now thought of him, house. William was standing at the door, eyeing the car as Nick parked it.

"Nice upgrade."

"Someone tried to kill me. They didn't succeed. My car took the brunt of it. This is a hire car while mine gets fixed. I need to talk to Larry. And is there a place I can plug this in? It's getting low."

"He prefers Lawrence. You've made progress?"

"Nothing personal, Billy, but I'll tell Larry. Not you. Where do I plug this in?"

"Get the cord. There's an outlet here."

Nick collected the charging cable and handed it to William. "Where's the old guy?"

William grunted and opened the door. "He's out back, getting some sun. Skin cancer really isn't on the top of his list of concerns anymore."

Nick pulled a chair up beside Lawrence's wheelchair. "Good evening, Larry. How you feeling?"

Lawrence pulled his oxygen mask off, hung it on the arm of his chair and looked at Nick with a steely glint. "It's Lawrence. Never Larry." He adjusted himself in his chair, wincing. "You must have news about my son, or you wouldn't waste your time driving out here."

"News about your son?"

"Well, yeah."

"You have two sons. Tell me about Tom."

Lawrence's face darkened. "There's nothing to talk about." He took a deep breath in through his nose, and let it out with a deep, rumbling cough. He wiped his mouth. "You don't know of what you speak." He coughed again. "Maybe this was a mistake." He put the oxygen mask back on his face.

"Gary told me about the car accident." Nick watched the waves cresting off the sandbanks. Seagulls banked off the air currents and dipped toward the water. Nick sniffed. "He seems pretty intransigent. He's living his best life, he says. Doesn't need your money. He's doing well enough on his own, and he'd like to keep it that way."

Lawrence sat in silence, watching the waves. He took a deep breath from the mask and lifted it off. "What's the boy up to?"

"He has a very successful tomato farm in the Blue Mountains." Nick chuckled. "Very successful."

"Good for him." He frowned. "That's hard work though. And not really the kind of money I'm talking about."

"He's been supplementing it with a, um, secondary product." Nick smiled. "A very lucrative secondary product."

Lawrence turned and realisation slowly dawned on his face. "Well. Not surprising considering." He nodded. "Actually, pretty smart. It'll be legal here soon enough. Good to get ahead of the curve, anticipating the market." He cocked his head. "How large is his nursery?"

"Very." He looked back at the waves. "Tell me about Tom."

Lawrence groaned and put the mask back on his face. He shook his head.

"Gary told me Tom was driving and survived the accident." He glanced at the old man. Still staring straight ahead. "Had a knock on the head but survived."

"No," he struggled to remove the mask so he could talk. "No. He didn't survive. My Thomas died in that car. The person who came out of the hospital after an eight-hour surgery and an induced coma was not my son."

William appeared like a wraith, his hands on the back of Lawrence's wheelchair. "Mr Harding, I think perhaps you should leave, now."

"Your boss and I were just getting to the interesting parts. Give us a couple of minutes."

Lawrence shook his head and pulled the mask back on.

"I think my boss is finished with this conversation."

Nick nodded. "Lawrence, I'll go back to Gary and see if I can convince him to talk with you, at the very least."

The old man dismissed him with a casual wave.

William followed Nick to the door. The charging cable was curled on the table next to the door. He handed it to Nick and opened the door. "I overheard you've located Gareth?"

"Gary? Yeah. Thanks for the interruption. I was just getting him to open up about Thomas. Or Tom, as the rest of the world calls him."

"I wouldn't worry about him. Where is Gary?"

"Up in the hills. Thanks for the charge." He paused before he got in the car. "Do you know where Tom is?"

"How would I possibly know where Tom is?"

Nick got in the car and watched William walk back to the house. He started the car and paired his phone. Scrolled through recent calls until he found Lucy, then called.

"Lucy speaking. Is this Nick?"

"I thought I'd give you an update. It's been taking longer than I hoped, but I am making progress."

"He's been that elusive? He's better than I thought he would be."

Nick grimaced. "I'll be up front. I'm working two cases right now; your deadbeat and the heir of a man on death's door. I've got Davie working the electronic search for the deadbeat, and he's really good at that and making great progress, while I've been working the time-sensitive heir case."

"I can't say I'm delighted by this, but I understand." Lucy sighed. "How much longer on the heir case?"

"The good news is I've found him. Gary Goulding. His father – "

"Lawrence. I'd heard he wasn't well. He banks with us. So you're finished that one then?"

Nick took a breath. "Essentially, yes. The son doesn't want to meet the father, but I've found him, and that's what was asked of me. I'm 100% on your deadbeat now. My call after this is with Davie to prep for a full-court press tomorrow morning. He's found a tonne of breadcrumbs. We'll have him shortly."

"Thanks for the call. Thanks for the update. Please keep me across everything that's happening."

"Absolutely. I'll call you late tomorrow." Nick terminated the call and sat back in the car seat. "Some days this job is just like being back in the office."

He reached for the gearshift and his phone rang. "Harding."

"Nickie, lad, this is DS Wallace. How are you doing?"

"You catch up yet?" Nick chuckled. "You're chasing my tail, aren't you? And I'm older than you. Lad."

"Do me a favour and hold the gloating, okay? We'd love to see you at the station tomorrow to compare notes. This guy is bad news. I'm worried for your safety."

"You're worried for your reputation." Nick paused. "Send me the address. I'll see you around 10."

Terry tapped his watch. A stupid action, since it was digital. He didn't want to wait the full forty-eight hours. He leaned back in the poolside chair and looked up at the underneath of the large patio umbrella providing him shade. "Tory. Tory. Tory. I'm Tory Gibson. Tory motherfucking Gibson."

Carol lifted her sunglasses and looked over at him. "Are you okay, hun?"

"I'm very uncomfortable here. I'm not going to be able to wait out this timeframe my guy is trying to keep me to. It's killing me."

His phone rang.

"That's your new phone."

Troy looked at the number. "Yeah. It's someone I know." He answered. "What?"

"Nice to talk to you too. Don't be a dick. I'm calling with information you might find useful."

"Okay, okay. What is it?"

"A private dick has tracked down your brother."

Chapter Seventeen

Nick had just left the beach house when his phone rang. "Davie, how's it rolling?"

"Where have you been? It's getting late. That car still have a charge?"

"Yeah, I'm at," Nick looked at the centre console display, "26%. That fuck William didn't plug me in. I'm on my way home. Have you had any luck sussing out who or where Terry is?"

"This is way worse than trying to find a needle in a haystack. This is a haystack with dozens of needles in it, and you're never sure which needle is the right one. Or if there are more. He definitely has inside help. I've tried getting into the credit reporting databases and they are impenetrable. To me, anyway. And if he's better than me at this shit, then there'd be much better ways to make money."

"Thanks. It was worth a shot."

"I'm not finished. Since this is internal to that company, I thought I'd do some digging in their less secure areas. I've got a trap on every person in the credit determination area, IT and governance. All of their emails are copied to my machine. I'll keep an eye on what comes through and let you know if I find anything."

"Watch your back."

"Don't worry," laughed Davie. "I'm invisible to them. I'm closing down for the night. I'll give you a call in the morning."

"After 10."

"Sleeping in?"

"Stopping by to talk with Wallace and Lin about the truck that smashed into me."

"It was stolen."

"Yeah. And maybe they can tell me who stole it."

"Wallace? Fat fucking chance. Good luck."

Terry was now fully Troy. Time didn't matter. He was good at this deception. He had to be to survive. He had a Medicare card, a NSW driver licence and a credit history in Troy Gibson's name of a quality that would be the envy of anyone.

And he needed a drink.

"Let's go." He grabbed his phone and wallet. Carol stayed in the chair by the motel room TV. "You coming?"

"I liked that house in Wyee."

"We'll find a better one. Come on. I need a beer. And a steak."

Carol groaned and pushed herself out of the chair. "Not too late. I'm beat." She pulled her T-shirt away from her chest. "I think I got too much sun." She grabbed her phone. "Where are we going?"

"Into the city."

"Jesus. That's an hour from here. It'll be time to come back as soon as we get there."

"We're not coming back here. I checked in as Terry. Terry is dead." He shook his head. "We're blowing this place. I need to hide in a crowd. Take what you need because we are absolutely not coming back to this fucking soccer mum hellhole."

Terry and Carol walked into a pub on Harrington Street in downtown Sydney. It was full and noisy and smelled of beer and Lynx body spray. He smiled. "I missed shit like this." He grabbed a table. "What do you want?"

"Chicken parm and some white Zin."

"Grab a table and I'll order."

Terry pushed to the counter and wedged himself between a tall biker and an old guy. He nudged the old guy aside to get closer.

"Get fucked, kid."

Terry looked at the old guy and grinned quizzically. "What the hell, old man?"

The bikie leaned forward. "You okay, Glen?"

"I can take the punk." Glen gave Terry a shove, catching him off guard. Terry stumbled backward into the bikie who grabbed him by the shoulders and shoved him back toward Glen.

Terry let the momentum of the shove work for him and swung a fist at Glen. The old guy bobbed out of the way and countered with a short jab to the gut.

He doubled over, then straightened with an uppercut that knocked Glen on his arse.

The crowd had moved away from the fight. Except for the bikie.

He grabbed Terry by the back of the neck with a tight grip and pulled him away from old Glen.

"Let go of me, you bloody ape." Terry flailed at the massive arm attached at the hand around his neck. He scrabbled at the meaty fingers. "Jesus, I'm blacking out."

Bikie let go and Terry collapsed on the floor. Bikie toe punted him in the ribs. "Might want to piss off, mate."

Terry pushed himself to his feet. He glanced briefly at the old guy who started this all and squared off against the bikie. "What do I call you, you fucking oaf?"

"Lucas. Grab your girl and get the hell out of here."

Troy snorted. "Or?"

Lucas balled his hands into fists and held them out. "Or these."

"I don't want a fight, you arsehole. I want a steak and a beer." Terry rolled his shoulders. "But I'll be fucked if I back down from a fight." He snapped out a fist to Lucas' gut and received zero response. He looked at his fist then at Lucas' slab of a stomach. Then back at his fist.

While Lucas was taking this in, Terry drove the side of his boot down Lucas' shin, followed up with an elbow to the side of his head. "Get down." He punched the big guy in the throat and kneed him in the groin. "GET THE FUCK DOWN!"

Terry was in a rage. Lucas had dropped to his knees and Terry was pummelling him about the head. Arms grabbed him and pulled him away from the fight. He struggled against them. Kicked backwards and connected with someone. He smiled when they yelled out and continued to strain against his restraints.

His head was throbbing again.

"Get off me, you fuck-puddles. GET OFF!"

He heard the familiar rattling of cuffs and was pushed face down onto the floor.

"Easy on, lad." The cuffs were ratcheted on his wrists behind his back, and he was pulled to his feet by his elbows. "You need to dial it down a bit. Ease up on the booze."

"I haven't had anything to drink yet, ya boof-head. That's why I'm here. Trying to get a bloody drink. Jesus. What kind of hell is this? Where am I going?" He looked across the room. Carol was watching him get dragged out. She shook her head and turned away. "Shit."

He was shepherded outside where one of the officers pushed him up against the squad car. "You have anything sharp in your pockets?"

"Get fucked."

He was shoved a bit harder. "I get stuck, you're going to be on the short end of a very hard baton." The cop patted

Terry's pockets, pulling out a set of car keys, a roll of cash and his wallet. He flipped the wallet open to his driver licence. "Troy Gibson." He pulled him by the elbow to the back of the car. He opened the back door. "Park yourself in there. Watch your head." He forced an unwilling Terry into the back seat. "Don't make it hard on yourself."

"Why am I being arrested?"

"You started a brawl with an old man. Sit back there and shut up."

The cop got in the front seat and entered the name Troy Gibson and the date of birth on the licence in his mobile terminal. He waited a minute for the digital response back from the base.

"You're clean. No priors. No arrests." He pulled the patrol car door shut. "A night in the holding cell should cool you off."

Troy leaned forward, straining against the cuffs. "No. I need to get home. And you left my girl in there."

"You don't make the rules, pal. Do yourself a favour and shut the pie hole and I won't charge you. Think of it as a sleep over."

Troy grumbled and sank back in his seat. He tried adjusting himself to get comfortable, but there wasn't a comfortable position with your hands shackled behind your back. None. "Shit."

Chapter Eighteen

It was another day. Nick lived up to the promise to himself of sleeping late. Except it wasn't 10 am, it was closer to 8, still late for him. He had a quick shower and skipped shaving. A bit of stubble wouldn't kill anybody.

It was one of those days that started off fresh and cool, but with a definite threat of heat on the way. The sky was the bluest blue and the grass and trees the greenest green.

He stowed the charging cable in the car, opened the windows and headed to the station.

Nick parked in a 30-minute spot half a block from his destination. His first stop of what would be at least half a dozen for the day. He pushed open the station door and entered the cool only taxpayer money AC could produce.

The woman at reception looked him up and down and plastered a mouth-only smile on her face. "Can I help you?"

"Looking for DSC Lin or DS Wallace. It's Nick Harding."

"You're in luck, Mr Harding. They're both still here. Another fifteen you probably would have missed them. I'll let them know you're here." She pointed at a chair. "Park there. It'll be a minute or two."

"They asked me to come in. I should hope they'd still be here." He eased into the utilitarian seat and leaned back; his legs crossed. He dug out his phone and had just opened a news website when the door to the back offices opened and Lin exited.

"Nick Harding. What a mess you have gotten yourself into." She moved to one side as Wallace came out behind her.

Nick stood and pocketed his phone. "Did you find out anything I didn't with either the video at the servo or from Jerry Sosa, the truck's owner?"

Wallace looked at Lin with a half-smile on his face. "I could ask you the same. Maybe we should pool our resources."

Nick chuckled. "I don't think we play that well together."

Terry had a headache that would be expected if he had been drinking the night before, but he didn't get that chance. He sat on the holding cell floor, head in his hands, elbows on his raised knees.

A uniform with a clipboard tapped it on the holding cell bars. "Troy Gibson. Up and at 'em. You're free to go."

Terry winced at the noise. He squeezed his head between his hands, then pushed himself to his feet. "About goddamned time, Jack. Where's my shit?"

The uniform raised an eyebrow. "Behave yourself. Follow me and we'll process you out. Go home, get some sleep, maybe think about some of your life choices." He winced as Troy left the cell and walked in front of him. "And maybe find yourself a shower. Or a deep soak."

Wallace inspected his perfect nails. "Oh, we definitely wouldn't play well together. But we might be able to work together."

A bellow came from behind the door. "GIVE ME MY SHIT!"

The three of them started. The door flew open, and a bedraggled man pushed past Lin and Wallace and out the front door.

Nick watched the door swing shut behind the receding back. "What in the hell was that?"

"Some guy, Troy Gibson, I think, brought in last night after starting a fight in a nice little pub in The Rocks. Sober as a judge. No priors. Clean sheet so he was kept here overnight to cool off," said Wallace. "Processed, but not charged."

"Yeah, that worked just great." Nick crossed his arms. "I really need to find the shit who drove into my car. Have you found anything?"

Wallace shrugged. "You've been to Wyee, so nothing new for you there. You talked to the owner of the house. You grabbed the video from Hardeep. You got the text from whoever rammed you. You talked to Sosa. Anything else we should know about?"

"You're doing a pretty thorough, and slow, job trying to find a car thief. What's the deal?"

"Have I missed anything?"

Nick looked at the floor and ran through the past few days. Separated the deadbeat work from the Gary work. He slowly shook his head. "No. That's it."

"Don't hold out on us."

"I'm not. Is this a two-way street?"

Wallace glanced at Lin and nodded. "Yeah. He was also at a motel in Parramatta. We're heading there in a bit."

"He won't be there now."

"No shit," said Wallace.

"You'll let me know what you find?"

"Maybe." Wallace and Lin left out the front door.

Nick watched them go, shook his head and followed them out.

Chapter Nineteen

Nick sat in the car and his phone rang. He punched the button to answer. "Harding."

"Sounds so formal. This is Lucy. Looking for an update on the deadbeat stealing all of our money, if you've got a moment."

Nick smiled. "We should probably do that face to face. I owe you a meal, I believe. Lunch at the same place?"

Lucy paused. "You have progress?"

"There's definitely been progress. Let me buy you lunch."

Another pause, then, "Okay. In an hour?"

Nick looked at his watch. "I'll see you there."

"Looking forward to it, Harding." She hung up.

Nick let out the breath he didn't realise he was holding. He placed a call. "Davie?"

"What's up?"

Nick drummed his fingers on the steering wheel. "Any luck pulling a face out of that video I sent you yesterday?"

"I'm doing just fine, Nicky. Thanks for asking."

"Don't bust my balls, Davie. I'm meeting the client for lunch. I'd like to have something concrete for her."

"You're making a very tenuous link between a burned-out house, torched truck and the skip trace? May not be anything."

"This is the guy." Nick glanced at the time. "I've got 45 minutes. How's it going?"

"I'll get right on it. I've been whiling my time away trying to crack the inner sanctum of the reporting agency. With no luck. I'll have a look at the video. Shouldn't take long."

Nick let out a breath. "Great. Text me what you whatever you call pull from it. I'm buying dinner tonight."

"Again."

A server topped up Nick's water glass. "Are you ready to order?" Nick was seated at an outdoor table under an umbrella. A cool breeze kept the heat at bay.

Nick checked his watch. "I'm expecting someone. Let's give it another couple of minutes." She was late. He started typing a text message to her, then stopped. He closed his phone and placed it face down on the table and sipped his water.

His phone buzzed. He flipped it over and read the message from Lucy. Terribly sorry to stand you up, Nick. My boss dragged me into a meeting and I couldn't text you until now.

I feel terrible. I'll buy you dinner, same place, tonight. Promise. Lucy.

"Ah, shit." He responded. Understood. No worries. See you here at 7.

He waved the server over. "Can I get a steak and chips and a schooner of Towhees? My guest had another appointment."

"How would you like your steak?"

"Medium rare. Thanks."

His phone chimed. An email from Davie. He placed the phone back down on the table without reading it and leaned back, trying to figure out next steps. The lack of resolution with Gary rankled him. One last crack at that while Davie worked the skip trace.

But the steak first.

The gate to the nursery was still chained shut. The signs still threatened dire consequences to anyone who even thought about trespassing. Nick decided to go for a frontal approach.

He got out of his car and approached the gate. There were no security intercoms visible, but Nick had a feeling he was being observed.

He stood back a few paces from the gate and looked up at the gum trees. "Hey, whoever is listening," he called, "Tell Gary that Nick Harding wants to speak with him again, and I'm not going to walk in this time."

He waited a minute and had opened his mouth to repeat the message when the gate swung outward a couple of metres and Charlie stuck his head out. "Yo. Mate. This way."

"I'm not walking, big guy. Open it." Nick backed up to his car, keeping his eyes on Charlie.

"Nobody drives in here."

Nick chuckled. "That would present a fairly serious logistical problem. How would your 'tomatoes' get to market?"

"Nobody without my approval."

"Let him drive," said a disembodied voice from the trees.

Nick smiled and waved at the trees. "Thanks, Gary." He nodded at Charlie. "Don't shoot me, okay? Open the gate."

Charlie scowled and pushed the gate open, continuously scanning for other traffic. When it was open enough to allow Nick's car through, he waved him in, hurriedly.

"Yeah, yeah." Nick put the car in gear and silently rolled onto the property. He slowed as he came along side Charlie. "You're not going to shoot me, right?"

Charlie's face remained deadpan. "You know where the house is. Don't stop to inspect the produce along the way or maybe I will."

Nick winked at him and saluted. "Yes, boss." He accelerated up the packed dirt road to the house. He was tempted to pull off to the side for a beat, just to get Charlie's reaction. But he'd seen the gun, and the risk wasn't worth it.

Gary was standing on the front porch, beer in hand. "You trying to talk me into this again?

Nick stepped out of the car. "That's what your father is paying me for." He nodded at the bottle. "Got one for me?"

"Sure. Come on in."

Nick followed him into the house and accepted the beer. "I had a long chat with your father yesterday. He's forgiven you."

Gary choked on his beer. "Forgiven me? Son of a bitch. I didn't do anything needing forgiving. Not then, anyway. I think meds are affecting his mental acuity."

Nick shrugged. "He's in a bit of pain. I'm sure some edibles would do him good."

Gary chuckled. "Fuck him. Grab a seat. Staying for dinner?"

"No. I've got plans." He closed his eyes. "Ah, shit."

"What's up?"

"I was hoping to have dinner with a woman who hired me on this other case, and I just remembered my partner is joining me for dinner. It's going to be a crowd."

"Life's a bitch, isn't it?"

"Tell me more about your brother."

"Tom? Nothing to tell. Haven't seen him or heard from him in five years."

"What was he doing five years ago?"

Gary scratched his beard. "Before he disappeared, he was working as a handyman for cash. He was getting really erratic. Violent temper. He was taking medication for a little while, but I'm pretty sure he stopped taking it. I keep my eye on the news, just in case a body washes up on the beach or is found in the bush."

"Did he have any friends he hung with?"

Gary sipped his beer, looking hard at Nick. "Why are you looking for him? You said my father hired you to find me and to tell me the old shit wanted to talk to me. You've done your job. You've done more than what's been asked of you." He belched. "Now I'm trusting you to keep the fact that my to-mato business is subsidised by my herb business a secret. Because I like you, Nick. You seem like a decent guy. I'd hate to have to send Charlie to visit you at your apartment in, where is it again? Right. Bondi Junction."

Nick paused his beer's journey to his lips. "Huh. You know where I live. Great. Come by for dinner sometime. I owe you." He put the still half-full bottle down on the table. "I'll pass your message back to your old man. And I don't care about the weed. It'll be legal here in a couple of years. I've got no problem with it. I envy you getting ahead of the market like you did." He cleared his throat. "I'll see myself out. Tell Charlie not to shoot me, hey? And keep Gloria on a leash."

"Davie, I'm sorry but I've got to reschedule dinner. I've double booked." Nick navigated a tight curve coming out of the Blue Mountains and back into Sydney.

"The longer you delay, the more money it's going to cost you."

"I know, I know."

"How was lunch with Lucy?"

"She couldn't make it. She's my dinner date." Nick stopped at a red light. "Apologies, but she smells nicer than you."

"No worries. Catch me up tomorrow. I did a pretty good job with the photo, though, right?"

The light turned green. "Haven't had a chance to look at it yet. But I'm sure it's great."

"It's a clear, face-on picture. I checked other businesses around that servo and found one with a security camera facing it from a different angle. Cracked it and got a perfect picture. Enjoy your dinner and we'll regroup tomorrow morning at your place, okay?"

"See you then."

Freshly showered and shaved, Nick liked the way he felt. He walked the block and a half to where he was meeting Lucy for dinner. This felt more like a date than a business meeting. He should have reigned in his expectations.

Lucy was at the same table in the back. Romanticism went out the window. She was wearing a severely cut suit and had a stack of file folders on the table in front of her. She had one open and was thumbing through the pages.

He slid into the seat and motioned for the server. "Can I get you a drink, Lucy?"

She looked up and closed the file. "Mr Harding. No, thank you. This is a business meal." She rested her hand on the files. "These are every transaction the twelve identities this person has used to defraud my organisation has made.

Hopefully it will provide you some assistance." She handed the folder over.

"I've got the highlights. Is there anything new in there that would be helpful?"

The server stood at the table, waiting. "Drinks?"

"I'll have a Towhees in a bottle." He nodded at Lucy. "And my colleague will have, what, a diet cola?"

Lucy smiled. "With a slice of lemon. And can you bring me a chicken Caesar salad please, dressing on the side?"

"And I'll have the chicken schnitzel."

He waited until the server had taken the menus and leaned forward. "My colleague Dave Sangster and I are making good progress identifying this man."

"We need more than just an identification. We need proof he was the many different identities that defrauded us. We need to account for every dollar defrauded. We need to be able to put this behind us once and for all."

Nick nodded. He smiled at the server as she placed the bottle of beer and a frosted stein in front of him. He dug his phone out of his pocket. "My colleague has cleaned up a surveillance photo of the man in question. We have a better face."

He scrolled through his email until he reached Davie's latest and opened the attached link. As Davie had promised, it was a clear photo. Of someone he recognised. He could place the face. He wasn't sure from where, but he knew he knew it. He frowned as he turned his phone so Lucy could see the image. "Do you recognise him?"

She took the phone and zoomed the picture, shaking her head as she did. "Better shot of the same guy we got photos of." She handed the phone back.

Nick looked at the photo again. "Oh, Jesus. He has a new alias now. Tory Gibson. Or Troy Gibson. Same initials. T. G. He was in custody last night for starting a fight in a bar in The Rocks." He sipped his beer. "I'll send you the photo. You should be able to match it with security footage at enough places to solve your immediate problem."

He forwarded the email and leaned back as his food was served.

"You still haven't told me how you linked this person to all of these other aliases."

Nick sat, frowning in thought. "T. G. All of the aliases have the initials T. G. , right?"

Lucy nodded. "That's what twigged us to the fact it was the same person."

"Shit." Nick found the number to the nursery and placed a call. Gloria answered.

"Hey, this is Nick Harding. I need to speak with Gary."

"Gary who?"

"I've been there twice. He served me dinner. This is very, very urgent. Get Gary."

"This is Gary. What is it now, Harding?"

"I'm going to send you a picture. I need you to tell me if it's your brother. I need a mobile number or an email address."

"This obsession with my brother is unhealthy."

"Mobile number?"

"Email. Mobile phones don't work up here. Remember?" Gary recited his address and Nick hung up. He forwarded the photo to Gary's email and called him back.

"Where did you get this?"

"Is that your brother?"

"What in the hell is going on?"

"Cases intersected. This person is the target of a different case. He rammed me, just luck I wasn't killed. Just say it. Is this your brother?"

"He's older. His hair is a lot longer and he's packed the weight on, but yes. That's Tom."

"Keep your eyes open. I think he's looking for you."

"Me? Why?"

"I think he wants daddy's money."

"And he thinks I'm in his way. Shit. Someone should tell him I don't want it." He was quiet for a second. "Can you come to the nursery tomorrow? I want to hire you to get some information and money to my brother."

Nick closed his eyes and leaned his head back. "Why not? It's already nuts."

"So you know who the deadbeat is?" Lucy leaned forward. "You've got him?"

Nick shook his head. "A little premature. A lot to tie up yet."

Chapter Twenty

Nick waved at Charlie and Gloria as he drove through the gate. Neither one of them looked pleased at the prospect of his visit. Once again Gary was on the front porch, this time with a large coffee mug in his hand instead of a beer.

Gary motioned for him to come in and entered the house without waiting.

Nick got out of the car and checked his phone. Still no service. "Hey, jammers aren't legal," he called as he walked up the steps. "How am I supposed to check Twitter? Jammers aren't legal."

Gary laughed, hard. "Jammers aren't legal? Yeah. Least of my concerns. How do you take you coffee?"

"Black. No sugar. Thanks." Nick looked at his phone again and slid it in his pocket. "Are you masking the operator's signals so your mobile phones can't be tracked?"

Gary smiled and handed him his coffee. "To business. Tell me about how it is you came to be looking for Tom."

He sipped the coffee and placed it on the table. "I try to maintain confidentiality when it comes to my cases," he held up his hand to stop Gary's protest, "but I think I can waive that for now." He cleared his throat. "But keep this confidential, okay?"

"I'm great at keeping secrets."

"Clearly. Your brother has figured out how to create near perfect credit reports. Gold plated. And he uses those stellar credit ratings to defraud a medium sized finance company." He shook his head. "He tripped himself up by not spreading that pain around, and by picking a new alias, whenever he needs one, with the same initials as Tom Goulding, T. G. Didn't help that the fake birthday he used is always the thirteenth of the month, increasing it by a month every instance. Like 13 January for the first one, 13 Feb for the next."

"How often would he do this?"

"Change identities? Whenever one got hot, I guess. It's been going back three or four years, as near as I can tell. He's just changed again. He's been 'Troy Gibson' for the last couple of days."

"He makes a lot of money doing this?"

Nick shrugged. "Not the kind of money you're pulling in, but enough. He'll lease a car, for example, drive it around for a month or two, while not making any payments, then sell it to a chop shop. High end cars. Maybe a chop shop, maybe they're shipped overseas. Don't know."

"Strange way to make a living."

"He'd also get personal loans and then default, transferring the money to multiple other accounts. Sign up for high limit credit cards, then suck them dry just before he changes identity."

Gary shook his head. "He wasn't that smart before he got whacked on the head."

"Yeah, he's getting help."

Charlie rushed into the room with his gun drawn. "There's a visitor coming in from the north. You need to get out of here." He looked at Nick. "Not you. Don't care what you do."

Gary hit a button on his remote and his TV came on to four quadrants of security camera feed. He scrolled through screens until he found one with an unkempt man approaching from the north between the greenhouses.

He switched cameras to follow the progress. "That's Tom." He paused the picture.

Nick leaned forward. The same face as the guy who stole the truck, sweating profusely. Gary restarted the video. Tom had a cricket bat in one hand, banging it against the sides of the greenhouses as he passed them. "He doesn't look happy, Gary."

"Let's get out of here," said Charlie. "The best fight is the one you don't have."

"It's one guy. I think we should talk to him," said Nick. "See if we can sort things out."

Charlie jabbed a finger at the screen. "That look like someone reasonable?"

Nick watched Tom, his thick legs pumping, a snarl on his face and sweat stains merging into one single dirty, greasy spot on his T-shirt. "You're probably right. How far away is he?"

"Minutes."

"But he's by himself, right?" Gary rolled his shoulders and pointed at the frozen picture on the monitor. "He's out of shape and no doubt very winded after running, what, almost two klicks from the north fence?"

Charlie nodded. "Seems really determined, though." He switched the camera to the front door. Tom stumbled up the steps and hammered on the front door with the butt end of the cricket bat.

"Open the door," Gary said to Charlie. "Nick, there's a way out the back if you want to leave."

"And miss this?"

Charlie yanked the door open a little faster than necessary and Tom stumbled into the room, the cricket bat clattering across the tile floor. He scrambled to his feet, sweaty, hair stuck to his scalp and a foul stink of days old perspiration wafting off of him.

He eyed the cricket bat, just out of reach. To get to it would bring him within kicking distance of Gary. "Hey, little brother. Helluva place you've got here. Pops know about it?"

"I haven't seen you in over five years and this is how you show up?"

"If I'd known you were sitting on this much pot, I would have been here years ago." He looked around. "Great house."

"Why. Are. You. Here?" asked Gary. "And your answer needs to satisfy the man with the gun." He pointed over Tom's shoulder.

Tom slowly turned. Charlie's revolver was pointing at his forehead.

Charlie motioned the barrel toward the sofa. "How about you lean over and place your hands on the back of the sofa and spread your legs very wide."

Tom hesitated and Charlie tapped his forehead with the muzzle. "Any time now, champ."

Tom growled deep in his throat and slowly turned. He placed his hands on the back of the sofa. Charlie kicked his legs apart.

"Jesus, mate. Take it easy."

"Nick, search him for me, would you?" asked Gary.

Tom straightened from the sofa. "You're Nick? You son of a bitch, I – "

Charlie grabbed him by the collar and forced him back to the sofa. "I told you not to move."

"You didn't, actually." Tom spread his hands on the back of the sofa and glared at Nick as he was patted down.

Nick had a sour look on his face as he worked his way down Tom. He pulled a wallet out of a back pocket and a set of Audi keys out of a front pocket. He tossed the keys on the sofa and opened the wallet. He took the driver licence out. "Troy Gibson. Son, you are a moron. January 13th birthday.

You know the only reason the finance company knew to look for something strange was all of the defaults to people with the initials T.G. and a birthday on the 13th of the month, right?" He shook his head. "How did you manage to keep this going for so long?"

"Greed."

"Yeah. Yours."

"No. Bank greed. They'll bend over backwards to shovel money to the 'right' people." Tom grunted. "Do you know how easy it is to look like the right person on paper?" He slowly stood and turned. He grabbed his wallet back from Nick and held out his hand. "My licence."

"You know the jig is up now, right?"

"The jig is up? What are you, my grandfather?" He stuffed the licence back in the billfold and held out his hand again. "My keys."

Nick looked at them and shook his head. He slid them in his front pocket. "It's not your car. I'll be returning it."

Tom lunged at him. "You fuck."

Nick danced out of his way and Charlie grabbed Tom from behind by his belt.

"And I think you should come with me and turn yourself in and work out a way of paying these people back." Nick sniffed. "But not in my rental. You reek."

Tom sagged against the sofa and dropped his head. "Shit."

Charlie slid the revolver in the back of his trousers and pulled his shirt over it. "You're not using my truck."

"I didn't ask, Charlie." Nick dangled the Audi keys. "I'll drive." He nodded toward the door. "We've got to talk, Tom."

"You want me to come with?" asked Charlie.

Nick looked at the sad, dejected image of Tom standing in front of him. "No, I think I'm good. I'll be back for my car. Gary, how far north of here to the road?"

"A couple of kilometres." He stared at Tom. "Are you sure you'll be okay?"

"Let's go, Tom. We need to talk."

Tom walked toward the door. "Like I've got anything to say to you. I'm taking my cricket bat with me." He leaned down to pick it up and was pushed off his feet by his younger brother.

"I'll mail it to you." Gary picked it up and leaned it against the sofa.

Tom pushed himself to his feet, puffing for breath and headed to the door. "Whatever. Jesus. Let's go."

Nick looked at Gary, who shrugged. "Let's go."

They walked north between the greenhouse huts, side by side, warily keeping an eye on each other, in silence for ten minutes.

Nick looked at him. "You had help, I'm assuming."

Tom grunted. "You think I'm too stupid to do this on my own?"

"I don't know you well enough to say that. But one of the best computer people I know couldn't get access to fake credit reports, so you had to have someone on the inside."

"Had to?"

Nick glanced at him and nodded. "Only logical."

Tom stopped walking and looked back from where they started. The house was small in the distance. He turned and looked toward their destination. The Audi was closer than the house was. More than halfway there. He faced Nick and smiled. "Idiot."

Tom's meaty fist slammed him in the face and Nick felt his nose break. He staggered back and Tom followed up with a hard body shot that dropped Nick to his knees. He got his arms up in time to block the knee coming for his head, but was knocked back onto his arse.

Tom shoved his hand in Nick's pocket and extracted the Audi keys. Rolled him over and took his wallet. "Thanks." He took the cash and tossed the wallet at Nick. He looked back at the house and smiled. Gary and Charlie were running toward them. "Really gotta run, Nick. Stay the fuck out of my business." He punctuated it with a kick to the ribs and trotted toward the Audi.

Nick wheezed himself to his hands and knees as Gary and Charlie reached him. "Let him go."

"He's already gone." Gary squatted beside him. "You look like a bad track of road." He helped Nick to his feet. "We need to get you to a hospital."

Nick pulled his arm free and bent down and picked his wallet off the ground. "No." He cleared his throat and spat bloody phlegm. "I'll get there myself." He touched his nose and winced. "Just need to clean up a bit." He wiped his hand on his trousers. "Your brother is a lunatic."

Gary headed back toward his house. "Yeah. I know." He glanced at Nick. "You okay?"

"No." He took a shallow, shuddering breath. "Couple of ribs, too." He held his phone above his head and moved it around, looking for a signal. "Jesus, you blocked coverage all over this place?"

"Security first. Why. Who are you trying to call?"

"The police. There can't be that many Audis up here. Got a chance of grabbing this guy." He looked at Gary. "At least one of my cases will be cleared."

Charlie skipped ahead and blocked the path.

"I don't think so," said Gary. He snatched the phone out of Nick's hand. "No cops." He smashed the screen against a rock and handed it back.

"You arsehole."

Charlie stepped out of the way with a half-smile on his face and invited Nick to continue his walk with a bow and a wave of his hand.

"You'll thank me later."

Nick sighed, winced at the pain from his ribs and continued trudging.

Chapter Twenty-One

Nick eased himself into the rental and dropped his phone in the centre console. He started the car and gave Gary a sardonic salute. He rolled past Charlie and Gloria at the gate. He gave them a smile and Gloria flipped him her middle finger. "What a sweetheart."

He watched the gate close behind him. The car chimed as his phone paired with it. "Huh. Hey Siri, call Davie."

"Hey, boss. How are things going?"

"Oh, just absolutely fantastic. I'm heading to the hospital to get my nose set and my ribs x-rayed. Can you get whichever police force is responsible for the Blue Mountains – "

"What the fuck happened?"

"Priorities. The cops."

"That'd be the Blue Mountains PAC, not surprisingly."

"Fine. Contact them and tell them there's a white Audi on the Bells Line of Road, heading toward Lithgow, I believe, with a boot full of cocaine."

"What?"

"The T.G. guy. Tom Goulding. Son of Lawrence and brother of Gareth. The two cases are inextricably linked and, well, just get the cops on him, okay? I've got to see a man about my face. And get a new phone."

"What are you calling me on?"

"It's my phone, but the screen is shattered. Siri is handling all my calls."

"Okay. I'll text you."

Nick glanced down at his phone with its smashed screen. "Don't bother. I'll call you back later." He pushed the disconnect button on the steering wheel. Took a breath and winced. "Hey Siri, where is the nearest hospital?"

Tom sat behind the wheel of the Audi and slammed his fist on the steering wheel. "SON OF A BITCH." He found the number in his phone and called. "Hey, it's me."

"You need a new ID already? That must be some kind of record."

"I need muscle."

The voice on the other end of the call laughed. "You haven't been in a gym since the day I met you. Why now?"

"No, you fuck. Meatheads. Grunts. Steroids in tracksuits. I need to take out a guy and I need some MUSCLE."

"You got the wrong guy. Don't call back. Ever."

Tom closed his eyes and shook his head. He'd called the wrong person. "SHIT." He tried to pull the right number from his memory. It wasn't coming. "Shit." He looked at his phone trying to manifest the phone number. "Wait." He scrolled to his text messages. Found the one with the candyman.

"Hey, need more blow? Or are you looking to offload more cars."

"I need some heavyweights to help me take out a guy."

"That's new."

"Can you do it?"

"I can do ANYthing for the right amount of money."

Tom sighed. "How much?"

"How many bodies, how soon, where, these parameters define the price."

Tom started the car. "Half a dozen, as fast as humanly possible and in the Blue Mountains. I'll drop a pin. How much?"

"You battling an army?"

"How. Much."

"That's a lot of people in a short time frame at a long distance. You've been a very good and reliable customer. Thirty grand."

Tom opened the map on his phone and sent the location. "How fast can they get here?"

"Earliest I can do is tomorrow morning."

"I just sent you the location. I'll get you the money today."

"Man, I hope it's worth it for you."

"It's worth a thousand times what I'm paying you."

The splint on Nick's nose was just barely visible to him. He normally never noticed that his nose was in his field of vision; it was a part of his face that became invisible because it was always there. Normally. Now there was an aluminium thing stuck to his face, driving him to distraction.

At least the ribs were only bruised.

He walked out of Nepean Hospital into the blue-sky, mid-day heat. He took his phone out of his pocket, looked at the destroyed screen and turned back into the hospital. He approached one of the triage nurses. "Quick question for you." He held up the shattered phone. "Is there an electronics store around here?"

She looked at his nose and at the screen. "You'd had a lovely day."

"Haven't I, though?"

She pointed vaguely east. "There's a shopping centre less than a klick that way." She took a closer look at his nose. "Whoever did that, did a spectacular job. It'll be barely noticeable after the splint comes off."

"Thanks for the help."

He took the opportunity to upgrade his phone. He signed the appropriate paperwork and had them insert his SIM in the new phone. When it powered up, he received a text message. Your father is back in the hospital. You should come.

"Oh, hell. I've got to run."

He called his mother from the car. "Did he have another heart attack?"

"No, Nicky. It was a pulmonary embolism this time. He dropped like a rock on the fourth fairway. First time he's golfed in months. He's in the hospital right now. They thought it was another heart attack at first."

Nick punched the hospital in his GPS. "I'm in Penrith. It'll be about an hour." He got in the car and looked at his phone. "Tell him I'll get there as fast as I can."

He pocketed the wired headphones and paired his new phone to the car. He entered the address and mapped a path to the hospital. Then he called Davie.

"Hey, how's it going?"

"You called the cops?" asked Nick.

"I did. They were more interested in me at first than they were in what I was telling them. But they eventually came around. How are you?"

"Ribs are bruised, nose is in a splint. And my father is back in the hospital. I'm heading there now."

"Damn, man. Sorry."

Nick shook his head. "Not a heart attack this time. Pulmonary embolism. He's getting treatment now. I understand the biggest risk at this point is a fragment of clot navigating itself to the brain causing a stroke. The doctors are good. He'll most likely be fine. But I need to get to the hospital. Can you reach out to Lucy, from the finance company, and let her know we're getting closer? I'll update her later tonight."

Traffic was stop-and-go into the city. He tamped down his frustration. Without a helicopter or a jetpack, there was little he could do about it.

He ran through the parking lot, every jarring step transmitted directly to the broken cartilage in his nose. His mother was waiting at the entrance of A&E.

She gave him a hug. "He's going to be okay. They're keeping him overnight." She pulled back and looked at the dull aluminium splint on his nose. "You get into a fight? That's not like you."

"I slipped. The clot?"

She frowned and looked at his face for another second. "They used some miracle clot dissolving meds. He's going to be on blood thinners, probably for the rest of his life, but he'll use that as an excuse to eat more fatty food." She smiled. "You want to see him?"

"I need to see him."

His mother checked her watch. "Visiting hours end in about thirty minutes. He'll be pleased you came."

Nick grunted.

"No, really." She patted him on his arm. "He loves you. You know that, right?"

As befitting a man of his financial means, George was in a private room. It was bright and airy, light streaming in the window. George was the one grey spot in the room.

"You don't look that well, old man."

George opened his eyes. He furrowed his brow. "Run into a door?"

"I'm going to grab a cup of tea," said Susie. "You two talk. I'll be back in a bit."

The hospital bed was against one wall, under a large window. The curtains were open, showing a stunning view of a mostly filled parking lot. A large, necessarily comfortable chair was at the foot of the bed, nestled into the corner, facing the bed.

Nick settled into the chair. He leaned back and crossed his legs.

His father pushed a button and the head of the bed raised so he could see his son. "You look like a racoon. What happened?"

"Forget about me. Are you okay?"

George waved his hand dismissively. "It'll take more than a blood clot to knock me down."

"That's funny. That's exactly what knocked you down."

His father adjusted himself and scowled at the IVs and sensors attached to him. "I think they're only keeping me in here to boost the hospital's revenue. I don't need to be here."

"You got a medical degree before you became a lawyer? I never knew." Nick frowned. "You really should retire, dad. You're not young, your firm is doing extremely well, and if you keep going, you'll work yourself to death."

"They prescribed rat poison for me. Not entirely sure that wasn't your mother's idea."

"What?"

"The blood thinner they've got me on. Warfarin. It's the active ingredient in those pellets you put out to kill rats and rabbits." He sighed. "Rodents."

"Lower dosage, I assume."

"Per kilo, yeah. I hope so." He pointed at Nick's face. "You going to tell me? Are you going to need legal help?"

"Maybe someday, but not now. Not yet." Nick scratched the corner of his eye. "You know I've got two missing persons cases, right?"

"That's what the cops are for."

Nick grimaced. "I've got two missing persons cases. One, Larry Goulding hired me to find his youngest son, Gary..."

"I hear Lawrence isn't doing too well."

"Couple of weeks, if that."

"Shit." George settled back against his pillow. "Good guy, Lawrence."

"Really? Because he implied Gary was his only son. Didn't mention Tom."

"Yeah," said George. "That's a rough tale. Poor kid got really banged up. Messed up his brain."

Nick leaned back. "You know about this?"

"I can't believe Gary did that to you. He's more of a peaceful hippy type. He was born a good thirty years too late."

"Let me tell you about my second missing persons case. A small finance company has been systematically defrauded over the past few years by someone creating, somehow, perfect identities, including air-tight, gold standard credit agency profiles. I can think of dozens of ways to steal which are easier. And always with the same financial company. It's like he was asking to get caught."

"I take it," George pointed at Nick's nose, "that wasn't Gary, then. You found the sociopath?"

"A couple of times. This was from the most recent engagement. Added twist to this whole thing is that this missing person is Tom, Larry's eldest son, the son he didn't tell me about."

George let out a slow puff of air. "That's shit. Does Lawrence know?"

"What, that he's alive? I'd bet anything he does and has cut him from the will. He probably doesn't know I've found him, though. Inadvertently."

"I wouldn't bet on it. Lawrence has a pretty good network of," George paused. "I was going to say spies. Informants? Something like that. He has both ears to the ground."

"That'd be something to see."

"What are you going to do?"

Nick caressed the dull aluminium on his nose. "I've got a couple of ideas."

"Violence solves nothing. At least not in the long term. Short term satisfaction, at most."

"I'll take it." He readjusted himself. "You didn't answer. Are you going to retire? Health scares are usually a pre-requisite for a serious consideration at grabbing the gold watch."

His father scowled. "I'd drive your mother nuts. Almost as fast as she'd drive me nuts. It's a non-starter."

Nick nodded. "Great idea. Work until you drop dead." He leaned forward. "I was serious. Cash out, buy a villa in Tuscany and split your time between the two places. Mum told me you both loved it there."

George emitted a non-committal grunt. The discussion was over.

"Okay. Great talking to you, as usual." Nick stood from the chair and gingerly stretched out the interstitial muscles between his ribs. "I should run. Things to see, people to do."

His mother met him at the door. "Stay for a hospital food dinner."

Nick shuddered. "I'm good. Got a date. I need to clean up." He gave her a hug. "I'll give you a call tomorrow."

"What really happened? You look like a racoon."

"No racoons in Australia, Mum." He held her gently by the shoulders and kissed her on the cheek. "I'll call you tomorrow."

Chapter Twenty-Two

Tom parked at a meter outside of the serviced apartment he had leased under the name Troy Gibson. He passed a young woman in the lobby retrieving her mail from her designated tiny mailbox. Tom didn't bother checking. This address was brand new. Anybody who knew this address he didn't want to hear from.

He was on the 8th floor, his apartment door directly across from the communal garbage chute. A thin young man was trying to stuff a couple of pizza boxes down the chute. He reeked of weed. Tom half smiled as he unlocked the door.

Carol was on the sofa, feet up on the coffee table watching an episode of The Sopranos.

"What are you watching that crap for?"

"This is the good one. Where they get lost in the Pine Barrens." She turned off the television. "Hey, babe. We need to get some dinner. Only thing here are a couple bags of crisps and some vodka."

"And you couldn't do that yourself?" He stopped and inhaled slowly through his nose. Let it out in a whoosh out his mouth. "Sorry. Stressed." He grimaced. "We'll eat at the pub, okay? The one up the hill has good food." He opened his phone and held it up to her. "This guy, this Nick Hardy Boys fuck, is looking for me. I need you to help me keep an eye out for him. The arsehole is everywhere."

"What do you want, Davie?" Nick pressed the earbuds in to block the surrounding noise.

"I think I found him."

He sighed. He stood at the entrance to the cafe. He could see Lucy at her usual window seat. She glanced at her phone, then looked around. "Where?"

"CBD. The Rocks, most likely. For now. He'll be somewhere else tomorrow."

"Shit. Get ready. I'll be there in ten minutes."

He nodded at the young man at the door and pointed to the back. "I'm with her."

"Nicky, I thought you'd never get here." Lucy smiled. Then looked puzzled as Nick continued to stand. "Sit. Please."

"I'm sorry." Nick held up his phone. "My partner just told me we've found the guy ripping you — your company — off. He's downtown. I need to run. Truly sorry. I promise I'll make it up to you."

"It has to be tonight?"

"This guy," Nick wasn't ready to tell her who he was, "moves around a lot. I know where he is tonight. That probably won't be where he will be tomorrow." He stopped a server walking by. "Tell Jimmy that Lucy's meal is on me, okay?"

"We get off at Circular Quay."

"Why'd we take the train, Nick?"

"Parking down here is insanely expensive. And it was only five stops."

They walked onto the waterfront. The evening air still held the warmth of the day's sun. The boardwalk was packed with tourists. Well-heeled ones were heading to or coming from one of the many expensive restaurants that lined the quay. The Sydney Opera House was lit up, drawing the less well-heeled tourists to it like moths to a flame.

Davie pointed toward the Sydney Opera House. "Always liked the way that looked at night."

"We're going the other way, though."

"How are we supposed to find this guy?"

Nick raised his eyebrows. "You were the one who told me he was down here."

"You have a better picture than the one I sent you?"

"Nah, that's it. And it's good enough."

Davie took in the teeming crowd. "I hope you have a plan. This is a big-arsed city."

"The guy is trying to lie low, so he won't be at any of the good restaurants. In fact, he'd probably avoid the good hotels, too. Too much surveillance. So, serviced apartments, hostels, motels. Eat at fast food places or pubs." Nick pointed up the hill from George Street. "There's a couple of serviced apartments up that way. Tons of pubs." He smiled at Davie. "Another reason not to drive here. So," he looked at his watch. "I doubt he'd be in for the night yet." He pulled Davie to a tourist map mounted on a light standard. It showed the immediate ten-block radius behind scarred plexiglass.

He placed his finger on the 'You are here' dot. "You head up George Street, towards Central Station. I'm going up the hill to Harrington, then over to York and Clarence. Let me know if you see him. Don't approach the guy, okay? He is fucking nuts."

"Let's meet back here at midnight."

"Agreed. Keep your beer receipts. This is going on the expenses."

Davie smiled, nodded, and turned south.

Nick waited for a trolley to pass then jogged across George Street and headed up Essex Street. It was a steep climb, and he was walking against pedestrian traffic. He noticed a couple of people glancing at the splint on his nose and smiling. He smiled back, silently cursing them to hell.

A queue was forming in front of the Italian restaurant at the top of the hill. He took a quick glance at those waiting to enter. None of them looked familiar. But the smell was intoxicating. He groaned. He should have eaten with Lucy.

The Cove Serviced Apartments were across Harrington Street. A Belgian Beer pub to its left. Nick shook his head. This guy was a pizza and domestic beer guy. Not peach or raspberry flavoured beer. The Canadian Consulate was to the right. The clubs around it catered to the international and diplomatic crowd. Also, not the kind of place he'd expect to find Tom.

He kept trudging up the hill.

Carol put down the menu and took a mouthful of beer from her pint glass. "I'm bloody starving, Tommy."

He leaned forward. "Tory, luv. My name is Tory." He looked around, then leaned a little closer. "Don't forget it."

"How much longer does this dance go on. I'm tired of always flitting about, not staying in one place more than a couple of months."

"The money's good though, right?"

She shrugged in acknowledgement. "It's been okay."

"Last few years, really good money. It can't last forever, though. You must know that."

"It's occurred to me that I can't see an endgame that works in your favour."

Tom raised his eyebrows and sat back in his chair. "Original plan: Run this scam, con, whatever you call it for another year or so — it's got legs — and stash enough money to live comfortable."

"How much have you stashed so far?"

"Half a mill. Not enough in a place this expensive. Was thinking about heading up to Mackay. Doesn't get as cold as this place, either."

"I've never been to Queensland."

"Really?" He drank. "Was thinking. Plans have changed."

"I thought your motto was 'Have a plan, stick to it.'"

Tom shrugged. "Good motto, unless something seismic comes along." He smiled. "Something truly seismic has come along."

"You going to tell me?"

Tom thought for a second. "Just between us. I'm trusting you explicitly by telling you this."

"Almost five years together, To -Tory." She licked her lips. "I haven't told a soul about the scams you've been running. That's something."

He nodded. "Something. Mice nuts compared to what's going to happen now." He paused, then made a decision. "My father is nearly dead."

"I'm so sorry."

"Fuck him. He's near death and my sources tell me that his will won't include a single penny for me." His face darkened. "Every bit of it is split between my punk-arse little hippy brother and some charity."

"Oh." A puzzled look took over Carol's face. "I don't get it. How is this seismic for you?"

Tom leaned forward again. "I get Gary out of the picture, and when the old dude croaks, I challenge the will. I've just got to get Gary out of the way without anyone knowing it was me."

"What do you mean, get Gary out of the way?"

Tom leaned forward, looked around, then drew his thumb over his throat. Then put his finger over his lips and smiled. "Shh."

"That's pretty drastic, even for you."

"I haven't told you how much my father's estate is worth." He tipped back the rest of his beer and looked at the bar. "Want another one?"

"How much is your father's estate worth, Tory?"

"Over 80 million. You want another beer?"

Carol sat back in her chair, stunned. "Fuck."

"Yeah." He stood. Let me get you another beer."

"I'm going out for a smoke. Order the food, already. I'll be back. We need to talk about this."

Nick realised he was in worse physical shape than he thought when he could feel his heartbeat in his nose before he crested the next hill.

He finally made it to the top. He turned right and walked north on Cumberland Street. It was a hidden pocket of City Sydney. The street ran parallel with the entrance to the Harbour Bridge. You didn't land on this street by accident.

At least it was a gentle downhill grade.

He stopped at a pub and showed Tom's picture to the bouncer at the door. "Seen this guy around?"

"Who are you, eh?"

"PI. Looking for this guy. He's got a bad habit of ducking out the back after ordering a large meal."

"You gotta pay at the bar here before they even start cooking. Not a problem here."

"You haven't seen him?"

The big guy shrugged, moving at least 20 kilos of shoulder muscle in the process.

"Cool. Thanks so much for your help."

The bouncer looked past him to the person standing behind Nick.

"Okay, fine. I get the message."

The Australian Pub was ahead. Almost as many seats on the outdoor patio as inside. Home of the kangaroo and emu pizza. A woman stood between him and the patio, lighting a cigarette. She was slightly taller than Nick. Dirty blonde hair with dark roots. A multitude of disorganised tattoos on her arms and a ring in her right nostril. A slight muffin top stuck out from under her crop top.

"Hi, excuse me. Have you seen this man around?" He held up his phone.

She finished lighting her cigarette and pocketed her lighter. "Let me see. Is he a bad guy?" She took the phone from Nick and squinted at it through a haze of smoke. Her eyes widened and she looked closely at Nick. "How do you know this guy?"

"You've seen him?"

"Nuh-uh. He looks like a lot of people I've seen. Non-descript, I think they call it." She handed the phone back. "Why are you looking for him? He owes you some money?"

"It's a private matter." He waved away some of the smoke. "Those things will kill you."

She turned half away from him. "Well, he's not in here. I've been here for a couple of hours." She looked at him. "On the prowl. About to give it up. You got any plans? Wanna party?"

"Yeah, no. You have fun. Be safe, okay?" He pocketed his phone and continued north.

Then stopped and turned back to the Australian. There was an empty table at the railing. He stepped over the railing and sat at the table. He pulled the menu from between the salt and pepper mills and slapped it on the table. "Fuck, I'm hungry."

Tom had a plate of half a dozen loaded potato skins and two more cold beer ready for Carol when she returned. "Those things will kill you, you know. You should quit."

"We're going to be here for a while." She glanced over her shoulder to the patio. "Recognise the guy sitting out there?"

"Who?" Tom scanned the tables, passing Nick, then coming back to him. "Oh, shit."

"Don't worry about him. We'll just wait him out. Tell me about the 80 million."

Tom couldn't pull his gaze from the PI with a nose splint sitting on the patio. "I broke his nose." He smile and clapped his hands.

Carol snapped her fingers in front of his face. "Focus. Don't worry about him. He's out there. We're in here."

"Well," Tom twisted in his chair until he found what he was looking for, "if he's got to take a piss, he's going to walk right past us."

"There must be a back door."

"There is. But we're not going anywhere until we've killed these skins." He handed one to Carol. "These are out of this world." He watched her glance back at the patio. "He just got here. Won't need the head for a while."

"Okay." She took a bite from the potato skin and smiled. Chased it with a mouthful of beer. "You think we've got enough time for you to tell me about the 80 million? More importantly, did you mean it about getting Gary out of the way?"

Tom stopped his beer halfway to his mouth. "Shit." He stood and waved for her to follow him. "I guess he needs to piss now."

Nick signalled for the server. "I'll be right back. I've done a lot of walking. Where's the men's?"

He pointed to the back right of the interior.

"Thanks." Nick held out his phone with the deadbeat's picture. "Have you seen this guy lately?"

"Yeah, he's in there with his girl. Big spender. You'll pass them on the way to the men's room."

"Thanks." Nick stepped into the cooler interior and started scanning for Tom. One quick pass and nothing. He slowed down, looking at each patron carefully. There was nobody who looked like Tom. There was, however, an empty table for two. There were four potato skins and two almost full pints of still cold beer left.

He hit the men's room then buttonholed the server on his way back to his seat. "The woman he was with - what did she look like?"

"They're not in there?"

"Doesn't seem like it."

"Shit."

"Not so much a big spender, just a big consumer. The woman?"

The server closed his eyes for a second, then snapped them open. "As tall as you, blonde, really tight jeans – "

"A white crop top, and a nose piercing?"

"You've seen her, then?"

"Yeah. Thanks." He handed the server $20. "Cancel my order."

He grabbed him as he turned away. "Is there a back way out of here?"

"Yeah." He pointed past the kitchen. "Why?"

Nick pushed past him and hit the door just as it was latching shut. He held it open as he looked up and down the street.

He lost them.

He called Davie as he retraced his steps.

"No joy so far, boss."

"I just missed him. And a girlfriend. Did you run across a female in your online searches?"

"Wasn't looking, actually. Heading back to the quay?"

Nick was now on the downhill slope that was so difficult to climb not half an hour earlier. He was almost falling over his feet. "Yeah. We should grab some food, too. I'm starving."

"You haven't eaten yet?"

"Would I be starving if I had?"

"I've stopped twice for food."

"There's an Italian place just up the hill from where we split up. Meet you there. We need to regroup."

Chapter Twenty-Three

"Nick Harding, are you awake?"

Seconds prior to the yelling at the door, Nick was indeed not awake. He pried his eyes open and cleared the night phlegm from his throat. "Yo, hang on." He grabbed the bathrobe hanging on his closet door. "Who is it?"

"Gary. I need your help."

Nick peered at his phone. "It's 6a.m., you dick. What the actual fuck?" He opened the door to a very haggard looking Gary, who pushed his way in.

"Sorry, I really need your help." He paced the lounge room.

Nick looked out the door. "Someone following you?"

"Maybe. Who knows?"

"Good point." Nick closed and locked the door. "What in the hell?" He yawned and scratched his chest. "I'm making some coffee. You want?"

Gary nodded while he paced. "Really apologise, but I got a disturbing phone call around midnight. I haven't slept. I want to hire you."

"You told me that. I was planning on stopping by later today. Why so impatient?"

Gary the stopped pacing and sat in one of the bar stool chairs at the kitchen counter. "I'm, frankly, a little scared. Terrified."

Nick placed a cup in front of him. "Tell me about the phone call."

"A little after midnight. It came from a blocked number. Someone told me that Tom was going to kill me to get our father's inheritance."

"Someone? Man or woman?"

Gary shook his head. "They whispered. But they were insistent."

"After yesterday, this surprises you?"

"Tom's unbalanced, but I'd never think he was going to actually kill me. A beating, maybe. If he got a lucky shot in."

"You don't need my help. You need to go to the police." Nick leaned on the counter from the other side. "I don't provide bodyguard services." He sipped his coffee and winced. "This woman, did she say anything else?"

Gary shook his head and pushed the cup away. "Just confirmed my name and told me what I told you. I don't need a bodyguard. I need you to help beef up the security at my place. I don't want the cops wandering around a few million dollars' worth of pot plants."

"You've got good security. You caught me sneaking in."

Gary shook his head again. "It's okay, but you shouldn't have been able to get in as far as you did. And you were only caught because Charlie happened to be looking at the cameras. And Tom got to the front door with what I have now. I want — need — something more mobile. More cameras. Some thermals. You'd probably know better than me. And I want to be able to access the feed from my phone."

"Your father only has a week or so to live. If you really don't give a shit about him, leave the country until he's dead. That defeats your brother's plan. Show up at the will reading and even if your brother does show, there's little to contest."

"I'm more than happy to split it with him."

"I can reach out to Tom." Nick shrugged. "But he's not going to believe me."

"That head injury really fucked him up. You'll help me out?"

Nick put down his cup of coffee and opened a mapping program on his phone. He mirrored it to his television and motioned for Gary to follow him into the lounge room. He centred the map on the nursery.

The entrance gate was at the southern end, a short drive off the main road. The main road curved east, then north bracketing his property. A side road, lined with trees formed the north boundary and a power line down the west side closed the loop.

"What surveillance do you have now?"

Gary pointed to the four corners and the front gate. "IR cameras here and buried sensors every 15 or 20 metres along the side of the roads. There's fencing, of course, but that doesn't stop many." He looked at Nick. "Any."

Nick zoomed and pinched and panned. Sighed a bit and panned and pinched and zoomed a bit more. "Okay. This isn't going to be cheap." He chewed the inside of his cheek, in deep thought. "I need a shower. Make yourself comfortable. I'll call my surveillance guy. He should be here by the time I'm ready."

"You guys don't have any big friends, do you?"

"What are you doing, Tom?" Carol squinted through the morning sun. "I thought we'd spend the morning in bed."

Tom grunted as he pulled up his trousers. "You can, if you want. I'm ending this today."

She sat up. "Ending what?"

Tom glanced at her, naked in the comfortable bed, and his resolve wavered a bit. As it should. He shook his head and pulled on his T-shirt. "Wait here. I'll be back tonight." He checked the time on his phone. "I need to get to a place and I'm late. Where are the keys?"

She slumped back in bed. "Wherever you left them. What shit are you going to get into today?"

"Better you don't know."

"And if you're not back tonight?"

He flicked her a glance. "I will be." He grabbed the car keys from the TV stand. "Hey, if I pull this off, no more changing names every two or three months. And money will never be an issue again."

Davie knocked and entered Nick's apartment. He carried a large sports bag, weighed down with everything Nick had asked for, plus a couple of additional items. He pulled up short when he saw Gary. "Hey."

"Hey back at ya."

Nick padded barefoot out of his bedroom tucking in his shirt. "Hey, Davie."

"You, of all people, should lock your door."

"Left it open for you." Nick lifted the bag out of Davie's hand and hefted it. "You got it all?"

"And a bit." He glanced at Gary, then back at Nick. "What's this about?"

"Gary has asked us to beef up security on his — his farm. His brother is making a play and, you know, forewarned is forearmed." He placed the bag on the counter, slid the zipper open and checked the contents. Satisfied, he closed it. "And he wants to know if we've got any big friends."

Davie burst out in deep, full-throated laughter. "We're the geek squad. A few of my friends are big, but not in the way you're thinking. More in the extra-large size bag of Doritos and two litres of Coke for lunch large." He hefted the bag off the counter. "Not what you're looking for."

Nick smiled and jabbed a thumb in Davie's direction. "What did I tell you, Gary? More brains than brawn in our crowd." He pulled on his shoes. "Let's get the surveillance in place before anybody shows." He handed the rental keys to Davie. "Follow us. I'll travel with Tom."

Two Subaru WRX's and a Holden Ute were pulled off the shoulder east of the nursery, angled a bit to the left. Tom parked behind them. He got out of his car, finger-combed his greasy hair back and tapped on the back fender of the ute.

A man the size of a rugby front rower got out of the driver's side, the ute rocking as it released his weight. An identically sized man got out of the passenger side. The truck sat a good five centimetres higher.

"You Tom?" asked the driver. It sounded like large gravel rattling around the bottom of a distillery barrel. "I'm – "

Tom held up his hand. "I don't want to know your names. Nothing personal. Just don't."

"Ya got to call me something." He looked at his travel partner and smiled. "I'm Mr Black and my buddy is Mr Pink."

"Fuck you," said Mr Pink.

Black laughed. "Four more in the two cars in front of us. What are we doing out here in the fucking sticks?"

"It's beautiful out here, though," said Pink. He took a deep breath in through his nose. "Smell those gum trees. Don't smell that in Parramatta."

The other four had exited their respective vehicles and stood in a semi-circle facing Tom, their arms crossed.

Tom looked at Black. He pointed to the trees to his left. "My brother owns this property. I want what's on it. I'm paying you good money to help me get it. I'm sure he has some security people, and," he scanned the trees, "I've got no doubt there are cameras."

"Your brother is definitely here?"

Tom nodded at Pink. "He lives here. A house on the grounds. Nice place."

"What's your plan?" asked Black.

Tom raised his eyebrows. "I thought you guys were the experts."

"We usually just do as asked, but I've got a couple of ideas." He turned to Pink. "You take the car and move about a klick farther up the road. Two of you half a klick, and two stay here." Black looked at his watch. "Give me ten minutes. Tom and I are going in the front door and cause a bit of noise. You five attack from the rear."

Tom and Black backtracked toward the front of the nursery. Tom pulled off the road a hundred metres from the entrance and checked his watch. "Five minutes from now."

"How are we going to get in?"

"I'm going to call him out."

Black chuckled. "Good luck with that. Why do you want this place so bad? Nurseries are a fuck of a lot of work."

Tom licked his lips. Drummed his fingers on the steering wheel and double checked the time. "You're here to take him out. Kill him. Nothing else is your concern. Am I clear?"

Gary, for all his weed-derived income, drove a piece of shit, sun-faded, brown van. The nursery name and logo were painted in white on both sides. Something rolled around the back whenever Gary took a corner, accelerated, hit a speed bump or was at anything other than a dead stop.

"Look, Gary, pull over and I'll tie down whatever it is that's driving me nucking futs."

Gary laughed. "We're almost there."

"You can afford something better, right?"

"Living the part, mate. Couldn't have a hard-working farmer driving around in a Lexus. What's in the bag?"

"Well," said Nick. "The cameras at your place are static, and you can only see the feed in your home. These digitally pan and scan, and the feed can be accessed anywhere. I'll install the app on your phone after we mount them. Only Wi-Fi at your house, obviously, but when you get out from under the jammers, you'll be able to check them from anywhere."

"That it?"

"I'm going out on a limb and guessing that you don't want your system tied to the cops. That's about half of what I can do for you. Audio alone," Nick looked at Gary, "well, that's a waste of time. Unless you want hours of recordings of Kook-aburras, Bellbirds and Butcher birds."

"Good point. Nothing lethal?"

Nick stared at him. "What?"

Gary shook his head. "Never mind."

They sat in silence as Gary's van fought its way up the long, winding hill to the nursery. His phone rang as they approached the gate.

He pulled to a stop and pressed the button on the garage door opener clipped to his visor. He answered the phone as the gate slowly started opening. "Gary Goulding speaking."

"Brother."

Gary looked at Nick and put the phone on speaker. "Tom? What do you want?"

Tom was leaned back in the car, eyes closed, phone in his hand, earbuds in his ears. "Stupid question, brother. We need to talk. Let me in."

Black tapped him on the arm and pointed. Tom sat up and looked. He could see the van stopped at the gate, and the gate slowly opening.

"We don't need to talk, Tom. You need to turn yourself in," said Gary.

Tom started his car and slowly advanced up the shoulder. "Yeah, that's not going to happen." The gate was fully open now. "Never mind. We can do this later."

He watched the shit-brown van lurch forward and drive on to the property. Tom accelerated as the gate started to close. He parked outside the entrance and he and Black ran through the gate as it swung closed.

He checked his watch. "This is working out better than I expected it to."

"When you say, 'take him out', were you kidding about killing him?"

The driveway gently curved to the left toward the large house.

"What's in the greenhouses?"

Tom shook his head. "Not your business. We're going to go through the front door and you're going to take care of Gary, and then we leave."

"Again, 'take care of him' means what?"

Tom raised his eyebrows. "Exactly what you think it means."

Chapter Twenty-Four

"I hope your friend knows to call when he arrives. I'd have thought he'd get here before us with that car."

"Knowing Davie, he probably stopped for food," said Nick.

Gary parked in front of his house. Nick got out, bag in hand and slowly turned, surveying the trees around the house with a different perspective. He was trying to get in before. Now he would be trying to keep people out. "You've got some muscle?"

"A couple. You've met them."

Nick nodded. "An old man and a bulldog woman. Excellent. What about people to help place cameras on top of poles and trees?"

"There's a cherry picker in the barn. We'll use that. How long will this take?"

"Better part of the day. Show me your security room. I need to get a feel for where the existing cameras are."

Gary led him into a room at the back of the house. It was sparse as security rooms go. Three monitors, a laptop on a desk and a file cabinet. An uncomfortable looking chair was rolled to a corner. He hit the spacebar on the laptop and the three monitors slowly blinked to life.

"Shit. Too late." Gary took a deep, resigned breath and let it out slowly. Two men, two very large men, were threading through the shrubbery at the north side of the property. Another was coming in from the north-west and a couple coming in from the east. He tapped a command on the laptop and one of the monitors changed vision to cameras near the front gate.

"Isn't that your brother?" Nick pointed at the smaller of two men coming in from the main entrance.

"He's really pissing me off. Why in the hell is he doing this?"

Nick turned and left the room. "You going to call the police now?"

Gary grimaced. "I'd rather not. Last resort." He looked around his house. "Really don't want cops. I've grown accustomed to this place."

"I don't know if you've really taken a good look at me, but I'd last about a third of a second in a fight with any of these guys. Except maybe your brother."

Gary raised his eyebrows. "You think you could take him?"

"I think I could outrun him."

Shouting from the north side of the house pulled their attention away from the immediate debate of who would win that footrace.

"Seems like Charlie met a couple of trespassers." Gary grabbed the cricket Tom had left behind on his last visit.

"Might have been Gloria." Nick grabbed a fire poker. "I'm going to charge you for personal security services if I make it out of this alive." He followed Gary out of the house.

"Sure. How much would that be?" He started jogging toward the yelling, bat out by his side.

"Still calculating the rate. I'll let you know on the other side of this. It's per bruise."

Charlie was valiantly defending himself against two of the biggest people Nick had ever seen. His jog slowed as their sheer size filtered through his consciousness. "Fuuuuck."

"Don't slow down, mate." Gary swung his cricket bat at the legs of the man closest to him. The square edge caught him on the side of the knee, and he buckled with a shriek just as Charlie unleashed a massive right hook. Charlie missed. The momentum spun him around, his face hitting the other intruder's fist.

Nick hesitated a second, then jabbed the poker at the intruder's thigh. It was a massive target.

The intruder was knocked off balance by the unexpected face hitting his fist and by the time the poker hit his thigh, his arse was where his thigh was. Not as quite as large a target, but still substantial.

"Son of a bitch, you prick." The man stumbled and fell beside his comrade with the shattered knee. He grabbed his butt cheek, pulled his hand away and looked at the blood. "Jesus, Chri-"

Gary shut him up with a short, sharp bat smack to the forehead. Shattered knee was whimpering on the ground beside him.

"Oh, shut up." Gary tapped him on the head, too. "You okay Charlie?"

"Yeah." He pushed himself up. "Thanks. I think I was winning though."

"The hell you were. Where's your gun?"

"Gloria has it."

Nick's head swivelled between the two as they talked. "Wait. You've only got one gun? Total? Securing this whole place?"

"Security really hasn't been an issue prior to this. Really could have used your friend. The more bodies, the better." Gary looked east. "Two others coming in that way."

"If you head off your brother, might shut the whole thing down."

"We'll get flanked. The two from the east first, then my brother." Gary nodded at Charlie. "Are you sure you're okay?"

"Yeah. I am. Why do you keep asking?"

"There's blood coming out of your left ear."

Charlie wiped at the side of his head. Looked at the red streak and wiped his hands off on his denims. "That's not coming from inside my head. One of those pricks, you busted his knee, has a ring on his right pinkie. Caught me in the ear." He shook his head. "I'm getting slow."

"You're walking away. He's not."

"Yeah. Into the next fight."

That next fight was only one greenhouse away. And they were barely needed. Gloria had shot one of them in the knee and was warily circling with the other, arm extended with the firearm not wavering a millimetre.

The one with the shot knee was curled up swearing a stream of imaginative ways for Gloria to die. As she circled around his body, she kicked him in the head, silencing him.

She gestured with the gun at the one still standing. "Get on the ground."

"I'd do as she says."

"Hey, boss," said Gloria. "What took you so long?"

"Helping Charlie out. You seem to be managing."

The big guy slowly kneeled, a snarl coming from deep in his throat. "Idiots."

Charlie stepped behind him, placed a heel between the guy's shoulder blades, and pushed. "You're not moving fast enough. Put your arms behind your back, dickhead." He held his hand out to Gloria. "Hand me a zip tie."

"I thought you had them." She tucked the handgun in the back of her trousers and took a big step forward and landed a hard kick to the side of his head with her heel. "That'll keep him for a bit."

"Well, we should probably still zip tie him, right? Who knows how long he's going to be out."

Gloria turned her back on him and headed back toward the house. "He'll be out at least thirty minutes, and when he comes to, he'll be useless for at least two days. This isn't the movies. He should check himself into a hospital." She cleared her throat. "This was too easy. Something else is going on."

Nick glanced at Gary and raised an eyebrow.

Gary nodded. "My brother came in with a big friend from the south. There's one more coming in from the northwest."

Gloria altered her course. "I'll take the fuck in the northwest." She looked over her shoulder, her expression dripping with resentment. "You handle your brother."

She upped her pace and broke into a trot, disappearing around a greenhouse. Charlie, Gary and Nick continued toward the house.

"She didn't look pleased," said Nick.

"She's a damned good horticulturist and I doubt she likes the way her life has turned out."

Nick caressed the aluminium splint on his face. "I understand the feeling." He trudged ahead.

Gary reached out and stopped Nick's progress. Charlie ran into the back of him. "Son of a bitch."

A column of smoke rose from behind the rows of greenhouses.

"SON. OF. A. BITCH." Gary started running toward the house, Charlie close behind. Nick tried keeping up, but every jarring footstep was transmitted directly to his fractured nose. He slowed to a trot, moving as fast as he could, bearing as much pain as he could, which wasn't much.

He caught up to Gary, Charlie, facing off against Tom and a large collection of muscle formed into a single human being just outside the house.

"Tom."

The brother looked at Nick and smiled. It wasn't a friendly smile. "Hey, did I do that?"

He and his hired muscle had the house to their backs. Gary tapped the cricket bat against the ground. Nick shifted the fire poker from one hand to the other, alternating wiping the sweat on his palms off on his trousers.

"What the fuck, Tom?" Gary shifted forward, an eye always on Tom's companion. "Why?"

Tom looked beyond Gary, like he was waiting for something. Or someone.

Gary shook his head. "Your friends are incapacitated. I'm not surprised. You manage to screw up pretty much everything you touch."

Tom's smile slipped a bit. "All of them?"

The crack of a pistol shot north of them echoed off the trees.

Gary nodded. "All of them. Except this guy. Mountain man."

"Mr Black."

"Excuse me?"

The big guy glanced to his left, in the direction of the shot. "Call me Mr Black."

Gary shook his head, irritated. "I don't really give a shit. Piss off before the gun shows up."

Nick tilted his head. "Do you hear that?"

Faint sirens slowly grew louder. "I think you're getting the wrong kind of attention." Nick jabbed the fire poker in the dirt. He noticed Gary shuffling, tapping the bat against his boot.

Tom looked back at the fire, then toward the gate. The sirens were almost on them. "Shit." He wiped his mouth and pointed at Gary. "This isn't over." He darted behind a greenhouse and ran toward the fencing on the east side. Mr Black hesitated for a second and followed him.

Gary watched them go and waited until they were out of sight then ran toward the house.

"Jesus. What are you doing?" asked Nick.

The house wasn't completely engulfed yet, but it wasn't far from it. Flames licked from the back windows. The east side of the house was burning, but there were no flames at the front entrance, only thick smoke.

Gary pulled his shirt off and wrapped it around his mouth. He ran into the house, smoke swirling around him.

Nick took a step forward and Charlie grabbed him by the shoulder. "Don't be an idiot."

"What the hell is he doing?"

Charlie didn't get a chance to answer before Gary ran back out, duffle bag in one hand and knapsack over his

226

shoulder. He tossed the duffle to Nick. "Yours. Won't be needing them now." He glanced in the direction of the front gate. "I need to get the hell out of here."

He ran in roughly north of the direction Tom ran, Charlie right behind him.

Nick sighed. "Jesus." He dropped the fire poker and loped after them. He tried his phone, alternately looking where he was going and looking at his screen. SOS only. Cell sites jammed.

He caught up to them at the trees just before the fence line, almost barging into Charlie. "What are we doing?"

"I'm keeping an eye out for police." Gary adjusted his pack. "This place is blown. I had to grab my go bag. Figured you wouldn't want a bunch of surveillance electronics with little shiny stickers on them advertising your company and phone number found on the site that is soon going to be a major drugs crime scene."

"Thanks." He checked his phone again. Signal. "You guys need a lift somewhere?" He sent a text to Davie.

Charlie shook his head. "I'm good. Got a friend just up the road."

Gary tugged on his earlobe. "Yeah. Thanks. I need to lie low for a bit. Did Tom seem a bit stressed to you?"

"Really not a great time to be joking. Where are you going?"

Gary contemplated his answer. "Damned good question. I'm going underground for a little bit. Maybe take your advice and get out of the country until I read the old man's obit."

Nick looked over his should at the nursery. "Not sure leaving the country is a good idea."

"Why's that?"

"The cops are going to be looking for you very hard once they inventory your crops."

Chapter Twenty-Five

Tom scrambled over the fence, catching his trousers on barbed wire and landing on his arse. "Shit." He rolled out of the way as Mr Black followed, almost landing on him.

"Hey, boss, where's your car?"

"No. You're on your own. Hike to wherever your buddy parked and hope he left the keys with it. I never want to see you again."

Black clenched his fists, his forearms bunching like over-fed pythons. "Ya prick."

Tom ignored him. He pushed through the undergrowth to the edge of the road. Traffic was light. He used his phone to determine his location and turned right, walking along the shoulder.

Black trotted up beside him. "Give me a lift to the car."

Tom stopped walking. He slowly turned to Black. "Listen, you over-fed pile of barely sentient muscle. Turn around and walk. You are on your own. You're a worthless piece of wombat turd swimming in a lake of emu piss."

Black narrowed his eyes and leaned forward. "Maybe I just take your car."

"You'd be dead before the sun went down. Who do you think I am? I have connections everywhere. My family runs this country. I'd know where you live, who your weaknesses are, and they'd be dead before dark." Tom was up on his toes now, spraying Black with his spittle. "You are lucky I don't kill you now. When your vast ineptitude is found out you'll never get a job in this line of work again. You'll be lucky to bounce at a country pub. Fuck off out of my face." He wiped the froth from the corners of his mouth and used Black's shirt to clean his hand.

Black looked down at him. He opened his mouth as if to say something, thought better of it and turned around and started walking.

Tom took a deep breath, watched him walk away, and pulled out his phone. "Hey, fucknuts!"

He took a picture as Black turned, then gave him the finger and turned his back. He sent the picture to the person who was supposed to have provided him with a team. He added a caption. "Fucking call me fucking right now."

He found his car where he left it. Pressed the fob and unlocked it. He was in the car and making a U-turn when his phone rang. He pulled over and answered.

"Took you long enough to call back." He put his earbuds in and continued driving. "You got the picture?"

"What in the hell is going on? I'm hearing things."

"Well, that's because things happened. You're going to give me every dollar back. What a useless group of halfwits." He drove past the entrance of the nursery. Two police cars were parked at the entrance and a fire truck was inside, heading toward the house. "This was a catastrophe."

"You need to be a bit more specific."

"What have you heard?"

"What happened there?"

"Your guys were as useless as eunuchs in a brothel. Six walked in, one walked out. Ran actually. Like a scared little rabbit."

"They met an overwhelming force, I heard."

"I don't know who's telling you that shit, but it was my brother, some geeky accounting schlep whose nose I'd already broken, an old man, and a bird with an antique revolver. Not at all overwhelming. Useless fucks."

Tom heard a long sigh on the phone line. "Well, you didn't give me much lead time."

"Who fed you this shit?" Tom glanced at his phone. "That Mr Black twat must have called you. Phones don't work inside that place."

"Mister who?"

"Arsehole called himself Mr Black. Travelled with a guy he called Mr Pink." Tom entered the freeway heading back toward Sydney. "Big, albeit useless, idiot."

"His name is Bert. According to him, there's a couple of concussions, and one of the team was shot in the leg."

"By the bird. With a revolver Ned Kelly would have thought was too old to use. Look, mate, I'm running out of time here. I figure I've got a week, probably less."

"Bert said there were a dozen or more laying in wait."

Tom took a breath and shook his head. "A couple of things. First, they weren't laying in wait, they're not fucking chickens. It's lying in wait. Second, there wasn't a dozen of anyone. Just the four of them, my brother being the most threatening, and he's a guy who plays with plants all day. I'm running out of time."

"I know. I know. Straight talk, you want to kill your brother, right?"

"As soon as possible."

"Where is he?"

Tom punched the steering wheel. "I don't bloody know."

"What's in it for me if I help, personally?"

"Let's meet. When's a good time?"

Tom listened to almost a minute of mobile phone network hiss before he got an answer. "There's a three-hour window starting in about forty-five minutes. Come here."

"Not there, mate. That would be stupid. Text me where."

Nick held up his hand and backed into the trees, puling Gary with him.

"What?"

Nick pointed. The large man who had left with Tom was walking up the shoulder. He passed without noticing them.

They stood and stepped out onto the road, watching him walk away. Nick held up his phone and took a picture of the receding figure. "He seemed pissed off."

The sound of rubber tyres rolling over loose gravel turned him around. Davie smiled at him and waved from the driver's seat.

"Our ride." Nick opened the driver's door. "Hop in the back. Gary and I need to talk."

"Thank you, Davie. Oh, you're very welcome, Nick." He got out and slid into the back seat, sitting in the middle. "You guys have fun?"

"No so much." Nick checked the car's charge. "Where am I taking you, Gary? I could take you to your father's place."

"Hell no. Penny's place, I guess."

"Not Patty?"

"Who?"

"I was led to believe you were currently living with a retro-chick named Patty."

"Oh, no. That was a short time thing. I ended it. She's still willing." He chuckled. "She's a bit off. Retro hippy. Take me to Penny's."

Nick checked the distance against the available range. "I can do that, but she'll need to let me plug in when I'm there."

Gary raised his eyebrows and half chuckled. "Sure. Why not."

Nick executed a tight U-turn. Davie slid to one side of the back seat, then grabbed the headrests and centred himself again. The electric car accelerated silently past the police cars and fire trucks streaming into the nursery.

"What the hell happened in there?" Davie rubbernecked as they passed the ever-enlarging column of black smoke rising from the compound.

"Shit happened. My brother wants me dead. When my father dies, Tom wants to be the only heir alive. Whatever my father's will says, he'll contest it."

Nick checked the police in his rear-view mirror. They were staying put. "And if your brother doesn't kill you, the cops will get you for possession of a hell of a lot more weed than would be considered personal use."

"You'd think I'd be worried about that, wouldn't you?" He shook his head. "My exposure is zero. Everything is owned by shell companies. Layers of them. But thanks for reminding me." He opened a banking app on his phone. "The accounts associated with this property's titular owner, a fictitious Norman Stormison, are about to be emptied and deleted." He entered a couple of commands. "Then the accounts that received Norman's funds will be emptied and deleted. Three more times and nobody will be able to find the money." He grinned at Nick. "Except me."

"And maybe me. That's the kind of thing I worked on in my old job with the AFP. We were pretty good then. I imagine they're better now, five years on."

Gary went silent for a few minutes. He tapped on the centre console. Looked over at Nick and opened his mouth, but before he could ask, Nick shut him down.

"No. I can't help you hide it better. I've got to draw the line somewhere. But I won't take it further. My job was to find you and deliver you to your father." He sighed. "I'm failing at that, though."

"Maybe you could tell me the kinds of things they look for?"

"One problem at a time." Nick checked the charge again. "The hills didn't do this car any favours." He glanced at Davie in the rear-view mirror. "The added weight in the back isn't helping, either."

"You arsehole."

"We're going to be coasting to Penny's at this rate. Are you going to call ahead?"

Gary shook his head. "And give her a chance to tell me to piss off before I get there? I'll negotiate face-to-face."

"Braver man than I," opined Davie from the back.

The car had 8% charge when Nick parked in front of Penny's house.

"She's let the garden go to shit," said Gary, a tinge of disappointment in his voice. He got out of the car and squatted by the flowering vines growing along a brick wall by the driveway. He rubbed one of the leaves between his thumb and forefinger and shook his head.

He stood and came face to face with Penny. "Oh. Hi."

Penny was wearing gardening clothes, a broad-brimmed hat and sunglasses. She crossed her arms. "What are you doing here? Trying to sell me gardening services?"

He pointed vaguely behind him, generally toward the flowering vine. "Someone should. You're using the wrong fertiliser."

"I'm not using any fertiliser."

"Then I guess that's what's wrong."

"Why are you here, Gareth? I thought we had an agreement. And I thought you were with Patty."

"The Patty thing ended almost as soon as it started." Gary wiggled an index finger in his ear and gave her a wan smile. "I'm in a bit of a pile of shit."

Penny looked past him to Nick and waved at him, giving him a small smile. "So I understand. What do you think I can do about it?"

"I need a place to lay low."

"Lie low. You're not a fucking chicken." She sniffed again. "But you're not lying low here, though. Chicken."

Gary looked at Nick, tilting his head, widening his eyes, beckoning. Maybe even begging.

"Penny, it's great to see you again. He does need to lie low. His brother wants to kill him." He held up the slow charge cable. "Can I steal some electricity from you for about an hour? I need a bit of a top up to get home."

She looked at Nick over her sunglasses. "An hour?"

He shrugged. "That will be enough to get me back to a decent charging location." He held up his hands. "Davie and I will stay out of your way." He looked across the street. Dora had a curtain pulled to one side. "We'll have tea with Dora."

"She'll like that." She turned back to Gary. "What's this about Tom?"

Nick strung the cable from the charging port on the car to an exterior outlet. "You'll like Dora, Davie. She's got great biscuits."

"Is that a gross euphemism?"

"No. Real, home-made biscuits."

Dora opened the door as Nick walked up the steps. "You're back. And who is your friend? Would you like some tea?"

Davie held out his hand. "My name is Davie. I'm a good friend of Nick's. He says you have amazing biscuits."

Dora narrowed her eyes and subconsciously moved her hands toward her breasts. "Nick, are you getting fresh?"

"I meant those shortbreads, Dora." He looked toward his car. "I've got to charge it up."

She nodded. "Great for the environment? At a cost." She led them into her lounge room. "I see you brought Gary by. Is he back for good?" She peered out the window. "The garden could use it. Tea? Coffee?" She smiled at Davie. "My biscuits?"

"Tea would be nice. And biscuits. Can we talk to you about Gary for a minute?"

"I'll grab the tea first, hun. You just wait here."

Davie sat back in the chair and took in his surroundings. Books. Everywhere. Stacked in the bookcases and lying on top of the stacked books. Stacked on the coffee table and the table the lamp stood on. "She likes to read."

"I think she wrote half of them."

Dora returned holding a silver tray. Three teacups on saucers, a large teapot and a plate of shortbread biscuits. There was a bowl of sugar cubes and a small pitcher of cream. "I only wrote seven of them. Working on number eight, but I'm getting hung up on the third act." She placed the tray on the coffee table and poured tea. "Cream and sugar yourselves. Tell me about Gary. Is he back? I think Penny is good for him, and he's good for her."

Nick leaned forward. "If we leave here and Gary stays, it's because Penny has allowed him to stay with her, lying low."

"Lying low from whom?"

"His brother. Tom. There's a bit of a beef between them. Pretty serious."

"Oh, you've got to tell me more."

"Listen, Dora, you can't tell anybody he's here. At least not for a few days until I sort this out."

She made like she was locking her mouth and tossing the key over her shoulder. "Mum's the word." She had a sparkle in her eye and fresh colour in her cheeks. "But you do have to tell me what this is about."

Nick smiled and poured some cream into his tea. "We've got an hour. Why not?"

Chapter Twenty-Six

Kids played on the beach, oblivious to the searing heat reflecting off the sand. A row of boards floated out past the swells, well outside the swimming area, waiting for the perfect one. Surf lifesavers scanned the water, looking for inexperienced tourists trying to drown. So far it had been a good day.

Tom stood on the beach, scanning for his contact. Sweat dripped down his back and pooled in the hollow above his belt line. Sweat beaded on his head and was staining his shirt under his moobs. He looked at his watch and clenched his fist. "Where are you, you prat?"

"That's not nice."

"What took you so long?" The familiar voice was behind him. Tom started turning around and was stopped by a firm hand on his shoulder. "No. We're not together."

"Why are we meeting here?" Tom plucked his T-shirt away from his expansive gut. "This is hell."

The chuckle behind him was light, but menacing. "Nobody on earth who knows you would expect to find you here. Ever. I felt this place was as good as any. Better than most." The voice paused. "I've got more information on the men I sent you. You've put a serious dent in my inventory."

Tom shrugged. "You sent idiots."

"I sent soldiers who expected better leadership than 'let's split-up and make us all easy targets'. Mate, you're a fucking mess."

"I need my money back. The thirty grand I sent you for those useless, barely sentient piles of 'roided out muscle." A hand tried to stop him from turning but he pushed it away and confronted the voice. "You sent crap inventory. I need a refund."

The man who sent the men, who took his money, his father's business manager, sneered. "Do you have your receipt?" In contrast to the sweaty mess that was Tom, William was the image of cool. His round sunglasses reflected sun into Tom's eyes. His pale blue polo shirt was clean, pressed, and fitted him like a glove.

Tom grabbed him by the front of the shirt, bunching the material in his fists, and pulled him closer. "You think you're a fucking joker? I need that money, cash, before the end of the day."

William looked around. "We really don't want to draw attention to ourselves. You, especially. I understand a lot of people are looking for you." He smirked. "Not your father, of course. Killing your mother puts a bit of a crimp in the old family relationships, doesn't it?"

Tom bunched tighter, pulling William even closer. "Shut your bloody mouth." He let go and stepped back. "I don't think that's what happened. I need money. You know that when my old man dies, I'm going to get his, so you know I'm good for it." He poked William in the chest. "And you know how close the old guy is to packing it, right?"

He looked around and leaned close. "Were you serious about helping me get rid of my brother?"

"Did I say that?"

Tom grabbed his shirt again. "You shit."

A young surf lifesaver approached. Young, and extremely healthy. He towered over both Tom and William. His close-cropped sun-bleached hair was damp. He wore a light nylon jacket over his bare upper torso, but that seemed to accentuate his muscles more than cover them. He smiled a fake smile. "Everything okay here, gentlemen? Lots of young families here. We don't want any problems."

Tom let go of William's shirt and turned on the lifeguard. "Why don't you pay attention to the brats in the water like you're supposed to be doing and mind your fucking business?"

William stepped between them. "My friend has just lost his father. I apologise for his outburst. We'll take this conversation to the parking lot." He grabbed Tom by the arm. "Let's go mate."

"Keep moving past the lot." The smile disappeared. "We've got the cops on speed dial, and they love an excuse to come to the beach."

Tom held up his hands. Surrendering. Something he hated doing. Backing down was a sign of weakness, but at this point, something in the back of his damaged brain was telling him to surrender. For now. "Right-o, buddy. We're leaving. Keep your pants on."

He trudged through the sand to the parking lot. He grabbed William by the arm. "My money or I'll tell my father how you've been skimming his accounts."

William wrenched his arm free. "Never happened, champ. And your father hates you. He's not going to listen to anything you say."

"I'LL MAKE HIM LISTEN!"

"Hey!" The lifeguard started walking up the dune toward them. "What did I say?"

Tom held up his hands again, then pointed at William. "Money."

The car interior was scalding hot. He rolled down all the windows, set the A/C to its coldest temperature and cranked up the fan. He peered out the windscreen at the lifeguard, standing with his massive hands on his hips, glaring at him.

Tom flipped him the bird, grim smile on his face. "Yeah, yeah. Whatever." He pulled the driver's door closed and leaned back with his eyes closed. His head was throbbing. The anger sat deep in his chest, a burning ball of fury with multiple targets.

But they were targets he couldn't see. His brother, he didn't know where he was. And his anger was strongest when pointed at him, and he really didn't know why. The anger was real. There was no question about that. He wanted to put his hands around Gary's throat and squeeze until the light left his beady little eyes.

But the thoughts swirling around that anger, the why of it all, were hard to grab. They flitted through his brain and were torched by the incandescent fury which permanently resided there.

He opened his eyes. The lifeguard was a couple of steps closer, finger pointed at him, mouthing something. He shook his head, shoved the gear lever into Reverse and floored it, just missing a woman carrying her son.

"Fuck." He threw it into Drive and left, the shriek of rubber on hot asphalt drowning out the cries from the little boy. He lost traction and swerved, glancing the passenger side of the car off a light standard. The window shattered, spraying the inside of the car with pebbles of safety glass.

He had a blinding flashback. The car accident. The one that killed his mother. Hitting the interior roof of the car, bouncing his head off the support posts, then landing in a heap on the ground. He was driving. He shook his head. Was he driving? Memories were like water spilling over cupped hands.

It didn't make a difference.

He had to find Gary and end this before the old man died. It had been years since they were on good terms. He didn't know where he would go now that his home was torched. There were limited options.

Wallace stood to one side and let the motel manager unlock the door.

"The room, uh, hasn't been cleaned since they left. I apologise." The thin, balding manager looked like he was afraid he was going to be arrested for sloth.

"That's perfect." Wallace held out his hand. "I'll take the key. You'll get it back when we're finished."

The manager hesitated, then pushed the key card into the detective's hand and scurried back to the motel office.

Lin pushed the motel room door open and wrinkled her nose. "Jesus. May my life never be so bad that I end up in a place like this."

The bed was unmade. Garbage was strewn around the bin on the floor by the TV table. Wallace wandered into the bathroom and immediately backed out. "You and me both. Anything useful, or do we just get the hell out of here?"

Lin pulled on a pair of latex gloves. She averted her head and spilled the contents of the garbage can onto the bed. Wadded up napkins with barbecue sauce mixed with empty crisps bags and soda cans.

And a couple of credit cards and a driver licence.

Wallace put his own latex gloves on and picked up the licence. "Terry Graves. Definitely the right place, Definitely on to a new identity."

Lin grabbed a pen from the bedside table and stirred through the rest of the trash. "What do you think the odds might be of this place having any kind of security system?"

"Let's find out." Warren dropped the credit cards and licence into evidence bags and slid them in his suit jacket pocket. "I'm not betting, though."

The manager had the nerves of a chihuahua in a thunderstorm. He scurried from behind his desk, flop sweat leaving stains under his armpits and on the collar of his T-shirt. "Y-yes, what can I help you with?"

"Relax. We're not here to bust you for anything." Warren looked around. "This time." He extracted the evidence baggies from his pocket and held up the driver licence. "You recognise this person?"

"T-that's Mr Graves."

"Sherlock, his name is on the card. Have you seen him?"

"Well, yeah. He and his girl were in that room for a couple days. Of course I recognise him. He still owes me money, so if you find him, let me know."

"What's the girl look like?" asked Lin. "Or was she a woman?"

The manager put his hands out in front of him, palms down. "No, no, no. None of that kiddie stuff happens around here. It was a woman. A bit taller than him. Blonde. Probably from a bottle because her eyebrows were so dark. Ink all over her."

"Like a sleeve? Can you describe it?" Lin held a pen over her note pad.

"Nah, it was really disorganised. Like anytime she scraped a couple of bucks together she'd get whatever popped into her head etched into her skin."

"You remember any of them?"

He shook his head. "Nothing memorable."

Lin closed her notebook and crossed her arms. "You have any kind of security system in this place? Cameras, specifically?"

"Yeah, of course. One in here and one outside the door."

"Nothing down by the room Graves was in?"

"The one outside the door is wide angle. Might pick up something."

Wallace pointed behind the counter. "We can access it here?"

"You have a warrant?"

Lin took a step forward. She wasn't a tall person, but she was still taller than the manager. "The video from the days he was here. On this thumb drive. In the next five minutes." She dropped the thumb drive in his hand.

"R-right. One minute." He offered a weak smile. "Not five."

The video was useless. Wallace and Lin were sitting in a small meeting room at the station, watching the grainy image of a hooded man walk briefly in front of the camera, forward and backward as the scrubbed the video back and forth.

"There's nothing here." Wallace pushed back from the table. "We're back at square one." He looked at Lin. "You hear me?" She was staring at the monitor, chewing the inside of her cheek. "Hello?"

"Let me see the driver licence again."

Wallace slid it across the table, still in the evidence bag. "Why? They were all wiped clean. No prints."

She tapped some commands and pulled up security video of the lobby. "I recognise that face. We've seen him before."

"Everybody looks like I've seen them before after a while."

"This one was memorable." She selected the video she was looking for and scrubbed it forward to when Nick Harding was in the station."

"Harding? It's not him."

"Wait." There was no audio. But the video said enough. She froze the image.

Wallace snapped his fingers. "Oh, hang on. That loud arsehole. Gibson. Troy Gibson. Right?"

Lin nodded. "We have his new name. And we have his prints."

Chapter Twenty-Seven

Nick checked the app on his phone then placed it face down on the table. "The car is more than half charged, Dora. We should get going."

Davie picked up three biscuits and wrapped them in a paper napkin. "For the road. These are delicious, Dora. You'll have to send me the recipe."

She smiled and clucked and flitted about them as they gathered themselves and made for the front door. "You must drop by more often, Nick. And bring your – friend – Davie with you."

"Oh, we are just friends."

"Certainly, love. It's all good with me."

Davie looked at Nick and smiled. "I'd be delighted to come back for a visit. If you promise more of those biscuits."

"Those are but a small sample of what I can do in the kitchen." She patted Davie on the stomach. "I'm sure you have very discerning tastes. Just give me a little warning before you come. I'm used to cooking for one. It'll take a bit of preparation." She winked at Nick. "You've got my number. Any time."

"Thank you, Dora. I'll take you up on that."

Davie removed the charging cable from the port on the back fender of the car and coiled it and placed it in the boot. "You think Gary will be staying here?"

"They went inside. That's a positive sign." Nick knocked on the front door. "You might get the front seat on the way back."

Penny opened the door and stepped to one side. "Come on in. I have you to blame for this."

Davie took a step back. "I'll wait out here."

Gary was seated in a chair at the kitchen table, both hands wrapped around a large mug of coffee. He smiled at Nick and pointed to a chair. "Want a cup?"

Nick sat across from him. "No, thanks. I've got to get Davie back to work, and I need to stop by the hospital to check in on my father."

"Sorry to hear that. Is he okay?"

"Mild heart thing. Too mean to die. They stuck a stent in somewhere. Then some clotting slowed him up. He's checking out this afternoon. He'll be throwing 3-irons in the water hazards by next week." He leaned forward. "It's cool with you and Penny?"

Gary smiled with half his mouth and raised an eyebrow. It looked like he had a stroke on the left side of his face. "Baby steps. She's letting me stay."

"For a week," said Penny. "And not a day longer." She stormed through the kitchen and into a back bedroom.

Gary looked over his shoulder then leaned forward. "I haven't told her exactly what's going on. Just that Tom has gone a bit psycho, and I need to lie low for a bit. Nothing about my father, okay?"

"She knows. I told her."

"Damn."

She returned from the bedroom with a stack of blankets and a pillow. "You sleep on the sofa. This isn't a reconciliation." She stopped them on the sofa. "Don't think it is."

Gary glanced at Nick, a we'll see look on his face.

"Okay." Nick placed both hands on the table, palms down, and pushed himself upright. "I only came in here to see if we needed to drive you home. And since we don't, I should get going. Still a lot of day ahead of me." He pointed at Gary. "We still need to talk about some things. I'll call you tomorrow."

Gary saluted him with his mug. "Looking forward to the call."

Davie pushed himself off the side of the car as Nick approached. "Just the two of us?"

"Yeah. He's going to try to reconcile with her and if he's lucky, she won't stab him to death over the next week."

Davie chuckled and settled into the very comfortable passenger seat. "Home, James. I've got to track down Tom's finances." He opened the napkin and looked lovingly at the shortbreads. "Don't ask. I'm not sharing." He tapped the screen on the console. "How do I get music in this thing?"

"Pair your phone, listen to whatever you want."

"You okay?"

"Penny's is a pretty obvious place to hide. I think it's a dumb idea."

Davie took a deep breath. "I don't get it. You've found the missing heir and he doesn't want to reconcile. Case number one, a bust. But you'll get paid. Plus, you know who the deadbeat is, his real identity, so go to the client, and the cops, and close this one out also. Two cases, both resolved, and you — we — both get a pocket of cash and head to the beach. With a cooler of beer."

Nick chewed the inside of his cheek as he navigated traffic onto the motorway. "I'm not finished. Something's not right and I need to find out what it is, or I will spend the rest of my life wondering about it."

"Not really the rest of your life." He stared at Nick. "Right?"

"Probably."

"Shit. You always do this. Just close them, man. You've done your job."

Nick shook his head. "Not yet."

Davie opened the Bluetooth settings on his phone. "How do you pair?"

Nick's phone rang through the car's speakers. "Hold off on that for a second." He answered the call. "Nick Harding Investigations. How can I help you?"

"It's Lucy, looking for an update, Nick. Any update. Can you tell me who has been defrauding us? And how? Is an arrest imminent? I need name and contact details so we can file a lawsuit to collect damages."

Nick looked at Davie. Raised his eyebrows. Should I tell her?

Davie nodded and pointed in the general direction of the centre console. "Yes."

"Yes what?" Asked Lucy.

Nick shook his head. "Not yet. Not yet, Lucy. I'm - we're - getting really close. My partner and I have travelled over a lot of regional Australia looking for this person. I'm close. Extremely close, but not there yet. Yet. Emphasis on yet."

"I have an exec meeting tomorrow morning. How far away are you, do you think?"

Nick looked at Davie and shrugged. He swallowed. "Sure, yeah. What time is the meeting tomorrow?"

"11:00 a.m."

"Cool, cool, cool. I'll have something for you before then."

"Please do. My career and your stellar reputation are on the line." The call disconnection sounded to Nick like it was more aggressive than usual, though with nobody actually slamming a receiver in a cradle anymore it was difficult to tell.

"Why didn't you tell her?"

Nick shrugged. "I don't know where he is, mainly. And that something else that's going on. I need to find out what it is."

An hour later, Davie back at his home office, had Nick parking, again, at the exorbitantly priced short-term parking at the hospital. He rushed in the A&E entrance, pushed the Up button at the lifts and his mother tapped hm on the arm.

"We're down here."

His father was beside her, in a pair of pyjamas, his bathrobe and a pair of hospital slippers. "Join us for tea?"

His father's face looked to Nick like it had more real colour than he'd seen in years. Not the third bottle of wine flush, but a healthy glow. "You're looking good, pops. You're leaving today?"

He shook his head and scowled. "One more night." Then he smiled at his wife. "One more sponge bath from the lovely Mildred."

"Mildred?" He looked at his mother, who was stifling a laugh. "Mildred? Who is Mildred?"

"I'm pretty sure she's older than me. She's got a thing for your father. I'm pretty sure he's going to give her a heart attack." She took him by the arm. "The cafe is this way. And the food isn't too bad."

The hospital had put some money into their facilities. The cafe had ten tables inside and six out on the patio. His mother had them sit while she got the tea and biscuits.

"You're looking good, pops."

"You said that already. You need money or something?"

Nick held up his hands and smiled. "No, no. I'm good. I meant it. There's real colour in your face. Whatever they did to you in here has done you good."

George tapped his chest. "Stuck a stent in. Cleaned out the pipes while they were in there. I haven't felt this good in decades." He nodded at the aluminium splint on his son's nose. "You getting into good trouble?"

"How well do you know the Gouldings?"

"We've golfed. Socialised in the same circles. Why?"

"Two cases. First one, Larry hires me – "

"Yeah, you told me. They've intersected."

Nick nodded. "Wasn't sure you'd remember. You're getting old. Lawrence engaged me to track down his youngest."

"Gareth."

Nick inhaled slowly through his nose. "Right. Gary. Old man Larry is about a week from becoming worm food and he wants to find his son to make sure he gets what's in his will."

"Ridiculous."

"Why's that?"

"He doesn't need to find him. His executor has up to a year after the death to track him down."

"Who am I to argue? He's paying me well."

"There's that." He pursed his lips. "And you've found him?"

"It took me a couple of days."

George smiled. "So that's good."

"I'm not finished. In a separate case, a finance company engaged me to track down a deadbeat who has been using a series of aliases to defraud them. Out of a crap load of money."

"Had to have someone inside, somewhere to help."

Nick nodded. "True. I'm still not finished." He held up his hand. "It's good. Let me finish."

Susie lowered a tray of tea in takeaway cups and a plate of pastries on the table. "Don't let me interrupt."

"I tracked down the deadbeat. Had some help from Davie."

"Oh, how is he doing?"

"He's great, Mum. Thanks for the tea." He glanced at his father who was smiling at him. "I'm going to finish this story though, okay?"

"Oh, don't let me stop you."

Another deep breath in through his nose. "I'm still sorting out the inside help, though I've got a pretty good idea who it is. I did find the deadbeat." He leaned forward.

"The other son. Tom. Gary's older brother. Yeah. I told you, you've already told me."

"Recapping, is all. Getting everyone up to speed."

George was shaking his head halfway through that sentence. "Thomas is dead."

"He is very much alive." He tapped, gently, on the splint. "This is courtesy of him."

"No, no. He died. in that car accident." George picked up a biscuit and took a bite. "Lawrence was heartbroken."

Nick slowly shook his head. "Dead to him, maybe, but not *dead* dead. Tom was driving the car that killed his wife. Gary couldn't take the strife and pissed off on his own and Tom was excised from the family."

George shifted in his chair. "Then Tom has a legitimate challenge to the will."

"And therein lies the rub. I think he's trying to kill Gary to eliminate the competition. And I'm in the middle of it. I've got to track down Tom, find out where he is, and get enough evidence to convince the cops to pick him up."

"Long way away from financial crimes."

Nick waggled his hand in a 'so-so' motion. "Financial crimes adjacent. It's been an interesting few days. But I stopped by to see you. What's the prognosis?"

"The doctors say he's going to live another twenty years, at least," said his mother.

"My luck." George smiled. "But I do feel better than I have in a long while." He reached across the table and took his wife's hand. "I think I might take advantage of this."

"If you don't run away with Mildred."

George winked at Nick. "Susie, I can confirm that Mildred gives great sponge baths." He held out his hand to stop her from replying. "But not as good as yours. However, if you want to keep that edge, you may have to practice more often."

"Oh, god, I think I'm going to lose my lunch. Look, folks, this has been a great catch up, but if you keep talking like this I'm going to have to leave."

His mother grabbed his arm. "Okay. We'll stop. You stay. Any improvement in your love life?"

Nick pretended to push away from the table. "Definitely my cue to leave."

"Never mind. Not my business."

Nick smiled at his mother. "I've been picking up some good vibes from a client. The deadbeat client. Lucy."

"You like her?"

"Susie, quit sticking your nose in." George reached for a biscuit and was met with a slap on the back of his hand. "Hey!"

"None for you, George Arthur Harding. These are butter cookies. Teeming with all of the bad cholesterols."

"Jesus." George sighed. "Might have been better if I died."

"Lots of tasty healthy food, pops." Nicks phone started vibrating in his pocket. He dug it out and held up a hand. "Carrots. Broccoli. Celery." He smiled at his father, and he answered. "Hey, Gary. She kicking you out already?"

"There's a crowd around the house. Somehow that FUCK found me. I need you to – " Nick heard a crash and wood splintering.

"Gary?"

"They've broken down the door." He sounded like he was running. "I'm heading to the back of the – "

There was another crash.

"Shit. Nick. I'm fucked."

Then the three tones indicating a terminated call.

Chapter Twenty-Eight

This time Nick really pushed back from the table. "I need to go. I have a client in trouble. I'm glad you're doing better, pops. I'll stop by the house in a couple of days and run the grill for you." He saw the look on his mother's face. "Chicken skewers. No red meat. Got it."

"Roo steaks are good."

"Something for another day." His phone started ringing again. "I need to take this."

"This is you, right, Nick?"

Nick waved to his parents and walked toward the entrance. "Dora. Things getting exciting up there?"

"You know?"

"Gary called me. He was cut off. What did you see?"

"Oh, it's a mess, Nick. You need to get up here."

"Did you see what happened?"

"Most of it's on my doorbell camera. I'll download it. Are you coming up?"

Nick slid into the car and paired his phone. Tossed it in the centre console and continued the conversation. "I'm on my way now. Get the download, that's good, but what did you see?"

"Four utes showed up. A bunch of guys poured out and kicked in the front door. I could hear the noise in there from all the way over here."

"I'm on my way up there. Are Gary and Penny okay, do you know?"

"They took Gary. I haven't seen Penny since they left. I'm going to go over and see if she's okay."

"No. Dora, don't do that." Nick accelerated onto the westbound freeway, edging the tolerances of speed cameras and radar guns. "You don't know if anyone stayed behind?"

"No, I think they all left. She might need help."

"Dora, please, no. Call triple-0 and tell the police what happened. Give them a copy of the doorbell video. Someone may be keeping a thumb on Penny to make sure Gary does whatever it is they want Gary to do. Please, just call triple-0 and tell the cops what you saw." He glanced at the GPS on the dash. "I'll be there in fifteen minutes. Promise me?"

"Okay. You make sense. Hurry."

Nick ended the call. "Siri, call Davie."

The ringing came through the car speakers.

"What's up, Nick?"

"I'm going to send you a video in about twenty minutes. It'll be poor resolution because it's from Dora's doorbell cam, so I'm not expecting miracles, but I'd like you to see how many faces you can identify."

"Sounds exciting. What's the background?"

"A bunch of people kicked in Penny's door and absconded with Gary. I think it's Tom, but I need confirmation, as well as anyone else involved."

"That's going to be difficult. From across the street those faces are going to not much more than fuzzy blobs, but I'll try."

"Thanks. Call me when you find out anything." He took the exit into Penny and Dora's suburb.

"You're on your way there?"

"A couple of minutes out."

"See if you can get some more of Dora's biscuits."

Nick laughed and hung up. He turned the corner to Dora's street and pulled to the kerb in front of her house. Two marked police cars, lights flashing, were parked on the street in front of Penny's house.

Dora came out on the front step and waved at Nick. Her face was pinched with worry. "Nicky. Thank you for coming. This was such a nice neighbourhood. I think I'm going to have to move now."

Nick gently closed the car door and walked around to Dora. He gave her a light hug. "This was a one-off thing." He looked across the street. "How's Penny?"

"I'm not sure. The coppers got here about five minutes ago. If she was hurt, I'm sure they would have called an ambo by now."

Nick gave her hand a squeeze. "You get that doorbell video for me, and I'll check on Penny. Make a copy for the police, too. It'll help."

She nodded and wiped away a tear. "Let her know she should come over here for tea if she's up to it."

"I will." Nick skirted the police cars and leaned in Penny's front door. He knuckle-rapped on the door frame. "Penny?"

A uniform came out of the lounge room and blocked his path. "She's a bit busy right now. Who are you?" she asked.

"Nick Harding. I'm a friend." He stepped to one side to let the officer see Dora's house. "There's a nice little old lady, scared out of her skin, in that house with doorbell footage of the attack. I'm sure you'd have gotten to it eventually, but I'm pretty certain she'd appreciate a uniform showing up to reassure her of her safety. Her name is Dora," Nick looked at the officer's name plate, "Officer Logan. How is Penny doing?"

Logan wrote Dora's name down in her pad and nodded Nick into the house. "She'll survive. Thanks for the tip." She closed the notepad and walked across the street to Dora's.

Nick found Penny and two uniforms in the kitchen. Penny had an ice pack on her cheek, just under her left eye. She saw Nick and gave him a half smile.

"I knew Gary would be bad news."

"What happened?"

One of the officers taking notes looked up. "And you are, sir?"

"He's a friend. Thanks for coming by Nick." Penny leaned down and looked at the officer's face. "Are we finished?"

"I still suggest you get checked out at the hospital. That cheek bone could be cracked. If you think of anything else, give the department a call." He nodded at Nick and walked out, his partner falling in behind.

Nick waited until they left. "What happened?"

"I'm sure you can guess. I was strongly conflicted about helping Gary. I should have listened to that little voice, screaming at me to kick him to the kerb."

"You know what's going on?"

"Some beef with someone."

"Someone. His brother," said Nick.

It took a few seconds. "Why in the hell would Tom do this?" She dropped into a kitchen chair. "I don't understand."

"Gary and Tom's father is very ill."

"You said."

Nick nodded. "He hired me to find Gary. He didn't mention he had another son. There are some family issues, I guess."

"I didn't know Tom well. He's older than us by a decade or so. But I never thought he was dangerous."

"Any idea where he might have taken Gary? Anything any of them said?" He leaned on the counter. "What actually happened here?"

"I need a drink." Penny tossed the ice cubes and tea towel in the sink and grabbed a bottle of wine from the fridge. She poured a healthy amount into a tumbler and sat.

"Nah, I don't want any. I'm driving," said Nick.

She sat across from him, scowling. "I really should have told him to piss off and leave me alone."

"Can't change history."

"I can learn from it." She took a large mouthful. "Except I'll probably never see him again."

Nick raised his eyebrows.

"I was in the middle of explaining to him that because I'm now a vegan, he can't bring any animal products into my house. We were discussing why any objection he had was wrong, and how the week would only be a day long if he kept up that shit when the door was kicked in. Six of them. One of them was Tom. I'm not sure who, because it happened so fast, but one of them knocked me to the floor when it all started. Gary yelled out at Tom something about not being such a dick as he was being bundled out."

She emptied the glass and poured another. "What now?"

"You finish that up and call an Uber to take you to the hospital. Your cheek isn't looking good." He stood. "And, uh, Dora wanted to let you know she wants you to go over for a calming cup of tea. She was projecting. I think the calming part was for her. She was pretty shaken up."

Penny let out a slow breath. "Right. That's fair. You going to see her before you go do whatever it is you're going to do?"

"Yeah."

"Tell her I'm okay and I'll be by in a little bit. Thanks for checking in. Find Gary, okay? He's an arsehole, but not that bad, push comes to shove."

"You bet."

Nick said goodbye and trotted across the street to Dora's. He raised his hand to knock, and she pulled the door open. "She's okay?"

"Hi Dora. Penny said she'd be by in a little bit. She's going to stop by the hospital to get checked out, I think." He pointed at his cheek bone. "She got hit. I think she's fine, but it's better she gets it checked out."

"Oh, dear." She motioned him in. "I'll put on some tea."

Nick checked the time. "I want to object, but I need to look at that video file, so I accept."

"Oh, and I gave a copy to that nice police lady. Thanks for sending her over."

The chair was just comfortable as Nick remembered it. "Davie loved your home-made shortbread, by the way." He looked up at her and smiled. "If you have a copy of that video for me, I'll send Davie a copy and see if he can get anything from it."

She handed him her phone. "It's stored in photos. Don't snoop. I'll get some tea." She smiled. "And biscuits."

Nick found the video clip stored in a folder filled with pictures of grandchildren and her garden. He watched the video. Davie was right. Fuzzy blobs, for the most part. But it was worth a try. He forwarded it to his phone, then sent it from there to Davie with a message. "You're right. It's shit. Do what you can and let me know what you find."

The tea came with her home-made shortbread biscuits. He thanked her, shared tea and reassured her that this wasn't a thing she should be regularly expecting. He bundled four of the biscuits into a piece of paper towel, for Davie, and thanked her.

"Tell Davie he can come up here any time he wants more of those."

"I will."

Davie called him as he was driving home. "Tom plus five. Not good enough to make out faces clear enough for any reliable facial recognition, but I got the rego from one of the trucks."

"That's actually very good."

"You get any of those – "

"Four of them. She says you need to go there on your own next time and have a cup of tea with her. I think she likes you. The rego?"

"Dude from Bathurst. Bruce Wallace. Big guy. Has had a number of arrests for affray. Want me to send you his address?"

"Don't bother. Gary's probably not there." He phone blurped with call waiting. "I've got another call. I'll catch up later."

"Sure thing."

Nick dropped Davie and took the new call. "Harding."

"This is William, Mr Goulding's assistant."

"Is he in? I need to talk to him."

"Have you located Gareth, yet?"

"I'll discuss my progress with Larry."

"It's Lawrence, and I'm deputised to speak for him."

"Don't care, Billy. My conversation is with Larry." Nick emphasised the names.

"I guess that's your prerogative. I should tell you that he is declining rapidly. The doctor was by today and gives him less than week, possibly as little as 48 hours. Your engagement was to find Gareth before Lawrence's demise. You have precious little time." He paused. "Or you don't get paid."

"Then I should probably stop by now." He paused. "My good friend James is the executor of Larry's estate. I'll get paid." He hung up. Changed his GPS destination to the Goulding estate and took the next exit off the freeway.

Chapter Twenty-Nine

"Where are you, son?"

Nick glanced at the GPS. "About fifteen minutes from Larry — Lawrence's — home. I need to meet him and bring him up to date. How are you feeling?"

"Your mother is driving me nuts."

Nick chuckled. "Serves you right. I can stop by after I catch up with Larry. But I need to see him first."

"Come by when you can. No rush."

"Okay. Why'd you call?"

"That thing you said about Gary and Tom's accident. The one that killed their mother. You said Tom was driving?"

"Yeah, that's the story I was told."

"No way. I don't believe it."

Nick sighed and turned on to the street where the Goulding residence was. "What am I missing, Pops?"

"That was Gary's car. He loved it. Babied it. Lawrence would tell me stories about that kid's obsessiveness. Maybe being the youngest, by yonks, made him that way. He wouldn't let anyone touch that car. Let Tom drive it? Never. Wouldn't let his best friend drive it. Wouldn't let anyone else even wash it. It was a power thing for him. Kind of dick-ish, if I'm honest. Something is not right with the narrative."

"Huh." Nick stopped at the entrance to the house. "Thanks. Interesting information. I'll catch up with you later and bring you up to speed with what's happening."

"Okay. Be careful. Those boys aren't stable."

Nick terminated the call and turned off the car. "Now I find out."

William met him at the door. "He's not well. You should be spending this time finding Gary."

Nick pushed past him, a little more aggressively than absolutely necessary, but the prick was due. "Found Gary. Need to talk to the old man."

William raced after him. "I can't let you see him. Where's Gary? You were supposed to bring him here when you found him."

Nick stopped and took William by the shoulders. They were larger than he thought they were. "Billy, lad, Larry pays me. You didn't pay me. I report only to Larry. And I would prefer to talk to him alone. He's in his usual place, yeah?"

He stepped onto the back patio and closed the door behind him, giving William the best menacing glare he could muster.

Lawrence was at the edge of the patio, looking over the harbour. He turned his head slightly as Nick stepped out. "William, bring the pitcher of water, please." The old man's voice was frailer than Nick had heard it.

"William is busy." He poured water into Lawrence's glass. "But I need to talk to you, if you're able."

Lawrence sipped the water, licking his lips. His face was sunken. Dark rings circled his eyes, and his skin was translucent. The wreath of hair around his bald pate had thinned and was unruly.

He looked like shit.

But he sighed, gave Nick a half smile and nodded. "You've found him."

"Gary? Yeah. I found him. A couple of days ago."

Lawrence took a breath, then scowled. "A few days ago? And you're not coming to me until now? And without him?"

"I also found Tom." He tapped his nose splint. "We got along like gangbusters." He moved his chair to face Lawrence head on. "Why did you tell me he was dead?" He inched forward, getting in Lawrence's face. "What in hell did you get me into?"

Lawrence recoiled and shook his head. He licked his lips and wiped the spittle from the corners of his mouth with a tremulous hand. "You inferred he was dead. I don't believe I ever used those exact words. Why were you looking for Tom?"

"That's not really the point, Lawrence. What don't I know that I should have known at the outset of this quest? Why is Tom not in the will and Gary is?"

Lawrence looked confused. "Who told you that Thomas wasn't in my will? Of course he is. That's not what this is about."

Nick stared at him for a minute, waiting for more. "Are you going to tell me before you die, or are you going to make me guess?" He held up his hand. "No, actually don't tell me. I'll see if I can guess."

He placed his elbows on his knees and clasped his hands, leaning forward. "There was a car accident, all those years ago. But Gary was driving, not Tom. How the accident happened is immaterial. Your wife was in the front seat. She died instantly." Lawrence winced. Nick continued. "Tom was sleeping in the back seat. He was thrown clear, but suffered a traumatic brain injury. Gary, the lucky little shit, somehow came out of the accident unscathed, other than a few bumps and bruises."

Lawrence reached out a shaky hand and took another sip of water.

"Then, because Gary is a bit of a sociopath and was unharmed, he told everyone Tom was driving. I'm surprised he wasn't questioned. Everybody knows Gary loved that car like a puppy. He'd never let anyone else drive it. Tom has no recollection of the accident, except for what he's been told. He's made those stories into his own memory. He fully believes it. He's convinced you've written him out of your will, punitively. I don't know who convinced him, but he believes it."

He licked his lips and leaned even closer. "Now he thinks Gary is the only person in your will and Tom is intent on killing him before you die, making him the only legal heir. Doesn't matter what's in your will, as far as he's concerned. He'll fight it, and as long as the seamier side of his life isn't exposed, he'll win."

"Oh, Jesus, Jesus." Lawrence drew a shuddering breath. "You know where he is? Tom?"

"He's got Gary somewhere. I'm assuming Gary is still alive, but no promises there. Do you know where Tom might go?" Nick stood and clapped his hands together once. Noticed that Lawrence flinched. "Is it true you've only got 48 hours or so?"

"They're guessing. I could drop dead right now. Long shot, I could last another month. The month is doubtful." He tried standing up and failed. "You need to get both boys to come here, as quickly as possible."

"Why? They're going to hash it out on their own."

"I need to talk to Gary. You can get to him, right?"

"Have you been paying any attention at all? Tom has Gary. Tom believes killing Gary will get him into your will because he doesn't know he's already in it. I expect he's holed up somewhere getting resources together to disappear him. Why did you only want me to find Gary? You knew Tom was alive, right?"

Lawrence sagged, if that was even possible. "I knew Tom was alive, and I've known for a few years he wasn't driving. I wanted Gary to admit to my face that he lied about it. I wanted him to know I didn't care. Past is past. I wanted them to reconcile. I wanted Gary to help with Tom's rehabilitation." He paused. Sighed. "I've fucked it all up. Tell me you'll help."

William opened the door and stepped out onto the patio. "Mr Harding, I must insist that you leave. Mr Goulding is far too frail for this continued harassment."

Lawrence turned in his chair. "Go home, William," he barked.

"I - I was - you hired me to take care of you. I'd be derelict — "

"If I hired you, I can fire you, right? So go home before I do that."

"Did I hear you say you found Gary? That's great news."

"Leave, William. Go."

William backed out of the patio and closed the door. He watched Nick pacing, talking with Lawrence.

He was confused. Tom wasn't supposed to be in the will. Not that he knew. The old man had lied to him. Killing Gary wasn't necessary. Tom had convinced him it was. He needed to call Tom off.

He walked down the hallway into the kitchen. He checked the patio. He could see Nick still talking, Lawrence protesting. He dialled the last number for Tom that he knew. It rang out to a generic voicemail greeting. He waited for the beep. "Tom, you have to call me back right away. It's not like you think it is. Let Gary go and call me back as soon as you get this."

He hung up. Held the top of his head while he thought. The old man had fucked up.

"My number one priority right now is to find Tom and keep him from killing your other son." Nick was approaching an anger he hadn't felt in years. He paced the patio. He wheeled and pointed a finger at Lawrence. "You could have been straight with me. Would have saved me a shit tonne of time and grief."

"Well, but — "

"Tell me, Larry, where would your eldest son go? Any properties you own that he might know about?"

Lawrence scratched the top of his head. He looked off to the far distance, colour leaving his skin. He sighed, slowly shaking his head. "No."

"What's that?"

"No. I don't know where he would be. I haven't talked to him in years. I don't own any properties that are abandoned. Empty. And they all have some level of security." He inhaled and seemed to grow a bit of steel in his back. "You say that you're good. Find Tom for me. I don't have long. I need to talk to him before I die. Let him know I know he didn't do anything wrong." He swallowed and took another sip of water. "Anything."

Tom was in a small rental unit on 20 hectares of land outside Orange, three hours west of Sydney. His nearest neighbour was over 5 km away and well out of earshot. He was nursing a beer, sitting backwards on a chair, leaning his elbows on the back and looking at his bigger, younger brother.

Gary sat on the floor, back against the wall, one arm handcuffed to the exposed pipe coming out of a disabled water heater. His wallet, car keys and mobile phone were on the table on the other side of the room. He rattled the cuffs. "Really? You've watched too many shitty movies."

Tom stared at him. Took a sip. Didn't say anything.

"What are your plans, big brother? You going to kill me?"

"I wasn't driving." He emptied the bottle and got another from the fridge.

"What?"

Tom straddled the chair again and twisted the top off the bottle. "I wasn't driving your car. When it went off the road and killed Mum and," he slapped the side of his head, "scrambled my brains." He stood and slowly walked toward Gary. "You were." He kicked the sole of Gary's foot. "You absolute son of a bitch. You convinced me, and dear old nearly dead dad, that I killed Mum."

Gary rattled the cuffs again. "I repeat. What are your plans?"

Tom returned to the chair. "Was planning on killing you and fighting the will." Tom belched. "To be fair, that's still on the top of my list."

"Fight the will? What in the hell are you talking about?"

Tom scowled. "Don't pretend you don't know little brother. I'm not in the will. Only you are. Do the math."

Gary shook his head. "Doesn't work that way, bruh. It would be proceeds of crime. You would end up in Long Bay and not a penny to your name." He pushed back against the wall, sitting a bit straighter. "Where you been? What have you been up to?"

Tom finished the beer and threw the bottle in the corner. "Don't go anywhere. I've got some errands to run. I'll be back in the morning. We'll finish things then. They won't be able to prove I killed you if they can't find a body."

"Seriously?"

Tom smiled.

"But I've got to piss," said Gary.

"So piss." The door slammed shut.

Gary slid the chain up the water pipe to the point where it met the wall. He stood as tall as he could, which amounted to a half squat. He could see the top of the table. His mobile phone lay there face up. He cleared his throat. "Hey Siri. Redial."

Chapter Thirty

Nick stood over Lawrence, leaning forward, his hands on the wheelchair arms. His face was centimetres from Lawrence's. "I'm going to find both of your sons. And I'm going to bring them here. And you're going to tell them what the hell is going on." He stood. "I guess money doesn't buy you brains."

His phone rang. He held up a hand. "Don't talk." He pressed the phone to his ear. "Harding speaking."

"Nick, this is Gary Goulding."

"Gary. Where are – "

"I can't hear what you're saying Nick. I hope I've gotten through. Tom has chained me to a hot water heater. I don't know where I am. It's rural. Past the Blue Mountains. Tom has left and is coming back in the morning to, I don't know. Kill me? Disappear me? My older brother is unstable. Try to find me. Please."

"Can you hear me at all?" Nick pressed the phone to the side of his head. Hard. The surf was high and making it difficult to hear. "Hello?" He heard the rattle of a chain and a sigh. Then nothing. "Shit."

He terminated the call and walked out. William met him at the car. "I don't want you coming back. Mr Goulding isn't well."

"Get fucked, Billy." He got in the car. Paired his phone. Pointed his GPS at home. Checked the battery charge — he had enough to get there. Just.

He called Davie as soon as he left Goulding property. "Buddy, how are you doing."

"Better than you, I bet. What's up?"

"Gary just called me. At my number." He read out the number from the recent calls list. "See if you can find a location for me?"

"He couldn't tell you?"

"We didn't really have a conversation. He talked, I listened. He's being held by Tom."

"Your other case."

"Weird shit, right?" Nick accelerated onto the freeway. "I've got until morning, apparently. Zero clues, except for a radius he might have travelled which covers way too many fucking square kilometres."

"I'll see what I can do. You owe me a pizza. Or two."

"I'm paying you. Buy your own pizza."

Davie laughed. "Fuck you."

Nick hung up and checked the charge. He eased off on the accelerator. Battery level was dropping.

He pulled behind a tractor-trailer and drafted. He might actually make it home. He settled back in the car and accepted the additional travel time as a necessary inconvenience.

Then his phone rang again. "Harding."

"It's Richard. Don't you have me in your phone?"

"Moffet? Late, for you. Did you find more fake profiles?"

"No, that's why I'm calling. And I apologise for the hour. I just received the final report from my team. The analysis was extremely thorough."

"No? What do you mean by no?"

"Not a single consumer credit report we've produced over the past ten years matches any of those names, or anything even remotely statistically like them."

"So just those twelve?"

"No, Nick. I know it's late, but listen to me. None. Not even those twelve."

Nick frowned. "Wait. You said the reference numbers matched."

"No. Not in our system. Matched the format of our reference numbers and they all pass the checksum tests, but they weren't in our databases. We checked three times, with three orthogonally different approaches. I'd stake my annual salary that they didn't come from us. They are just really, really good forgeries."

Nick nodded. "Okay. I believe you. Email me something I can add to my report to my client. Thanks." He cut off Richard's response to answer another incoming call.

"Harding."

"Is - is this Nick Harding, Private Investigator?"

"It is, but my calendar is full right now. It'll be a couple of weeks before I can take another case."

"I think this relates directly to one of your existing cases."

Nick sat up straight, paying more attention. "How's that?"

"My name is Carol. We've met. Outside the restaurant at The Rocks."

Nick dug through his memory. "Tall blonde, lots of tatts?"

"Yes."

"I was looking for Tom Goulding."

"He was going by Troy Gibson then. One of his many aliases."

"Do you have information about Tom's whereabouts?"

"Tom and I are - maybe were - a couple. But he's gone troppo. He's holed up somewhere with his brother."

Nick's interest waned. "I know that already. Any idea where?"

"Not a clue."

"Then why are you calling me?"

"The poor boy's got TMI. Got this massive scar down the side of his skull. Under the hair. He's not right in the head. Help me find him, okay? I'll pay you well. I've put a lot of money away."

Nick was silent, thinking.

"Are you there?"

"I'm thinking." Nick thought.

"Don't think too long. This is serious. He's gone over the edge."

"I can't take your money. I'm already engaged to find him. But I will take any information you might have that would help with that."

"I don't know what I can tell you."

Nick took the exit off the freeway. "Any remote places you know of where he might be?"

Nick could hear Carol tapping her nails on a surface. He let her think.

"He was supposed to meet me at the apartment in The Rocks. I can't reach him. The only thing I can think of is that he'd go out west sometimes for a couple of days."

Nick frowned and pulled to a stop in front of his apartment building. "What, like Perth?"

"Like out towards Orange." She cleared her throat. "Look, I'll help you however I can. You can call me on this number. Just don't let him know, okay?"

"What does 'out towards Orange' mean. In Orange? This side of Orange? Can you narrow it down?"

"Sorry, that's all I know. Call me if you find him, okay? I'll call you if I think of anything else."

"Thanks." Nick ended the call and ran the charging cord to an outside outlet. "There are annoying disadvantages to having one of these cars. They either need longer battery life, or a lot more rapid chargers spread around the place." He locked the car and set the app on his phone to alert him when the charge hit 75%.

His phone rang as he opened his apartment door. "Davie. Let me guess. You triangulated his phone to somewhere west of here. Near Orange, perhaps?"

"What? Jesus. How in the hell do you do that?"

"How close can you get me?" Nick dropped the car keys on the kitchenette counter and grabbed a bottle of water from the fridge. He stifled a yawn as he twisted off the top.

"Well, turns out not that close. The towers up there are pretty spread apart. Couldn't get a GPS signal from it. Had to estimate it based on tower signal strengths. It's a roughly 3 sq km long potato shape just east of Orange. Heading up tomorrow morning?"

Nick stretched. "No. I'm going to grab a few hours and head up tonight. Running out of time. You up for an adventure?"

"I'd love to, but I've got to go into the office tomorrow morning. The actual office. I need to be presentable and rested."

"No worries. Send me a map. Point me in the right direction."

The hot shower eased the tiredness from his muscles. He wiped away the steam from the mirror. He needed to shave his head. The stubble was getting soft. The splint on his nose was loose, the steam degrading whatever adhesive was keeping it on his face. He gingerly pulled it off and left it on the counter beside the sink. He leaned closer to the mirror and inspected the damage. The bruising had graduated to an ugly yellow stain around his eyes.

He checked his email and the map Davie had sent him. Davie had been right. The area was impossibly large.

But he had to start somewhere.

And he needed sleep, first.

Nick set the timer on his phone for three hours. 10 pm. There would have to be enough charge in the car by then.

Then his phone rang. "Jesus Christ. I'm fucking TIRED." He took a slow, steadying breath and answered. "Harding speaking."

"Nick, this is Lucy."

He leaned back on his bed and closed his eyes. "Good evening, Lucy. It's late. I'll give you call tomorrow and bring you up to speed, okay?"

"That 11:00 meeting has been pulled forward to 9:00 am. I need to have an update before then. You've bailed on me a couple of times, Nick. I need the information tonight. I need a compelling enough story to keep both of us from getting fired."

"It's 7 pm, Lucy."

"Nick, I need this. We need this. I'm at the place we've tried to meet, what, three times now? I've ordered your food. I know you're a five-minute walk away. I'm not taking no for an answer."

Nick heard the three tones telling him she'd hung up. "No money is worth this."

But he pulled on a T-shirt and a pair of shorts. Grabbed his phone and wallet and went for the five-minute walk.

He nodded at the server at the front who pointed over her shoulder to a table on the back patio. "You staying this time?"

Nick shook his head. "I don't think I have a choice."

He weaved through the tables to the back. Lucy was facing him, picking apart a dinner roll.

"You showed. Sit. Don't leave until we're finished. If you don't want to eat, you're going to have to watch me. I'm starved." She waited a beat. Nick remained standing. "Sit. You look exhausted."

He sat. "I don't know how much I can tell you." A server placed a plate of pasta and meat sauce in front of him. A basket of rolls complimented the food. He dipped a roll in the sauce and took a bite. "Thanks for the food, but I'm afraid you're going to be disappointed."

"Look, I'm not an idiot. I know that you can't always dictate the schedule of things like this, but it's been days. You've given me nothing. If I don't have a substantial update for my manager tomorrow morning, she's going to insist I cut you loose."

"Well," he shook Parmesan on his pasta. "I can tell you I've identified who the person is. Definitively." He held up his hand to stop her asking the obvious question. "No, I can't tell you yet. I know the who, looking for the where, and," he smiled, "if you compile a detailed list of all of your company's losses, there's a fair chance I can get full restitution."

Lucy's fork stopped halfway to her mouth. She looked at the food on it, then lowered it to her plate. "That's a bit hard to believe."

Nick shrugged. "No guarantee, but more likely than not."

"Can I take that to the meeting tomorrow?" She picked her fork up and continued eating.

"I'd hold off until it's a bit more certain."

"But you can tell me who it is, though, right?" She leaned forward. "I'm assuming his initials are T. G., right?"

"They are, but again, I don't want to reveal his name yet. I have one more thing I need to do." He picked at his food. "Your meeting is at 9?"

"Yeah. Will you be able to tell me by then?"

He shook his head. "I'd be pushing it, but let them know I'll be giving you an update by noon."

"But will you?"

"Absolutely. Maybe. Look, tell them you'll have something by the end of the day. That's definite. I hope it'll be earlier. I'm really sure it'll be earlier. Better safe than sorry though, right?"

Lucy put her fork down and pushed her plate back. "I'm losing my appetite, Nick." She sighed. "You sure know how to show a girl a good time."

He spun his fork in the pasta. Gathered a good portion. "Lucy, I think you have a bigger problem."

"It's either in my shop, or the reporting agency."

Nick held up his fork, punctuating his point. "It's inside your shop." He cleaned off his fork and spun some more.

"Shit. Why?"

"If it was me, and I had a head inside the credit reporting agency faking up reports for me, I'd spread it around, take the business to multiple financial institutions. As near as I can tell, this TG fella has only ripped off you folks." He put his fork down. "Plus, the credit reporting agency has not been able to find any record of the twelve reports you shared with me." He watched her face. She slowly acknowledged his suggestion.

"Double shit."

"So, who?"

She thought for a minute, her index finger shifting back and forth like she was pointing at heads on an org chart. The realisation dawned on her face. "For the right level of approvals to get these loans banked it would have to come from one office."

"Have I met him?

She nodded. "And he's in the meeting tomorrow morning."

"That's going to limit the amount of information you share tomorrow." He furrowed his brow. "Maybe."

"Maybe? Definitely. He can have me fired. I let on that I know he's the person behind the fraud without cast iron proof and I'm out of the building before lunch. His word against mine. And he seriously outranks me."

Nick dipped his garlic bread in the pasta sauce. Chewed on a bite. "But maybe if you had enough supporting information they would believe you." He dabbed bread in the sauce again. "I know you've said the meeting was pulled forward, but do you think you can get them to reschedule? Come up with some kind of excuse like a flat tire or an emergency dentist appointment? I will make sure I get enough to you by noon."

She nodded, slowly. "Yeah. But you better have something for me."

Chapter Thirty-One

Gary leaned against the wall, more than half asleep. The cabin was dark. He had no idea what the time was. He pushed himself up the wall and looked at his phone on the table.

He smiled. "Hey Siri, what time is it?"

"It's twenty-three hundred hours and three minutes."

He yawned and rattled the chain connecting the cuff to the water heater. Stopped. Looked up at the ceiling and groaned. "Shit. I'm a fucking moron. Hey, Siri. Call triple-0."

"Emergency Services Do you need police, fire or ambulance?"

"Oh thank god. Police."

"I'm sorry, I can't hear you. Can you speak up?"

"POLICE."

"What's the nature of your call?"

"I'M BEING HELD IN A CABIN IN THE BLUE MOUN-TAINS. I DON'T KNOW WHERE."

"Can you check the coord -" Beep beep beep.

"HELLO?" Gary moved as close to the table as he could, his arm stretched back toward the water heater. "HELLO!?" The phone screen was black. The battery had died. "Son of a BITCH."

He retreated to the wall and slid to the floor. He leaned his head back against the wall, looked up and screamed. Took a deep shuddering breath and a closer look at what he had as inventory in the cabin. He got back on his feet and stretched the arc from the pipe as far as he could reach. Tom was smart. Nothing other than a worn floor mat was within his reach. Even if he stretched to the point of pain.

He heard the sound of wheels crunching over gravel. "Hey! In here!"

The door swung open and bounced against the outside wall. "Bro. We're at least five klicks from anyone. Yelling is a waste of time." He picked Gary's phone off the table. "Almost forgot this. You've got smart friends, especially that PI, the little shit. He can track it."

"It's dead."

"Maybe. Bet it can still be tracked if it's dead." He pocketed the phone. Then took it out and grabbed it with both hands and grunted as he twisted. His forearm muscles bunched and his face grew red.

"You, brother, are a fat slob," said Gary as he stood. "Here. Give it to me. I'll break it for you."

Tom dropped the phone on the floor and smashed it a couple of times with his heel. He pulled a revolver from the small of his back. He pulled the hammer back and aimed at his brother.

Gary sat back down and held up his hands. "Whoa, bro. Take it easy." His entire focus was on the matte black muzzle pointed at his face. It was shaking, amplifying the tremors in his brother's hands.

"All these years? You had me think I killed Mum." He shook the revolver at Gary and bellowed a scream. He stepped back and held his hands on top of his head, pressing the side of the revolver against the scar on his head. "You were always the good brother. The cool brother. You're a real good actor. You're a shit bag."

He swung the revolver back down and jerked on the trigger. The explosion filled the small cabin.

Gary instinctively squeezed his eyes shut and tried to make himself tiny, jerking his head away from the shot. He was lucky he jerked left.

Wood splintered and sprayed his cheek. His ears were ringing. He opened one eye and peered at Tom. Then glanced at the hole in the wall, centimetres from his head. "Are you a shit shot, or was that a warning?"

Tom shot again, to the other side of Gary's head. He nicked the water pipe Gary was chained to. Water sprayed Gary's arm. He scrambled to his feet and tried to get out of the way of the flood.

"You son of a bitch." Tom's hand was steadier. He took a couple of heaving deep breaths. He scratched his head with the muzzle and threw the gun when the hot metal touched his scalp. "Ah, shit."

Gary laughed. "Fucking idiot." He stood with his cuffed arm extended as far as he could to stay out of the rapidly enlarging pool of water. "You're a joke, bro. Not even a funny joke."

Tom snarled and scooped the gun off the ground. He tested the heat of the barrel, and when satisfied it wouldn't cause injury, tucked it in his belt at the small of his back. "Joke?" He took slow steps toward his brother. "Says the idiot cuffed to a pipe." He stood just out of Gary's reach. He took deep breaths. His sweaty hair was stuck to his scalp.

Gary wrinkled his nose. "You could take a step back. Maybe two. You're a bit sour." He cleared his throat. "You going to kill me or what?"

He could see the indecision wander over Tom's face. Then it settled into steel determination. "I still have those errands. Got to get supplies. I'll be back in the morning." He nodded at the water pooling on the floor. "You might want to do something about that."

The door slammed behind him. Gary heard the car start and its wheels crunch across the gravel. He had maybe four hours before his brother came back and he was pretty confident Tom wouldn't miss the next time.

"But that's a tomorrow problem." Water was still gushing out of the water pipe. It wasn't hot, but it was still wet.

The pipe he was cuffed to was the output of the water heater. To stop the flow, he'd have to turn off the water coming in. He sloshed to the tank and felt around the top until he found the incoming feed. Twisted the faucet clockwise until it was off.

The water continued to flow, releasing another four hundred litres before it emptied. He looked around. Water everywhere. Not a dry piece of floor within his limited reach. He sighed and slowly eased into the pool, saturating his trousers.

Tom's heart raced. The arteries in his neck throbbed and he felt light-headed. He slowed the car, rolled down all the windows and took long, deep breaths. He had to keep it together for another couple of days. "Almost. Almost. Almost. Almost."

The streets were quiet, and he had no desire of attracting potential witnesses. He rolled his car slowly up Penny's driveway and turned off the ignition. The clicks of the cooling engine blended nicely with the chorus of cicadas and tree frogs. He pushed the car door open, wincing as the hinges squealed, and stood beside the car.

The front light turned on. Penny stepped onto the front step in a bathrobe and a scowl. "Get in here before the neighbours see you," she hissed.

She held the door for him, scanning the neighbourhood. It was past midnight. Unlikely anybody would be watching, but better safe than sorry.

She followed him in and closed the door. "What in the hell are you doing here? And where is Gary? I swear to god, if you've –"

"I need to –"

"Shower. I know. Trust me, I know. Go. I'll make some coffee."

Tom stripped as he walked, stepping into the shower and sighing as the hot water hit him. He closed his eyes and tipped his head back. He let the hot water wash over him. The soap smelled like lavender and the shampoo smelled like strawberries, but he didn't care. It had been days.

He rinsed off and turned the water as hot as he could bear. Turned and let the steaming water beat off the back of his skull. He found the steaming needles hitting the outside of his scalp countered the overwhelming pain usually present on the inside.

When the water started to cool, he turned it off. Stood in the steam-filled cubicle for a couple of seconds, then dried off and wrapped a large towel around his waist.

Penny handed him a mug of coffee and sat at the kitchen table. "What's going on, Tom? Where's Gary?"

He sat across from her and saluted her with the mug. "Thanks. I need this." He sipped and winced when it burned his tongue. "Hot." He smiled at her. "Gary who?"

"Seriously. I hope you haven't done something stupid."

Tom took a long deep breath in through his nose. "Seems all I do is stupid stuff." He shook his head. "Gary is stashed somewhere. He'll keep."

Penny rubbed her brow. "What in the hell do you mean, stashed? What are you doing?"

Tom reached across the table and took one of her hands in both of his. "I'm righting ten years of wrongs. Believe me, I know what I'm doing."

Penny gently pulled her hand free. "Tommy, I've known the both of you since we were kids. Not once in decades did you know what you were doing." She patted his hand. "You have always been the loveable oaf." She swallowed and sat back. "Until the car accident. You really need to see somebody. The spiral is getting darker."

He pulled his hands back. "I'm on the right track. And I'm not a loveable oaf." He clenched his fists. "There's nothing loveable about me."

"Tom, that's not true."

He pushed back his chair and dropped his towel. Pulled on his clothes and grabbed the coffee. "Thanks for the java. I wasn't here, right?"

Penny stood in the door and watched him leave. She scrolled through the contacts on her phone and called Gary. It went straight to voicemail. "Gary, I'm worried about Tom. He's spiralling hard. Call me when you get this."

Chapter Thirty-Two

Nick jolted awake. It took him a second to remember why his alarm was set for 2:00 am. He rolled off his sofa and grabbed the phone. Blinked the sleep out of his eyes and turned off the alarm just as a meaty fist banged once on his door.

He opened the door and stood to one side as Davie walked in. "Thanks."

"Coffee."

Nick pointed to the kitchen. "Two travel mugs in the cupboard above the sink. Make one for me too. I need to piss." He ran his tongue over his teeth. "And brush my teeth." He pointed at Davie. "Extra strong."

He thought about a plan of attack as he cleaned the fuzz off his teeth. They had to find Gary. And all he knew was where he wasn't. The process of elimination was going to be way too slow. He needed hard data. "Hell, I'll take any data."

Davie handed him a travel cup as he left the bathroom. "I was just thinking the same thing. What do we know?"

"Tom took Gary. That's about it." He smiled at his friend. "I thought you had to work tomorrow."

"I'm going to call in sick. We know more than that about Gary. We know from where he took him. And when."

"A starting point. The video quality was crap, though." He smiled. "So, we go to the source."

"It'll be almost 3:00 when we get there. She's going to be pissed."

Nick held the door for Davie and followed him out. "She'll get over it."

She didn't look like she'd get over it. Penny stood at the door, robe wrapped tightly around her, arms crossed. Nick pointed at the doorbell camera. "Good morning, Penny. We need to see the video from when Tom grabbed Gary."

Davie narrowed his eyes. "Why didn't you call the police when that happened?"

"I don't have the video."

"Bullshit." Nick grabbed the camera and tested the mounting. "You can either let us in and download a copy for us, or I'll rip it off the wall and my IT genius mate will extract it."

Penny glanced across the street at Dora's house. She sighed and stifled a yawn. "Fine. Jesus. Come in." She pointed them at the kitchen table. "Wait there while I get my laptop."

"Hey, I've had a bunch of coffee. Can I use your — "

"Down the hall, on the left. Lift the seat."

Davie nodded and smiled and trotted down the hall.

Penny entered and slid the open laptop across the table toward Nick. She sat across from him.

Nick spun it around. It was open to the doorbell app and the video of Gary's abduction was queued up. He tapped the spacebar. Saw the trucks roll up. Saw Tom and five of his friends pile out of the trucks and storm the door. He tapped the spacebar and paused the video. "Why didn't you call the police?"

Penny rested her elbows on the table and cupped her head in her hands. "I've known the Gouldings since I was a little kid. Tom was older and like a big brother. For a little while. Gary and I hung out." She sniffed and sat up straighter. "Tom and I lost contact after the accident. He took it horribly."

"Tom wasn't driving."

She nodded. "I know, now. I think that's what triggered him. Maybe."

Davie returned from the bathroom, sat beside Nick and reached over and tapped the spacebar. The video resumed. Audio of a scuffle followed by Tom and two others strong-arming Gary out of the house and into one of the trucks. He tapped the spacebar again as the trucks left rubber. "I don't see how this can help us. I've already seen this from Dora's angle. I can get a better view of the faces, but I'm not CSI, or the cops. Or Facebook. I don't have a neat and nifty facial recognition program I can use."

Penny sighed and spun the laptop toward her. She tapped a couple of commands and spun the laptop back to Davie. "Tom was here an hour or so ago. He had a shower and a coffee and left. He was driving a different vehicle. Maybe that will help. You've got to stop him."

Nick pulled the laptop closer and started the video. It began with Tom walking up the front walk, looking like he'd been on the wrong end of a rough week. "I can't see the rego on his car."

"Keep watching."

That video stopped and the next one started as Tom left. He trotted down the walk and got in the car. The headlights flared in the camera as the car backed out, then left from the direction it came. Nick backed it up until the front licence plate was clearest. He magnified the screen and looked at Davie. "Got it?"

Davie had an app open in his phone. He entered the registration and looked at the screen again. "Streetlights really throw off the colour. It's a 2020 red Holden Commodore. Rego expires in about 4 months." He shook his head. "I would have sworn on the stand it was a dark grey from the video. Penny, those doorbell cameras are crap."

"It does the job. So you know what type of car it is. So what?"

"So," said Nick. "We know the car he's driving — it's probably not his, but that doesn't matter — and we know he's taken Gary to, and I quote, 'past the Blue Mountains'. Carol said he had a place out near Orange. Davie pinged his phone in a fairly large area outside of Orange. There aren't that many properties out there. We just need to find one remote enough with a bright red, late model Holden in the driveway."

"Needle, fucking haystack." Penny stood and grabbed her laptop back. "I'm going to kick you both out and go to bed. Don't bother me again until you've found him. Them."

Nick pulled into a truck stop just outside of Orange. He backed the car into a rapid charging station and plugged in. They'd been driving two hours, Davie glued to his laptop screen.

"You know Google doesn't update maps that often. And Tom probably stole that car no more than a week ago. If that."

"Not using Google." Davie mentioned a near real-time survey company. "Council planners use this. Fire control. Flood plain management. Data is typically no more than a few days old. They use drones and low flying aircraft." He closed the laptop and got out of the car. He slung the laptop case over his shoulder and stretched. "What time is it? I need sticky buns and coffee."

Nick grunted in assent. They found a booth near the back and Nick bought coffee and pastries while Davie tethered his laptop to his phone.

He looked up when Nick returned with the goods. "Thanks." He devoured a bear claw with two bites. Took a tentative sip of coffee. He looked at the time on his screen. "Almost 4. I'm getting too old for this shit."

"And reductive. How's the hunt? What percentage have you covered?"

"Depends on the size of the search area."

Nick peeled the top off an orange-poppy seed muffin. "I thought you were containing it to the polygon you thought the phone was in."

"If we're limiting it to that, about 85% complete. Nothing yet. You know this is a real long shot, right?"

"Only shot we've got." Nick switched sides of the table and sat beside Davie. "Where next?"

Davie slid a clear piece of acetate out of the laptop case and taped it to the top of the screen. It barely held, the tape had been used so much. A fine grid was marked on the clear sheet of plastic, as well as the major highways. The majority of the squares on the grid were crossed off with a red mark.

He zoomed the map back until the highways on the map aligned with those on the acetate. He picked one of the few remaining un-checked boxes on the grid. He flipped the acetate out of the way and zoomed until that area filled the screen.

Nick leaned over and pushed Davie a bit to one side. "Nothing in that grid."

Davie cocked an eyebrow, gently pushed Nick back and increased the zoom. A small cabin resolved. It was a kilometre, at least, off the main road and at least ten kilometres from the nearest property. The road leading up to the cabin looked like a dirt road. Davie zoomed in on the cabin.

"No red car," said Nick.

"Not at the cabin." Davie panned the map and followed the road back to the highway. "There." He pointed at a car turning off the highway onto the dirt road. "That look like a 2020 Holden Commodore?"

"Enhance," said Nick, with a small smile.

"Enhance? What the fuck? You think I'm NCIS or something?" Davie caught the smile on Nick's face and pushed him away. "Prick." He zoomed in as close as he could, nodded at the image got larger. "Yeah. That's it."

Nick flipped the acetate back and did a quick count. "Still ten grid blocks you haven't checked."

Davie sighed. "We're on a clock, right? I could take a couple of minutes and calculate the probability of finding another car exactly like the one we're looking for in the remote bush of Australia, but I can tell you right now, there's more of a chance of you winning the lottery tonight." He hovered the cursor over the cabin and wrote down the coordinates on a napkin and handed it to Nick. "You can enter coords in your GPS, right?"

Nick snatched the paper from Davies hand and slid out of the booth. He grabbed his coffee and a donut. "Let's go. Time's a-wasting."

"Jesus." Davie closed his laptop, slid it into its case, grabbed two pastries and his coffee and trotted after Nick. "Hey. Wait up."

Nick unplugged the car and stowed the cable. "Not sure we gained much in the charge department."

Davie stood outside the car scarfing down sweet, sticky rolls as Nick entered the coordinates off the napkin to his onboard GPS.

"'Hey, you finished carb loading?"

Davie dusted his hands off on his trousers and got in the car. Placed his coffee in the cup holder. "How far?"

Nick looked at the massive map displayed on the centre console. Then he looked at Davie. Then back at the map. Then at Davie. The route was displayed, including estimated travel time.

"Right." He checked the route. "Fifteen minutes? Shit. That's great."

Nick nodded. "We get there, grab Gary and piss off out of there. Take him to the old man in the morning."

"It's a plan." Davie twisted in his seat and looked at what passed for a back seat in the Dvorak electric car. "I get dibs on the front seat when we pick him up. No fucking way I'm going back there again."

Nick chuckled and pulled out of the truck stop, accelerating onto the freeway. "No problem. Gary's a head taller than you. He'll love it back there."

They rode in silence until Nick slowed and turned left off the main road onto gravel.

"We're getting close."

"Half a klick up this road."

Davie thought for a minute as Nick eased the car over the shitty road. "You think this is safe?"

Nick shrugged. "If there's a red car there, we might be fucked."

"Great."

Nick slowed as he got closer. The map on the display showed a sharp hairpin turn just before the cabin. He was down to a crawl as they approached the corner. "Now or never." He eased around the corner and slowed to almost a stop.

The cabin sat in front of them. By itself. No vehicles. Davie let out an audible sigh of relief. "I really didn't want a confrontation."

Nick pulled the car up to the cabin's door and got out. He looked at Davie, still sitting in the car. He motioned him to follow. "Come on."

"Fuck." Davie got out of the car and immediately turned a full 360 degrees scanning the night bush. "He might be here, waiting for us."

Nick chuckled and tested the door. It opened easily. "Come on," he said again. He pulled the door open and walked into the cabin. Pools of water covered the floor. Nick stepped in and kept to the edge of the room. "Damn."

At the far end of the room was a water heater with a broken pipe.

And the cabin was empty.

"Fuck."

Davie stepped in and immediately stepped back out. "That's a lot of water."

"Get back in here. The place is empty."

Davie walked along the edge of the room until he got to Nick, standing beside the water heater.

The exit pipe was broken. Nick looked closer at it. "Look at the rubbing. He was cuffed to this." He followed the pipe up to the break. A piece was missing. "And it looks like someone shot it, weakening it."

"Gary's not here."

"No, but he was." Nick held up his hand. "Hang on." He held a finger to his lips. "Someone is coming," he whispered.

He moved to the back side of the door. He could hear wheels crunching over gravel. Davie stood on the opposite side of the door.

"What are we supposed to do? I don't have a weapon."

Nick winked at him. "Fake it."

The crunching stopped. They heard a vehicle turn off. The door slowly opened. Davie cocked a fist and was about to swing when he saw who it was.

Nick stepped out from behind the door. "Carol? What are you doing here?"

"How did you find this place?" asked Carol.

"I asked first."

"I'm looking for Tom. Have you seen him?"

Chapter Thirty-Three

Gary walked backwards down the road, watching for traffic. He stuck his thumb out as headlights approached.

The car didn't even slow for a second look.

"Don't blame you, really." He turned and continued walking. He had a map in his head, and he wasn't sure how accurate it was. All he was certain of was that it was going to be a long walk.

The handcuff smacked his leg as he walked, so he grabbed the loose end and held it in his hand. Breaking the water pipe, once Tom had shot it, wasn't difficult. His phone was destroyed beyond repair. And at what he guessed was around five in the morning, getting a lift from a stranger, while wearing torn clothing with a handcuff strapped to his wrist had odds approaching zero. It would be a very long walk.

The road in front of him brightened from halogen head-lights approaching from behind. He sighed, turned and stuck out his thumb. Approaching zero doesn't necessarily equal zero.

The car slowed, passed him, then stopped. It reversed back toward him, stopping alongside. The passenger window rolled down and Gary leaned down and looked in. Tightened the grip on the handcuff. Just in case.

The driver stifled a yawn and squinted up at Gary. "What the fuck are you doing walking along this road at this time of day?"

"Trying to get a ride. It's a long walk. It's been a helluva night." He held up the handcuff and chuckled. "She got a bit too freaky."

The driver laughed. "I'm going Parramatta. I can take you that far. Hop in."

"Much appreciated." Gary got in. "Name's Gary. Don't have to go that far. I'm heading to Bilpin."

"Fair enough. Half an hour down the road. Let me know where you want to get dropped. My name is Rick." He glanced at the cuffs. "Freaky?"

Gary glanced at the cuff still on his wrist. "Yeah. I'm going to need a locksmith to get these off me, and that's going to be an embarrassing convo."

"So, how freaky?"

"Mate, I didn't wait to find out. Bolted as soon as she tried to cuff me to her bed. I mean, she was eager enough, but I was getting a real bunny boiler vibe off her."

"You could have called an Uber."

He grimaced. "Left my phone there, so I'm going to have to see her again anyway."

"Oh, mate. That sucks. Just tell the coppers it was stolen and get a new one."

Gary nodded. "Yeah. Probably best bet."

He settled back in his seat, keeping an eye on the driver. Making sure he stayed awake. Last thing he needed was another car accident.

He leaned forward to tell Rick to stop as they approached the curve before the nursery.

"This the place?"

Gary shook his head. There was a police car parked across the street from the entrance. "Half a klick ahead. On the left. Just drop me on the side of the road."

Rick glanced at the police car as they passed. "No worries, mate. Understood." He glanced in the rear-view mirror. "Just around this corner?"

Gary nodded and removed his seatbelt. "Perfect. Thanks." He waited until the car stopped on the shoulder and got out. He leaned down and looked through the window. "Much appreciated. Take care." He nodded. "And thanks."

He walked through the bush, between the strands of barbed-wire fencing at the perimeter and wended his way through the greenhouses to his home.

It wasn't completely burned to the ground. The stench of charred contents filled the back of his throat. He tripped on the front step in the dark and stopped his fall palms first.

The wood was wet. He peered at his hands. Wet and sooty. "Shit."

The door was off its hinges and canted to one side. He pushed it out of the way and stepped into the foyer. The construction was double brick exterior and concrete cladded single brick walls for the interior. The contents were torched, but the structure was still standing and would for quite a few more decades.

Feeling around the house in the dark was time consuming and tedious. He needed to find somewhere dry he could crash for the night. He stepped out the back of the house to the shed. It hadn't been touched by the fire. Just inside the door was a large torch. He turned it on, squinting in the sudden bright light and placed his hand over the lens. The light was dampened enough he knew the cops on the street would never detect it, but still bright enough to find his way around without tripping over debris.

He played the light around the house as he walked to the far end, furthest from where the fire had been lit. The guest room was largely unscathed. The tile floor in the en-suite was still damp, but other than that and the pervasive smell, you could almost imagine nothing had happened in the house.

He dropped on the bed, closed his eyes and almost immediately fell asleep.

Nick paced the cabin. He pointed to the bullet holes on the wall. "Two shots. No blood. You think he missed, or he was just trying to scare Gary?"

Carol shook her head. "He wouldn't miss from this close if he wanted to shoot him."

Davie picked the shattered phone off the wet floor. "This was going to be my way of finding Gary."

Carol leaned against the wall by the door, her arms crossed. "I don't care about that arsehole. I want to find Tom." She chewed on a thumbnail. "He isn't right in the head right now and I need to settle him down."

"How did you find this place?"

"I've been looking since I called you. I knew it was out here somewhere."

"We may be looking in the same direction. Tom took Gary. Stuffed him in a truck. By the looks of the busted pipe, he'd secured Gary to the pipe somehow, left for whatever reason and Gary escaped." Nick looked at floor in thought. "Hang on a sec." He grabbed Davie's tablet and opened the map. He pinched and zoomed and turned to orient himself. "We're in the middle of the bush. Once he walks to the main road, such as it is, there's fuck all anywhere around here." He pointed to his tablet. "Except his nursery. I'd lay even odds he hitched a ride there."

"Long shot," said Davie.

"Well, he sure as hell isn't walking the roads at this time of night." He looked at the time. "Morning."

"Agreed. But if he hitched a ride, he could have gone anywhere."

Nick shook his head. "He's a clever guy. Maybe not that smart, but clever. He's going to think his place is the last place anyone will look."

"You boys fill your boots. I need to find Tom. He won't be at Gary's house, I know that."

"How?"

Carol took a deep breath in her nose and let it out slowly. "Let's put it this way. If he was at Gary's house, Gary would be dead by now. And Tom would be long gone. Be a waste of time." She pushed off the wall. "I'm heading back into the city. He's probably gone back to the flat." She pointed a finger gun at Nick. "Call me if you hear anything."

Davie watched her leave then turned to Nick. "Okay, Gary's pot farm."

The police car was still parked across from the open entrance to the nursery. Nick didn't slow. "Shit."

"You think if we asked real nice, they'd let us in?"

Nick chuckled. "I'm not sure what they're there for. They aren't securing the place. We can just walk through the bush around the corner. I've done it before. A couple of times." Nick rounded the corner and pulled over on the shoulder.

"I'm not walking through bush at night. Have fun." He settled back in his seat.

"Well, I sure as hell can't drive in the front gate with the cops parked there." Nick thought for a minute. Smiled. "Show me a map."

Davie handed him his tablet. "What are you looking for?"

"This thing is fast. Gonna give the sleepy cops a bit of excitement." He pointed to a side road about half a kilometre beyond the entrance to the nursery. "There." He got out of the car.

"Hey, where are you going?"

Nick pointed at the bottle of water in the centre console. "Muck up the back plate, Davie. Enough so their cameras can't make it out. I've got the front."

Davie grunted and pushed himself out of the car. "You're driving." He grabbed a fist full of dirt. Put it in a pile. Scooped a bit more out of a hole and poured some of the water in the hole. Dropped the dirt back in and stirred it up. He moved to the back of the car and scrubbed the mud over the plate. Made sure some of the letters and numbers weren't visible. "Not sure how long this is going to last."

Nick brushed dirt off his hands. "Only needs to work a couple of minutes." He grinned. "Hop in."

He turned the car around, checked the map again where the side road was and nodded. "Brace yourself." He hit the accelerator hard, barely made the corner heading toward the nursery without hitting the gravel shoulder and sped past the parked police with the speedometer passing 120 km/h on the way up.

He dropped the speed and pulled hard on the steering wheel, left, into the dirt road.

"Lights," said Davie.

Nick turned off the headlights, applied the emergency brake and took his foot off the brake pedal. He kept his eyes on the rear-view mirror.

They waited a full minute in silence before the police car sped past, roof lights flashing.

Davie let out a held breath. "I was beginning to think they wouldn't bite."

Nick grunted, put the car in reverse and ease back out onto the road. He moved the gear stick from 'Reverse' to 'Neutral' before he breached the tree line and rolled quietly, and stealthily onto the macadam. He looked up the road in the direction the police car had travelled. The red and blue lights were visible, but at a distance. And still receding. "They're making good time. How long do you think we've got?"

Davie shrugged as Nick pulled the car into gear and pointed back toward the nursery. "Half an hour, maybe a bit more. They'll give up the chase in a little, take the opportunity to refresh their coffee and snacks and eventually come back to one of the more boring posts they've had in years."

"Let's set the clock at thirty minutes, then." Nick navigated the car through the partially open gate. The police tape slid up the bonnet and windscreen as he drove under it.

The only sound from the car was wide, low-profile tyres crunching over the dusty, dirt road. The headlights splashed across the burnt-out porch, eliciting a sharp intake of breath from Nick. "Worse than I thought it was."

They were sitting in the stopped car, taking in the damage, when Gary stepped out on the front porch with a shotgun in his hands. He held it across his body. Not threatening for the moment, but less than a split second from spraying them with buckshot.

Nick turned off the headlights and stepped out of the car. "Gary. You don't need that." He turned on the light on his mobile phone.

"Nick?" He squinted past the torch light. "How'd you find me?"

"You want that," Nick nodded at Gary's left hand, "that, um, cuff removed?" He stepped slowly onto the porch, his hands out to the side and empty, save for his phone. "Everything okay?"

Gary took a step back. "How did you find me?"

Davie got out of the car and stretched. "Put that thing away, Gary. Easy to find you. Tracked where your phone was before Tom heel-crunched it, took a look at a map and odds were better than even that you'd be here."

Nick frowned. "Better than even? You told me even. Better than even, I would have driven faster." He smiled at Gary. "You got any food here?" He didn't wait for an answer. "Pretty ballsy." He nodded to the car. "Leave the gun here and get in. The cops will be back in a few minutes, and we need to get you out of here."

Gary shook his head and walked back into his house. "I live here. I'm not going anywhere." He held the shotgun low, index finger inside the trigger guard and his thumb just behind the hammer.

Nick took a deep breath and followed him in. "Come on. We distracted the cops and they're going to be pissed when they come back." He checked the time. "And I need to get you to your father's place. He's almost gone and wants — needs — to see you before he dies."

"I'm not hearing a compelling reason so far. Get the hell out of my house." He lifted the shotgun slightly. "Now."

Davie held up his hands. "Not cool, man. At least let Nick get that cuff off your wrist. It can't be that comfortable." He looked at Nick. "You can pick a handcuff, can't you, Nick?"

"I need a hairpin, a bristle from a steel brush or broom. Something like that."

"Paperclip?" asked Gary. He put the shotgun on the sofa and pulled drawers open on his desk until he found an oversized paperclip.

"That should work." Nick held out his hand. "Come here."

Gary handed him the paperclip and held out his wrist. "This take long?"

Nick straightened the paperclip and stuck one end in the keyhole a couple of millimetres. "Hold your wrist still." He held the shackle with one hand and bent a 90 degree corner on the end of the paperclip, making a little hook. He used the hook to release the double lock bar, then moved the lock bar out of the way and pulled the ratchet teeth out, releasing the cuff.

"You've got to teach me that."

"No, I don't." Nick tossed the paperclip on the table. "You, however, need to see your father."

"I appreciate what you've just done for me, but I've told you before, I don't want his bloody money."

"Trust me, that's not going to be a problem." He held up his hand to forestall an interruption. "Seriously. Let's get going. You need to close things out with your father. And if you stay here much longer, you'll be doing that from behind bars."

Gary gave it a minute's thought. Then he nodded. "Fair point. Let's wake him for breakfast."

"Shotgun." Davie held up his hand. "But I'll pull the seat forward so you've got legroom.

Chapter Thirty-Four

Tom pulled off the road and onto the driveway to the cabin. Tyres crunched over gravel, and as the headlights splashed across the open door he swore.

"Fucking HELL."

He knew it was closed when he left. He hadn't locked it, but shit, his brother was cuffed to a pipe. He braked hard and ran up the steps into the cabin. He didn't spend much time there. The pipe was broken, the floor was still soaked, and Gary's smashed phone had moved from the floor to the table.

"Dammit." He picked up a cheap wooden chair and threw it across the small room. Kicked the edge of the table with the bottom of his foot and sent it skittering across the floor.

He ran out and slammed the door behind him. It hit the doorjamb and bounced back. He got his hand up just in time to keep it from slamming into his face.

A thought occurred to him. "Shit. He's going to the old man."

Gary sat sideways in the back seat of the rental. "Bloody hell. Nice enough from the outside, but you couldn't fit an average teen back here." He adjusted himself, in vain. "How much farther?"

Nick rolled his eyes and Davie laughed.

"What's so fucking funny?"

"You sound like every eight-year-old I've ever known." Nick glanced at the GPS screen. "About an hour. We'll get there near about 6:30." He looked at Gary in the rear-view mirror. "Just in time for breakfast."

"When was the last time you saw him?"

Nick thought for a second. "Yesterday, I think. Time is kinda messed up. I'm running on far less sleep than I'm accustomed to."

"How was he?"

"Frail. Still sharp as a whip, but his body was failing fast. Too bad brain transplants aren't a thing."

Gary raised his eyebrows. "Yeah. Could've helped a lot of people." He adjusted his legs and winced. "Jesus, this is an uncomfortable car."

"You're going to have to put up with it for another hour."

Tom floored the Commodore's accelerator as he turned off the driveway. The V8 engine's throaty roar echoed through the gumtrees on either side of the road. He clenched his jaw as hard as he pressed his foot to the floor. It was a ninety-minute drive in most situations, but at 5:30, with little or no traffic, he thought he could make it in a bit over an hour. He reached 130 kmph on the M4, blowing past two mobile speed cameras. He didn't care. It wasn't his car.

A Highway Patrol car coming at him in the opposite lanes lit its blue and red roof lights up as they passed each other. He glanced in the rear-view mirror and watched as it bounced across the grass median behind him and took up the chase.

"Shit."

He accelerated as he reached the offramp to Penrith. He was still over half an hour away from the old man's house and now he had to deal with this. He turned off the car lights and took an immediate right off the main drag, then a left and another right then pulled over in front of small bunga-low. He turned off the engine and the interior dome light and quietly got out of the car. He closed the door slowly, pushing it until he heard the 'click'.

Blue and red flashing lights moved slowly down the cross street. He squatted beside the car until the police and their lights had moved on.

He still needed wheels, though. He trotted down the mid-dle of the street scanning left and right until he found the perfect car. Late 70s. Some tire wear so he knew it ran. Best of all, it looked exactly like Gary's car, before it was totalled.

He smiled. He knew this car inside and out. He checked the doors first. No point making a mess if the owner was generous.

The owner wasn't. All of the doors were locked.

The front garden had a low wall made of loose-fitting stones. He picked one with a sharp corner and moved to the driver's side of the car. He took off his shirt. He bunched the shirt on the small backdoor window, took a firm grip with the rock and tapped the sharp corner against the glass.

The safety glass spiderwebbed. And in the very early morning it sounded very loud.

Gary brushed the glass out of the way with his shirt and reached through to unlock the driver's door. It was a manual transmission. He put the car in neutral and rolled it out of the driveway and onto the street before he got in. Hot-wiring a car this old, with no steering lock, took less than three seconds. He quietly made his way back to the M4 and pointed to Sydney.

He was twenty minutes behind schedule. Unfortunately, this car couldn't hit the speeds the Commodore could. He pushed it as hard as he could.

"Wallace, the prints came back. Terry Graves is Tom Goulding." Lin scrolled through the report on her monitor. "Goulding. He's that rich guy, right? Mining?"

Wallace rolled his chair over to her desk. "If it's the same Goulding."

"Based on these reports, It's the same Goulding. Was in a car accident about ten years ago. Nothing prior to that. A lot of minor infractions since then. Minor, but escalating for a couple of years, then nothing."

"Nothing for how long?"

Lin counted off on her fingers. "Fifty-four months."

Wallace nodded. "Let's see if we can figure out where the black sheep of the family is hanging out now."

Nick slowed as he navigated the narrow roads in Vaucluse. "You awake, Gary?"

"How in the hell could I sleep in this tin can?" He looked out the side window. "He still lives out here?"

"How would I know 'still'? He lives out here. Just around the corner." He drove through the open gate and stopped at the front door. "Yes, we're there yet."

William answer Nick's knocking, wearing a robe and slippers. "It's 6:30. What in the hell are you — ? Gary. Surprised to see you."

"Billy. Still a leech. Where's the old man?"

William stepped outside and closed the door behind him. "He's sleeping."

"Time enough for that in a couple of days, if the rumours are true. I need to talk to him."

William shook his head. "He's only got a few days. Let him rest."

Gary smiled and took a step closer to William. "Listen, Billy, you over-fed, hind-tit sucking waste of oxygen. I'm going in this house, finding the old fuck and waking him up. Then we're going to have a chat. You have a choice: He's woken by your screams of pain, or he's gently woken by his youngest son tapping on his forehead." He took a step closer. "Your choice."

William stifled a yawn and stepped out of the way. "You've been a bully since you were five. Wake him up. I don't care anymore." He followed Gary into the house.

Nick tapped Davie on the arm and leaned close. "Anything in your research find out that these two knew each other?"

"Nothing."

"We going to wait out here like a couple of outdoor dogs?"

Nick chuckled "Let's follow them."

Davie skipped into the house. "This isn't a house. This is a bloody palace." He looked up at the high ceilings. "How much stupid money do you need to afford a place like this?"

"If you have to ask..." Nick followed Gary and William into a bedroom with more floor space than his entire flat.

Lawrence was asleep on his back. The head of the customised hospital bed was elevated. Heart rate, blood pressure and oxygen level monitors read performance metrics through a cluster of cables attached to his frail body. A nasal cannula pumped oxygen into his nose.

His eyes flickered open. His eyes moved from William to Gary to Nick to Davie. His gaze stayed on Davie. "Who are you?" His voice was a wheezy raspy leaf across sandpaper. "Do I know you?"

Davie gave him an aborted wave. "Um, David Sangster, sir. Friend of Nick. You can call me Davie."

The look of dismissal from Lawrence was immediate.

Nick smiled as the old man's attention turned to William. He leaned close to his friend. "Don't worry about it," he whispered. "The old guy is extremely direct."

Lawrence cleared his throat and pressed a button on the side of the bed. The head raised more, until he was almost completely sitting up. "William. What in the hell is going on? What time is it?"

"I can answer, Larry," said Nick. "You hired me to find your youngest son, and here he is." Nick glanced at Gary. Noticed for the first time the fury on his face. His hands clenched into fists. He stepped closer and slightly in front of Gary. "He's — "

"Shut up," said Lawrence, feebly waving him away. "You haven't said a word since you stepped in here, son." The distain layered on the last word was clear to everyone. "I know what happened that day. How you lied. I'm pretty sure you're a grade-A sociopath. Don't worry about an inheritance. I changed the will a few years ago." He looked to Nick. "I needed to be sure you'd find him."

"As long as you're still paying me."

Lawrence ignored him. "Gareth, you're on your own. Get out of my house."

"You, miserable son of a bitch. I'm a sociopath? You are twisted. You're not good enough to be a sociopath." He half raised his clenched fist. "I should have beat the shit out of you when it would have been a fair fight."

"I SAID GET OUT!" Lawrence's face reddened. He coughed, his chest heaving. William rushed to his side, patted his back and got his oxygen mask.

"Gary, we should go." Nick nodded toward the door.

"Yeah. You fucking near killed him." Davie had already made his way to the exit. "Shotgun, again."

Gary stood at the foot of the bed, clenching and unclenching his fists for a few seconds.

"You're out of here in one minute, son, or the cops will be asking you questions about a weed nursery."

That snapped Gary's fugue state. He grunted and stormed out of the bedroom.

Nick pointed at Lawrence. "I'll be in touch about my invoice." He jogged out of the room after Gary. He found him and Davie at the front door, shoulder to shoulder, blocking the exit.

"Hey, dickwads, out of the way." He pushed through and came face to face with Tom's gun.

Chapter Thirty-Five

Tom pulled the hammer back on the revolver. "Jeez. The whole fucking group in one place. Makes my job easier." He moved the muzzle off Nick and pointed it at Gary. "It's just him I want to waste, though."

"You don't have to do that," said Nick.

Without taking his eyes off Gary, Tom lashed out with his left fist and smashed Nick in the nose. "Shut the fuck up."

Nick fell back on his arse and grabbed his face. "Man. Jesus." Blood flowed through his fingers. "What the hell? This was just starting to heal. You absolute twat." He pushed himself to his feet and tilted his head back. "Fuck."

Tom stuck the muzzle in Gary's chest and pushed him into the house. "We're going to talk to the old man."

"Come on, mate." Gary took a half step back and Davie jumped out of the way. "I was just in there. I'm not in the will. He was fucking with my head." He pushed his chest against the muzzle. "What are you going to do about it, you fat fuck?"

In a smooth, fast motion Tom smashed Gary on the side of the head with the revolver. "Into the house, little brother."

Davie held out his hand and stopped Nick. "You're not thinking of going in there, are you? We need to get the hell out of here."

Nick pushed his hand away. "We can't leave." He ran into the house. "That guy has problems."

They ended up back in the bedroom. Lawrence had a full oxy mask on now, the bed was flat again, and the monitors were singing the tale of a very ill man. Tom stood at the foot of the bed, alternating between pointing the revolver at Gary, William and Lawrence.

"I wasn't fucking driving that car, dad." He jammed the muzzle in Gary's back. "This little shit would never let me drive his car. So, ipso facto, q.e.d., I did not KILL MUM." Tom took a deep breath. "But I'll kill Gary here to keep him from getting a red cent from you."

Lawrence fumbled with the oxygen mask, eventually letting William remove it. "Garth is getting no money. He's not getting anything. No house, no stocks, no cash, not a fucking penny. Put the stupid gun down."

"I DON'T BELIEVE YOU. If I kill him, he can't get anything." He spun Gary around. "Between the eyes." He cleared his throat and swallowed. "Should have finished you in the cabin." He pulled the hammer back and Nick caught him broadside in a tackle that would have him signed to any professional rugby squad.

Nick and Tom hit the floor and rolled. The revolver skittered across the tile and stopped at William's feet.

He looked at it for a second, then scooped it up and pointed it at Gary. "I never thought I'd say this, but I agree with Tom. You're a sociopath who needs to go away."

"The safety is on, arsehole."

William smiled. "I'm not a moron. I'm not going to fall for that. Revolvers don't have a safety mechanism." He took a step closer to Gary. "I hate these things, but they're awfully handy. Throws a good-sized chunk of lead at you at a respectable velocity. I can lodge that lead in your brainpan. End you forever. End my nightmares."

"Oh, come on, Billy. It wasn't that bad. We were just having fun." Gary held his hands out, trying to corral William. "You don't want to do this."

"I've dreamed of it." William took a step back. He waved the revolver toward the back of the house, facing the water. "The sliding patio door. Out there. On the rocks."

Gary planted his feet. "Not going anywhere until you tell me what you're going to do.

"I'm going to get you to stand on one of the tallest rocks, wait until the tide is high, and execute you."

"Wow. You're not the smart one in your family, are you? Dawn is cracking, and high tide is at least three hours away. You're going to shoot me, elevated, in broad daylight?"

"Oh, would you put that stupid thing down." Lawrence signalled for Tom. "Help me into my chair, Tommy."

William shifted his position to keep both Gary and Tom in view.

Davie started taking small steps backward, toward the bedroom door. He nodded at Nick to follow him.

"No. I'm staying," said Nick. "You should too. Calmer heads, and all that." He took a step toward William, who pivoted and pointed the revolver at him.

"Back it up."

Nick held his hands up. "Billy-boy, you're in a no-win situation." He glanced at Tom helping Lawrence into the electric wheelchair. "The geometry is getting tricky for you. And there's only one real road out of here. You start shooting and Davie calls the cops as he hauls his arse out of here and you've got no way out." He pushed his hands down toward the floor. "Just lower the gun. Take the bullets out and make it a useless tool."

Gary chuckled. "Just like Tom. Useless, piece of shit tool."

"Shut up, you fucking punk." Lawrence was trembling with rage. "I should have taken you out back and cleaned your clock when you were a teenager. You're an entitled narcissist with delusions of grandeur. Unquestionably a sociopath." He wiped spittle from the corners of his mouth. "I've known for years. I should have said something to Tom when I knew. Should have helped you with whatever the fuck is wrong with your head, son."

He shook his head and idly brushed back his thinning hair with a trembling hand. "Gary, I'm really sorry I let this go last as long as it did. Your mother is dead. That's behind us now. I can forgive you, but I can't forget what you did. Especially to your brother."

He held out his hand, still trembling. "William, give me that fucking thing."

William still had the revolver trained on Gary. He clenched his jaw. Squeezed the grip hard enough to whiten his knuckles, then finally let out a breath and lowered the weapon. He let it spin on his index finger and held it out to Nick. "You're the sanest one here."

"Pretty low bar, if you ask me." Davie smiled looking at the others in the room. His smile slowly disappeared. "No-one asked. Right."

Nick fumbled with the cylinder release and spilled the shells onto the floor. "Shit." He squatted, picking them up and Tom took his chance and lunged at Gary. He caught him off guard, crash tackling him at waist level and driving him into a tall floor vase filled with dried plants. It smashed into the wall and shattered, Gary and Tom immediately following it.

Tom's phone fell out of his back pocket and skittered across the floor and stopped in front of Davie. Nick looked at it, then at Davie and nodded. Davie squatted like he was tying his shoe and scooped up the phone.

Gary rolled on top of Tom and grabbed him around the throat with both hands. He was taller than his brother, and heavier, but Tom had a decade more of dirty fighting experience, and was making use of it.

Lawrence tried standing from his chair. "STOP! This is what I wanted to stop. You are brothers!"

Nick pushed Davie out of the way as Tom grappled Gary into the wall right beside them.

Gary hammered down on Tom. He was reducing older brother to a gelatinous, bruised mass of pain when he saw his father. He was on his back, grasping at his left shoulder, gasping like a salmon on a riverbank. William was on his knees beside him, ripping the packaging off a portable AED.

Gary stopped and pushed Tom away. He ran to his father and dropped to his knees beside William. "You know how to use those things?"

William nodded and tore open Lawrence's robe. He stuck one of the pads under on the old man's upper right chest and the second one on the opposite of his body below the left nipple. "Hands off him." He pushed Gary aside and depressed the 'Shock' button on the controller. He waited until the device checked for a heartbeat, then discharged. When the shock passed he started CPR.

Tom had crawled over by them. "He dead?" He sat back on his heels. "It's over?"

"Is what over?" asked Nick.

Davie pulled his phone out of his pocket and backed out of the room.

"Hey." Nick grabbed Tom by the arm. "Is what over?"

"I've spent the last how many years with this man on my back over something I didn't do." He pointed at Gary. "And this piece of shit knew. From day one. I've been living with guilt I didn't need to own." Tears were streaming down his face. He sniffed and pushed himself to his feet. "Fuck this. If you get a single penny from the old man, I'll be fighting it in court."

Sirens sounded in the distance, growing stronger. "That's my cue." Tom ran out of the house and got in the stolen car and left, slowly, trying to maintain control.

He didn't make it to the gate.

An unmarked sedan with red and blue strobes in the front grill blocked his exit. He accelerated toward the car, then stopped short, head down, hands up. "Shit."

Wallace got out of the passenger side and Lin got out of the driver's side, guns drawn.

"Tom Goulding," called Wallace. "Reach out with your right hand and open the door from the outside."

Tom complied, awkwardly. Turned and pressed his hands on the bonnet of the car. "Ya got me, copper. I'll go easy." He did a fairly passable imitation of Bogart.

Warren holstered his sidearm while Lin covered him. "I'm going to pat you down. Do you have anything in your pockets that might stab me? Open knife? Needles?"

"Nah, mate. The knife is closed." He flinched as Warren patted him down. "Hey, watch the nads."

"You should be so lucky." Warren cuffed Tom and put him in the back of the unmarked car. "Sit there for a bit. I've got to talk to some people. Make yourself comfortable. You've got a lot to answer for."

Nick and Davie approached the car. "Hey, Wallace. You've been looking for Tom, too? You finally caught up with us. You should have said something. I've known where Tom's been for yonks. Almost a good friend, I've known him so long." He touched his re-broken nose. "Almost. What do you have him for?"

"Multiple vehicle thefts, many multiple aggravated assaults, arson. Twice."

"Twice?"

"The house and the truck."

Nick nodded. "He's also guilty of at least 12 cases of fraud over the past three or four years. Millions of dollars' worth."

Lin flipped open her notebook. "Details, boy."

"I'm older than you, Lizzy. It's Nick. Maybe even Mr Harding. I'm meeting the client shortly. I'll give you the details after I tell them."

Chapter Thirty-Six

The sun was starting to burn a path across the sky as the coroner's van drove away with the remains of Lawrence Goulding. Uniforms asked a few perfunctory questions of Gary, William, Davie and Nick. There wouldn't be an investigation. The man was old, had very advanced cancer and died of a heart attack.

Nothing was mentioned about the shattered floor vase.

Rich people are special.

The last cop left and Davie visibly relaxed. "Glad that's over with."

"You were worried? There was nothing for you to worry about." Nick pointed at Gary. "That guy, on the other hand, if they knew what he owned, he'd be in the back of one of their cars."

"But they don't know, do they?" Gary dropped into a sofa and crossed his legs. "Billy, get me a coffee, would you?"

"Get fucked." William grabbed a broom and started sweeping up the mess in the bedroom.

Gary tipped his head back and laughed. "Well, this is over." He sighed. "I guess I should get out of here. I've got a business to rebuild, and none of daddy's money to help me."

Nick opened his wallet and took out the old newspaper photo. "Answer me this, Gary." He pointed at the four people in the photo behind Gary and Penny. "That's Tom and William in the back, right? Who are the other two?"

Davie dropped Tom's phone in the centre console before he buckled in. As Nick pulled out of the driveway, Davie opened his laptop and connected Tom's phone. "I'm assuming this is what you want me to do?"

"See if you can unlock it."

"Done. Give me something hard."

Nick glanced over. "You unlocked it that fast?"

"You can do doors. And handcuffs. I can do phones." He tapped a couple of keys. "He's been messaging someone about drugs and selling hot cars."

"William."

"And someone else about new identities."

Nick smiled. "Perfect. Have that number ready." He looked at his GPS. He depressed the call button on his steering wheel and said, "Call Lucy."

The phone was Bluetoothed to the car. The ringing came through the car speakers. Nick thought it was going to go to voicemail just as Lucy answered.

"Lucy speaking. Who is this?"

"You don't have my number in your phone? I'm shocked." Nick pulled onto the freeway. "Can you pull that meeting forward? I have what I need."

"Long night?"

"Very. But we're finished."

There was silence on the phone for a few seconds. Nick checked to see if the call dropped. "You still there?"

"My office, 9:30. Does that work?"

Nick smiled. "Davie and I will both be there."

"Done. See you then."

"Thanks." Nick dropped the call and glanced at Davie. "You tired?"

"Absolutely fucking knackered."

"We're almost finished. Stop at my place, shower and go to this thing. Then I'll buy you the biggest breakfast you've ever had."

"Screw breakfast. I need sleep."

Lucy met them at reception. "This is going to work?"

"Fingers crossed." Nick accepted the visitor's pass and put the lanyard over his neck. "Everybody going to show up?"

"Yes." Lucy fidgeted. "I mean, how sure are you?"

"Nothing is ever 100%, but I've got a pretty good track record."

She nodded. "Okay. How do we do this?"

"Tell them it was important that you pull the meeting forward, and that Davie and I have an interim update."

"Interim? I thought you'd finished. I need you to be finished."

Nick smiled and rested his hand on her arm. "I am. I just need one specific person in the audience to have their guard lowered. Can you do that?"

"I can." Lucy checked her watch. "We're down two floors. The meeting starts in three minutes."

She led them down the stairs and held the door to the conference room, letting Nick and Davie enter. She followed and pointed them to their seats. She remained standing. Present at the meeting were the same people Nick had met when he first signed on to the case. Lucy's manager, Catherine Ross, was sitting back in her chair watching her boss, and Nick's old friend, Scott Smith, and the head of compliance, Brad Williams argue the merits of VAR — video assistant referee — in topflight football. She glanced at Lucy who knocked on the table.

Nick nodded to Davie who opened his laptop and connected it to the monitor on the far wall. When the room turned to look at what was on the screen Davie slid Tom's phone out of the laptop case and placed it in his lap.

"Good morning. Thanks for coming on short notice. Nick and Davie tell me they have some interim results for us."

Nick watched the faces. Catherine watched Lucy. Scottie looked concerned and Brad leaned forward. "Interim?"

Nick stood.

"Good morning. I echo Lucy's thanks. I called her before 6 this morning, asking that she pull this meeting forward. I very much appreciate you taking the time."

"So what have you found?" Brad was spinning his pen on his knuckle.

"Let me give you some background."

Davie tapped his spacebar and an array of twelve identities filled the monitor. He tapped the bar again and a thirteenth filled the middle of the screen.

"Thanks, Davie. Finding the guy wasn't too hard."

Brad nodded. "So your job is finished. Excellent work." He stood and extended his hand. "Fantastic work. Send me the invoice personally and I'll walk it through the system."

"Settle down," said Nick.

Brad held out his hand for a few more seconds, glanced at Lucy, frowned and slowly sat. "What do you mean?"

"I got curious. This person — his name is Tom Goulding, by the way — managed to successfully defraud a mid-level finance company for years with a bunch of well-established fake identifications. The reported credit score on all of these was good. Really good. Like I would kill for numbers that good."

"Exactly. Excellent fake identifications. Fooled me," said Brad. "And full credit to Lucy for finding the pattern that exposed the fraud. I've had my team review their methodologies to make sure this kind of thing doesn't slip through the cracks again."

Nick smiled and nodded. "Yeah. Here's the thing. If I had a way of creating such good, no, what did you call them, excellent identifications, why would I only target you, a smallish, mid-level financial company? No offense."

"None taken," said Catherine. "Frankly, I thought the same thing. You, I take it, have a theory."

"You bet I do." He nodded at Davie. "I think that the credit reports were filtered through someone here."

A phone rang. Brad reached into his inside suit pocket. He frowned and declined the call. He slid the phone back into his suit pocket and it rang again. He declined the call again.

Davie lifted Tom's phone off his lap and placed it on the table. He called again. Brad's phone rang again.

"Hey, Brad," said Nick. "You were Tom's contact inside of the company. You set up the identities, made sure the credit agency bought the lie and swindled millions out of this business." Nick shrugged. "I don't know why. I don't know what you, specifically, got out of enabling a clearly mentally damaged man, but that's not why I was hired. Someone else can figure out why you're such a shit."

He nodded at Davie who tapped the space bar one last time. An old, grainy picture filled the screen. "Gary is the little tyke. Eight years old. Tall for his age, but still a youngster. Right behind him is Tom. He's eighteen in this photo. The girl is Penny. We've met. Next to Tom is you, Brad. I'd bet my fee on it. Beside you is the guy who I believe Tom gets his drugs from. William. Was Tom's father's business manager." He waved his hand. "But that's none of my concern at this point."

He slid a file folder across the table. He weighted it perfectly. It stopped just in front of Catherine. "Lucy already has a copy. All the details are in there, including some suggestions on how to tighten up the compliance part of your business. Clearly it needs tightening. It should provide a solid basis for civil action against who I expect will be your former compliance manager. I'll be handing Tom's phone and a version of the report over to the police as soon as we leave. I expect there'll be criminal action also. Against a lot of people."

Davie closed his laptop, stashed it away in its case and stood beside Nick. "Great meeting you all. He's promised me a huge breakfast." He started toward the door. "And I'm starving."

Nick raised his eyebrows and nodded. "I did promise him that. Lucy, thanks for reaching out to me in the first instance. I believe I owe you a proper dinner. I'll call you later today, okay?"

Chapter Thirty-Seven

The service was graveside. Attendance was low. There was Lawrence, of course, in the box. Nick was there. Davie tagged along. Gary and Penny attended but didn't seem to be paying much attention. William hovered but was avoiding everybody.

And Tom was there. With Carol. And two cops flanking him. An ankle monitor was just visible below the cuff of his too-short trousers. A few others were attending, all dressed in suits too warm for the hot weather and all, except William, looking like they didn't want to be there.

The minister finished his words and stood back from the casket. Carol and Penny each stepped forward and put flowers on the casket.

Nick slid his hands in his pockets and wandered over to Gary. "Not a cent, I hear."

"What's that?" Gary looked Nick up and down. "Right. You. Not a sweet cent." He shrugged. "Doesn't really matter. I'll be set up again in a couple of months." He chuckled and punched Nick lightly on the shoulder. "Lots of demand for my product. And lots of loyal customers."

"They're not going to wait a couple of months. They'll find someone else," pushed Nick.

Gary leaned forward, conspiratorial look on his face. I'll be fine, lad. Don't go telling, hey?"

"Lad? You're fucking ten years younger than me." He took a breath. "How is it you seem to have escaped all legal consequences for everything you've done?"

Gary held his hands out and looked for an instant like the shrug emoji. "Clean living, I guess."

"Far from it. Your luck is going to run out one of these days and the snapback is going to be an almighty bitch." Nick shook his head and walked away. Tom was talking to one of his constable friends, his hands flying around like a Frenchman.

"Everything okay?"

"I was just telling this moron that women's football is just as good as men's, just a bit slower. Great skill in those squads." He threw his hands up in despair. "This troglodyte is an NRL fan."

Nick nodded. "How are you doing?" He tapped the side of his head. "Up here, I mean."

"Still get the headaches. I'm on some different meds though. Working with a real good head doctor. Psych counselling, cognitive therapy, some relaxation techniques. And Carol has been good for me. And to me." He reached out and took her hand for a second.

"Will you do time?"

"I'm already doing time. Remanded until trial. I have a public defender, which is brutally stupid. I have millions now. Tens of millions. But they're tied up for at least another couple of months."

"So you couldn't afford bail, either," said Davie.

"Even if I could, the judge declined it. Pre-emptively." He grimaced. "I've got a bit of a history."

"Why so long for the money?" asked Davie.

"James, the executor, has to go through all of the old man's accounts, make sure all bills are settled, accounts are closed, that kind of thing, before he can disburse."

Nick nodded. Tapped the side of his head. "You're keeping it tamped down?"

Tom saw Gary and turned his back to him. "As long as I don't see, hear or smell that prick I'm fine."

Nick chuckled. "Your mate Brad is in a bit of a pickle."

Tom shrugged. "His pickle. Not mine. But," he hesitated. "But I may be assisting my friends in uniform as they put together the case against Brad." He tapped the side of his head. "Not everything up here is broken."

"Is your free lawyer any good?"

"Meh."

"I'll see what I can do to help. I know some people."

Tom scuffed the ground. "Hey, that girl we talked with, Lucy?"

"Yeah?"

"Let her know that once all the knots are untied with my inheritance I'll make full restitution, okay? Might even keep me out of Long Bay."

"I'm having dinner with her tonight. I'll let her know. She'll be delighted."

"Thanks. I appreciate that."

The service was over, and the attendees were dispersing.

"You can find your way back, Davie?"

"I was hoping to get a ride, but yeah, okay. If that's what it has to be."

"I'm stopping by my parents' place. Need to talk to them alone."

Davie nodded. "Fair enough. I'm good. Catch you later."

"Thanks." Nick got into his car. His car. The rental had been returned and his Mazda, shiny with a new paint job, was a poor second choice to the EV. But it was clean, ran well and, from the outside, looked brand new. And he didn't need to plug it in at the most inopportune times.

It was a short drive to his parents' house. He travelled on autopilot, thinking about what he was going to say. He had no recollection of the intersections he'd driven through, whether the lights were red or green, if pedestrians had jumped out of his way.

He pulled into his parents' driveway and turned off the car. Sat there for a minute.

His mother opened the front door and stood on the small porch. "Nicky?"

Nick grunted as he got out of his car. "Hey, Mum. You okay?" He walked up to her and gave her a kiss on the cheek. "Dad up?"

"Why in the hell wouldn't I be?" His father was walking up the hall to the front door. "You think I'm an invalid or something?"

"You should be sitting down, George." His mother ushered his father to the patio. Nick followed. His father was slower than he remembered him.

He pulled up a chair and sat beside his father. "How are you feeling, pops?"

"Fit as a fiddle. That stainless-steel mesh stent stuck in my arteries to keep them open is working a treat." He smiled "I'm feeling better than I have in years. The only thing slowing me up is the fucking stitches in my leg where they went in. Still hurts like a son of a bitch. Want to see them?"

"Oh, hell no."

George laughed. "How are you doing?"

"Closed out both cases. Thanks for your tip about Gary's car, by the way. Was the missing puzzle piece."

"Do I get a cut of your fees?"

Nick laughed. "5%. Of next to nothing."

"You enjoy this work?"

Nick took a deep breath in through his nose and let it out slowly. He nodded. "I really do. It's never the same. I don't have to sit in an office all the time. Some cases the money is really good."

"Some."

"Yeah, some. Others I do just to help people who need help. Makes me whole. You get that?"

George nodded. "I actually do." He grabbed Nick's hand. "Hey. I've taken your advice. As soon as this bloody hole in my leg heals, your mother and I are heading to Florence. Taking a couple of months to explore and find a nice retirement villa."

Nick raised his eyebrows. "Really? I'll have a place in Italy to crash?"

George waggled his hand. "We'll be going there to hide from you, son."

"Oh, fuck you very much. You don't think I can find you? I can find anyone."

About the Author

Tony McFadden is a displaced Canadian now calling Australia his home. He and his wife and two children live near the beaches where he spends as much time as possible writing.

More about Tony and his writing can be found on the interwebs at
TonyMcFadden.net/mybooks, Facebook
and Twitter.

Also by Tony McFadden

G'Day LA • G'Day USA

Matt's War • Daly Battles: The Fall of Pyongyang • Target: Australia

Book 'Em - An Eamonn Shute Mystery • Unprotected Sax • Family Matters

Have Wormhole, Will Travel • Killing Time

Mac D: Private Investigator • A Step Too Far (A Mac D Case) • Hunter/Prey (A Mac D Case)

The Murder of Jeremy Brookes (A McGinnis Investigations Case) • Number Fifteen (A McGinnis Investigations Case)

Batteries Not Included (A Nick Harding Case)

9 780648 562863